Ian Watson was born in Tyneside in 1943. He studied
English at Balliol Coll
fiction stories were stir
lecturer in Japan. In 196
story, was published i
then his stories have a
anthologies. They hav
in three previous collec
Sunstroke and *Slow Birds*.

Ian Watson's first novel, *The Embedding*, was published
in 1973 and received enormous critical acclaim. His second
novel, *The Jonah Kit*, became a British Science Fiction
Award winner as well as confirming his position in the
front rank of contemporary writers. He has been features
editor of the journal *Foundation* since 1975 and a full-time
writer since 1976. His most recent novels are *Chekhov's
Journey* (1983), *Converts* (1984), *The Book of the River* (1984)
and *Queenmagic, Kingmagic* (1986).

By the same author

IAN WATSON

Evil Water

and other stories

GRAFTON BOOKS

A Division of the Collins Publishing Group

LONDON GLASGOW
TORONTO SYDNEY AUCKLAND

Grafton Books
A Division of the Collins Publishing Group
8 Grafton Street, London W1X 3LA

Published by Grafton Books 1988

First published in Great Britain by
Victor Gollancz Ltd 1987

ISBN 0-586-020193-9

Printed and bound in Great Britain by
Collins, Glasgow

Set in Bembo

ACKNOWLEDGEMENTS
'Cold Light' first appeared in *The Magazine of Fantasy and Science Fiction*, 1986; 'When the Timegate Failed' first appeared in *Interzone*, 1985; 'The Great Atlantic Swimming Race' first appeared in *Isaac Asimov's Science Fiction Magazine*, 1986; 'The Wire Around the War' first appeared in *Isaac Asimov's Science Fiction Magazine*, 1984; 'When Idaho Dived' first appeared in *Afterwar* edited by Janet Morris, 1985; 'On the Dream Channel Panel' first appeared in *Amazing*, 1985; 'The People on the Precipice' first appeared in *Interzone*, 1985; 'Skin Day, and After' first appeared in *The Magazine of Fantasy and Science Fiction*, 1985; 'Windows' first appeared in *Isaac Asimov's Science Fiction Magazine*, 1986; 'Evil Water' first appeared in *The Magazine of Fantasy and Science Fiction*, 1987.

Contents

Cold Light

Doubtless it is one of life's typical ironies that a man with defective eyesight should have spent many long years studying the history of artificial lighting. However, my friend John Ingolby was also a prominent churchman. By the time his book appeared John was well advanced in the hierarchy of the Church of England. He was Bishop of Porchester.

Now, at this time the Church was in a certain amount of disarray. On the one hand it was waning due to apathy. On the other, it was beset by fundamentalist evangelism which seemed unpleasantly frantic and hysterical. Between this Scylla and Charybdis a new liberal theology was being steered which it was hoped would inject new life and modern, humane thought into a seemingly dying institution.

Not, however, without resistance!

Already one new bishop – who publicly denied the doctrine of the virgin birth – had been enthroned amidst scandal and protest. Within two days of his enthronement, the venue – an ancient cathedral, finest example of Gothic architecture in the land – was blasted by lightning and its transept gutted by fire. Reportedly the bolts of lightning came from out of a clear sky; so fierce were they, that the lightning conductors were overloaded.

Immediately the popular press pointed gleefully to the hand of God Himself as source of the miraculous lightning; and some traditionalist clergy endorsed this explanation of the meteorological hazard. The cathedral had been polluted by such an enthronement; here was God's sacred reaction. Yet God, of course, was also merciful. Having first set His house ablaze, He then permitted the massed fire brigades to quench the flames and save the majority of the edifice.

Liberal-minded churchmen issued statements explaining the fire as a coincidence, and deploring popular superstition. The same cathedral had, after all, been severely damaged by fire thrice already during its history – the most recent occasion, a hundred years earlier, being incidentally a case of arson provoked by another theological dispute.

Yet the noisiest single critic of the new bishop from amongst the ranks of ecclesiastics bitterly denounced such pussyfooting explanations. In disgust he publicly quit the English church and embraced the Greek Orthodox communion. The Greek Orthodox Church, as its name implied, was a staunch guardian of doctrine, ritual, and liturgy.

Some months later scandal struck again.

A radical-minded dean and lecturer in theology had been hired as presenter for a major new television series called *The Quest for God*. As the date for screening the first episode drew near, this dean revealed in interviews that he did not believe in an afterlife; nor in the Resurrection of Christ; nor for that matter did he even accept the 'objective' existence of a God. 'God' was a personal construct of the moral consciousness of humanity, said he.

A wave of protest arose.

And of course that first instalment of *The Quest for God* was blacked out nationwide by a lightning strike . . .

Of the industrial kind. TV engineers seized this opportunity to protest certain changes in their duty rosters.

The industrial dispute was soon settled; and two nights later the TV network transmitted the blacked episode in place of a football match. But by now newspaper headlines had trumpeted: *Lightning Strike Blacks Atheist Dean*. Even though the smaller print below explained the nature of this particular bolt from the blue, editorials in bolder black type suggested that God may move in a mysterious way His lightning to direct.

Such publicity hugely swelled the viewing figures for a programme which many people might otherwise have felt disposed to ignore; so much so that the 'atheist' Dean was obliged to preface his second prerecorded appearance one week later with a brief personal statement in which he quipped endearingly that if God did not exist, He could hardly have thought of a better way to draw the nation's attention to the quest for Him.

It was in this fraught climate that John Ingolby's book was published, surprising me (for one) by its title – then by its angle.

Religion and the History of Lighting: that was the title. The last word is quite easy to confuse with 'lightning'; and indeed the printers had done so at least a dozen times during the course of three hundred pages without John – with his poor eyesight – noticing the slight though substantial difference whilst he was correcting the proofs. However, this is a mere incidental irony. The primary shock of the book came from the manner in which, like some seventeenth-century metaphysical poem, it yoked together two apparently disparate things: a scholarly history of artificial lighting – and theological insights.

I admit that my first reaction was that an exuberant editor had persuaded John to rewrite his whole volume, giving it a new commerical slant.

Let's be honest. Suppose you happen to be an *aficionado* of beer-mats, then their history is a consuming passion – to yourself, and to a few hundred other like-minded enthusiasts. However, your *History of Beer-Mats* must inevitably lack the kind of popular charisma which sells a million copies.

Likewise with the history of lighting.

Blazing sticks in Neolithic caves; grease and wick in a

bear skull; Phoenician candles of yarn and beeswax; Roman tallow lamps; Elizabethan lanthorns; candles of spermaceti scented with bay-berry; rushlights; Herr Wintzler's lighting up of Pall Mall with gas; Welsbach's incandescent mantle; De la Rue's dim electric light of 1820; Sir Joseph Swan's carbonized cotton filaments; Humphrey Davy's carbon arc; Edison at Menlo Park; mercury vapour; neon; acetylene . . . Fascinating stuff! Yet how many of the general public would wish to read three hundred pages about it?

John set the tone from the very outset. 'We wanted light,' he wrote, 'so that we should not feel afraid . . .' He went on to parallel advances in religious awareness with the developing technology of artificial lighting: from early shamanism to paganism, from the 'light of the world', Christianity, to medieval mysticism, from the Dark Ages to the modern enlightenment of radical theology. He suggested a direct link between the two: with lighting influencing religious beliefs, and religious beliefs influencing the technology of light.

John made great play with the fitful glimmering of candles and the haunting, soul-like shadows which flitted around rooms as a result; with the smokiness of oil lamps and the bonfires of the Inquisition; with the softly restful, comparatively brilliant glass chimney lamp of Swiss chemist Aimé Argand which climaxed the Age of Reason; with the clear steady paraffin lamp of Victorian pragmatic Christianity.

He harvested a rare crop of quotations to prove his point, from such authorities as Saint Augustine and Meister Eckhart, Jakob Boehme and Kierkegaard, Tillich and Hans Küng. His chapter on medieval stained glass and the visionary cult of the millennium was masterly, and prefaced – anachronistically, I thought at first – by this famous passage from Shelley:

> Life, like a dome of many-coloured glass,
> Stains the white radiance of Eternity . . .

Then the finale to the chapter completed the quotation (which not many people know beyond its first two lines); and I understood.

> . . . Until Death tramples it to fragments.

And what of late twentieth-century lighting – not to mention fibre optics, laser beams, and holography – and the new radical, atheistic, afterlifeless theology?

And what of the future? – a future which John saw as lying in the harnessing of 'cold light': the bioluminescence of bacteria, the phosphorescence of fireflies and the fish of the abyss, which generate an enormous amount of chemical light with minimal energy input, and without heat? What of the cold light of the next century which must surely follow on from the bright yet hot and kilowatt-consuming light of our present era? What of the theology of *that*?

My first assumption, as I say, was that the publisher had prevailed on John to jazz up his volume.

My second assumption, when I delved deeper into John's religious musings, was that he had decided to throw his cap into the ring of radical theology; that he had chosen to run up his colours as one of the avant-garde of the Church.

Or had he? Or rather, on whose behalf was he running up his colours?

During the many years that I had known John – since college days, a time of life when brainstorming sessions are quite common – he had never to my knowledge spoken heatedly about the validity of the virgin birth, or of Christ's dead body walking around, or of the afterlife, or of a God in Heaven; or any of the crunch points of the new clear-vision theology which was even then taking shape. Indeed I felt that John had entered the Church largely as a reliable career – one in which he thought he would excel, since he was a good Latin and Greek scholar, but one in which his actual belief was nominal.

Let me be more specific. John did not doubt his vocation; but nor did he question it. He was more like a younger son of the eighteenth or nineteenth centuries to whom becoming a clergyman was a matter of course; and like several such who became better known as naturalists or geologists or amateur astronomers John had his own parallel, genuine passion – namely the history of lighting.

John's father had been a vicar. His uncle was a bishop. The step was natural; advancement was likely. Without a doubt John was good-hearted; and was to prove excellent at pastoral duties. Whilst at college he involved himself in running a boys' club, and in serving hot soup to tramps of a winter's night. However, he seemed uninterested in theological disputes as such.

Could it be that John was deeply traditional at heart – and that his book was in fact a parody of the new rational theology? A spoof, a satire? Was he intending to pull the carpet out from under the feet of the church's intellectuals – like some Voltaire, but on the other side of the fence?

Had he been so annoyed in his quiet way by the new trends in theology that he had sacrificed to God all of his private research work into the history of lighting – his consuming hobby – so that by using it satirically he could defend the faith?

Would he watch and assess reactions to his book, then announce that *Religion and the History of Lighting* was in fact a holy joke? One intended to demonstrate the credulity of unbelief? To show up the trendy emptiness of today's scientific theology?

Or was John Ingolby entirely innocent of such guile?

Was he a true innocent: the stuff of saints and geniuses and the dangerously naïve?

Or was he simply short-sighted and afflicted with a species of tunnel vision which had compressed his two diverse occupations – the Church, and the history of lighting – absurdly yet persuasively into the selfsame field of view? Maybe!

At any rate, in the wake of the cathedral fire and the televised *Quest for God* the publicity department of John's publisher dangled his newly-minted book under the noses of the media; and the media gladly took the bait.

Here was more 'new theology' from a bishop; more (apparently) rational probing of 'superstition' as a kind of slowly vanishing shadow cast by improving human technology, a function of blazing brands and paraffin lamps and neon and lasers; and an analysis of mystical insight as an analogue of candlepower and lumens – with the possibility, thrown in, of new illuminations just around the corner.

And did not Bishop Ingolby's book have something to say (at first glance) about holy lightning? Lightning which suddenly was humanized – into the sodium-vapour lamps on motorways, the neon strips over shop fronts – by the deletion of a single letter, 'n', like the removal by a clever trick of an unknowable infinity from an equation?

Yet – to reinject a note of mystery – did not the possibility of cold light remain? Here, John's fancy soared poetically.

The newspapers excelled themselves. Bishop Ingolby was a debunker – and should be defrocked forthwith! Bishop Ingolby was a scientific mystic, striving to yoke technology to divinity! He was this. He was that.

Certainly he suddenly became notorious. *Religion and the History of Lighting* sold a lot of copies; a good few, no doubt, were read.

T-shirts appeared bearing the icon of a light bulb on

them, and the legend: *S.O. & S.* Switch On, & See. (With a punning undercurrent of Save Our Souls.) These T-shirts seemed as urgent and arbitrary as their sartorial predecessors which had instructed people to RELAX! or FIGHT! or BREATHE!

Switch On, & See. But see what? See that there was nothing in the darkness of the universe? Or that there was everything? Or that there was something unforeseen?

Thus, by way of prologue to the strange and terrible events which happened subsequently . . .

The 'Bishop's Palace' in Porchester is, in actuality, a large Georgian house set in modest grounds of lawn and shrubbery standing midway between the railway station and the ruins of Porchester Castle. The west wing of the building was devoted to the administration of the diocese. The east wing was John's own domain, where the domestic arrangements were in the hands of a housekeeper, Mrs Mott, who arrived every morning bright and early and departed every evening after dinner; for John had never married.

Most of the domestic arrangements were Mrs Mott's province: cookery and cleaning, laundry and such. The lighting styles of the various rooms in the east wing were John's own choice; and it was in this respect that one half of his palace resembled a living museum.

The kitchen was lit by electric light bulbs; the small private chapel by massive candles; the dining-room by gas mantles; the library by brilliant neon strips. Innumerable unused lighting devices stood, or hung, around: Roman pottery oil lamps, miners' safety lamps, perforated West Indian gourds designed to house fireflies . . .

When I arrived to visit John at his urgent request on that early November evening several months after publication of his book, the whole of the east wing which met my gaze was lit up in its assorted styles, with no curtains

closed. As I walked the few hundred yards from the
railway station, a couple of anticipatory rockets whizzed
up into the sky over Porchester and exploded, showering
orange stars. This was the day before the country's children would celebrate the burning at the stake of the
Catholic Guy Fawkes for trying to blow up a Protestant
Parliament – an earlier religious feud. John seemed, meanwhile, to be conducting his own festival of light.

I . . .

But I haven't mentioned who I am, beyond the fact that
I was at college with John a good many years ago.

My name is Morris Ash, and I am a veterinary surgeon
turned homeopathist. I live in Brighton, and cater to the
more prosperous sectors of society. My degree was in
Biochemistry, and I had originally thought of going into
medical research. A certain disenchantment with my
fellow human beings – coupled with dawning ecological
awareness of the soaring world population and the degra-
dation of the natural environment – had shunted me into
veterinary studies.

I had done well in my profession, though I never
practised to any great extent rurally with sheep and horses
and cows, which may seem a contradiction (of which life
is full). I had become an up-market urban vet, doggy
doctor, a pussy physician, renowned among my patients'
owners for my compassionate bedside (or basket-side)
manner.

Twenty years on, I had five partners working with me
(and for me); and was more of a consultant in difficult
cases than a routine castrator of tom-kittens. My thoughts
turned once more to biochemistry and to medical research,
but with a difference: I interested myself in homeopathy,
in the theory of treating disease by means of minuscule,
highly diluted doses of substances which would ordinarily
cause disease. I began to investigate the possibility of
treating animal ailments likewise, and within a few years I

was supplying a wide range of home-made homeopathic remedies to the pets of my clientele, should the owners prefer this approach – and a gratifying number did. Homeopathy worked startlingly well in a number of recalcitrant cases; and word of my success spread quickly. I soon found that I was treating my erstwhile patients' owners homeopathically, too – though not, I hasten to add, for mange or distemper!

Now, there's nothing illegal in this. You need no medical qualifications to practise as a homeopathic doctor; and it's a curious fact, as I discovered, that a good few human beings would rather have their ills tended to by a vet than by an orthodox doctor.

A doctor is often cursory, reaching quickly for his prescription pad to scribble upon it in illegible Latin. A doctor is frequently inclined to treat his human patients as examples of blocked plumbing, or as broken-down cars – this is the common complaint by patients. Whereas a vet must always fondle and gentle his patients (or else the vet is likely to be scratched, bitten, and kicked). A vet seems more sensual, more full of curative love. He is seen to cure – to a certain extent – by a laying on of hands, whereas a medical doctor metaphorically jabs a fist into you.

Also, people might prefer to confide in a vet because his trade isn't viewed as a mysterious Freemasonry. A vet has no cryptic knowledge or secret records.

Finally, the doctor appears to have the power of life or death over you; yet he will never exercise the power of death mercifully. Indeed the law forbids him to do so. Death can only come after a long, humiliating, and dehumanizing process of medical intervention which often seems experimental to the wasting patient and his relatives. The vet *does* possess the power of instant death. He can give lethal mercy injections to distempered puppies or crushed cats. Yet it is the instant *mercy* of this, not the lethal aspect, which is noted primarily.

(Did I mention love? I have admitted that I did not overly love my fellow human beings compared with the furry and feathered folk of the world. So in common with John – though for different reasons – I too never married. As a result, to many pet-owning widowed ladies I seemed impeccably . . . shall we say, eligible? Which was perhaps another of my homeopathic attractions. I had diluted and rediluted my spouse potential over the years till I became, to some hearts, devastating.)

John and I had remained firm friends for many years – as I say – and we met perhaps thrice every year, one of these occasions invariably being our college reunion supper; the other occasions variable. We seemed to have much in common. We were both confirmed bachelors. As regards charitable acts John perceived me as a kind of lay St Francis of Assisi, ministering to the world's chihuahuas and gerbils. I had told John, at some stage, all I knew about the enzyme-catalysed chemical reactions which coldly light up fireflies, deep-sea fish, bacteria, and fungi; and how one day we might learn to light our homes and cities similarly – information which had surfaced, theologically mutated, in his book . . .

I was welcomed to the palace. We drank excellent pale sherry. We spoke of homeopathy. We talked of John's book and of its lightning success (*de scandale*). He mentioned an upcoming television interview to be filmed in his variously lit home, during the course of which he would stride from room to room and thus from firelight era to neon era, expounding, concluding his performance in the candle-lit chapel; but he was rather vague about these plans.

I tentatively broached the puzzle (to me) of the true intention of his book. Surely an old and discreet friend was privileged to know – especially since I myself had no religious axes to grind? John sidetracked me, to admire a

lanthorn from Shakespeare's day which he had recently
bought at auction and which now adorned the mantel shelf
of his lounge.

Then Mrs Mott served us dinner in the next room, to
faintly hissing gaslight.

It was a tasty meal but a queer one. We commenced
with *escargots* and giant champignons, both cooked in
butter; and John obviously had some difficulty distinguish-
ing which of the spheres were snails, and which were
mushrooms. He attempted to slice through one snail shell
and then to prick out the meat from within a mushroom.
Had he commanded this menu as a deliberate tease to his
bespectacled self?

A turbot steak in béchamel sauce followed. Next, in
sentimental homage to a shared taste from our student
days when we had both patronized the same cheap whole-
some dive of a café, we tucked into tripe and onions
accompanied by mashed potatoes.

Afterwards, came a meringue concoction; followed by
a slab of Wensleydale cheese, and white coffee.

Mrs Mott departed homeward, leaving us alone.

It occurred to me that the whole meal had been white,
or at least creamy-grey in colour; and served upon white
plates. Even the wine we drank with it was Liebfraumilch
– 'milk of a beloved woman' – not that I should have
fancied a robust Burgundy as accompaniment to the meat
dish in question! Had we drunk Burgundy or some other
red wine, it might have looked as though our glasses had
miraculously filled with the blood so visibly absent from
that part of the cow's anatomy.

An all-white dinner. Why?

Had Mrs Mott gone mad?

'Will you pour the port?' asked my host; and I obliged.
The port, at least, was a rich purple-red; a contrast on
which I forbore, for the moment, to comment, though
my curiosity was by now intense.

John tasted his wine, then at last confided in a low voice, 'I'm going blind, Morris. Blind.'

'Blind?' I repeated the word stupidly. I stared at John's round, rosy face and at the thick round spectacles thereon, which from some angles made his eyes seem to bulge. His cheeks were faintly pocked: a bad reaction to a childhood bout of measles, which I knew had nearly killed him and which had certainly impaired his eyesight. The dome of his head was mostly bald and smooth. His skin, and remaining strands of hair, were somewhat greasy. A lot of talcum powder would need to be patted on to him prior to any television appearance; or else he would seem shiny on screen.

I decided that it was high time to broach the matter of the meal – without insulting it, however, since my taste buds had relished every morsel even if my eyes had not had much to feast on.

'Er, John . . . the dinner we just ate . . . splendid fare! Mrs Mott is to be congratulated. But, hmm, there wasn't a scrap of colour in it. Everything was white from start to finish. White food on white plates. Highly ingenious! But, um, that doesn't mean that you're going blind – just because you couldn't see any colours. There weren't any to be seen.'

John uttered a few staccato laughs.

'Oh Morris, I *know* that!' he declared. 'Mrs Mott has always been a great admirer of yours. The white dinner was in your honour.'

'Was it? Why's that? I don't quite follow.'

'You see, that's her understanding of how homeopathy works. In this case, a homeopathic cure for failing vision. Take something as essential to the health of the body as a well-cooked meal. The smell and the taste play a major role in stimulating appetite. So does the look of the meal: the contrasts, the colours.'

'Oh, I see! Mrs Mott imagines that by reducing the colour content to almost nothing – '

'Just as the homeopath reduces the drug content of a medicine virtually to nothing, by repeated dilution. Exactly!'

' – thereby your visual faculty will be stimulated, rather than dulled? Your brain will strain to discriminate the tiny traces of colour remaining? My word, what an imagination that woman has.'

'The white dinner was also served as a broad hint in case I didn't bring myself to ask your help, Morris.'

Ah.

Now I could put two and two together.

Here was another instance where someone hoped for medical advice from a vet rather than from a doctor. A vet who was a close friend. A vet, moreover, who had no special bigoted axes to grind regarding a certain radical bishop who had reduced the visions of the saints to an absence of adequate light-bulbs.

Doctors often had axes to grind. My patients' owners had complained to me thus more than once. Male doctors – most are male – harboured gynaecological obsessions, obsessions about the 'hysteria' of female patients. They nursed obsesssions about plumbing and pills and tranquil-lizers. They held political views, often of a right-wing stripe, which they allowed to colour their medical person-alities. Or else they had religious obsessions – about, say, birth control or woman's role as a mother. There was no such thing as an objective doctor. Personal beliefs and prejudices always flavoured diagnosis and treatment. By contrast veterinarians could easily be objective – and at the same time loving – because (to put it bluntly and very generally) animals had no politics, and no religion.

'What do you think's wrong with your eyes then, John old son? Cataracts?'

John emptied his glass of port, as though to fortify himself.

'I'm going blind within,' he said. *'Blind within'*.

'Now what do you mean by that?'

'The blindness is like a shadow inside of me. This inner shadow is spreading. It's growing outward, ever outward.'

I thought for a moment. 'I'm no eye specialist,' I said, 'but it sounds to me – if you're describing this correctly – as though your optic nerves are inflamed. The pressure of the swelling could make the nerves atrophy gradually. The blind spot would seem to enlarge. Part of the retina would go blind.'

John shivered. 'It's more than that.' He struck his forehead a blow. 'This blindness has taken root inside me like some foul black weed!' His voice faltered and hushed. 'It's because of my book, don't you see?'

'*What?*'

'I've prayed, of course. One does. I pray on my own in the chapel every morning for half an hour. Prayer clears the mind. The day organizes itself. Not that I pray for myself personally! I pray that the whole world shall see the light of goodness.' John seemed embarrassed. He had never mentioned private prayer to me before. 'Meanwhile my own light grows dim. *Vilely* so.'

'In what way "vilely", John?'

'There's a taint of corruption to this blindness. A moral miasma is creeping around in me, spreading its tendrils.'

'You blame this on the publication of your book? It's as though you're being . . . punished?' I refilled his glass from the decanter. 'I hate to say this, John, but a tumour is a remote possibility. If a tumour presses upon the visual centres of your brain there could be emotional repercussions. You might even sense the tumour as something dark and evil growing inside your head.'

'Oh no I wouldn't. If I had a tumour, I would suffer

from a steady grinding headache for at least a few hours every day. Every now and then I might see complex hallucinatory patterns; or else an aura of flashing lights. You might suddenly look like an angel to me! Or Mrs Mott might. I *do* have a number of books in my library which aren't about technology or theology. Medical books. I've checked up on tumours. I've checked up on eye troubles – I can still read, with spotlight and magnifying glass. Under normal circumstances what afflicts me would most likely be what is known as toxic amblyopia.'

'Ah. Really? You'd better explain. Obviously I'm not the best fellow to hold a consultation with!'

'Oh but you are. Now listen, will you? Toxic amblyopia involves a reduction in the acuteness of vision due to a toxic reaction of the optic nerve. I have the symptoms of this exactly. The *commonest* cause is overindulgence in alcohol or tobacco. But I don't smoke; and I don't ordinarily overimbibe. Quinine can also cause the condition; but I've never been near the tropics. I'm not one of your malarial missionaries of yesteryear. Other causes are prolonged exposure to various poisons, principally carbon dioxide, arsenic, lead, and benzene. One thought immediately springs to mind: am I being poisoned by these gaslights in here, or perhaps by the candles in the chapel? By something in this very palace which is directly connected with my hobby-horse? That would be ironic, don't you think?'

'Maybe you've already solved the puzzle, John.' In which case why had I been invited? And why had Mrs Mott cooked the all-white repast?

My friend shook his head. 'I've had the gas-mantles checked. They're perfectly safe. As for the chapel, ever since I began to suspect candles as possible sinners I've only lit one on each occasion. No remission! I've thought carefully of every other oddity of lighting. All systems are innocent. And my vision is getting worse. The affliction has no cause; unless of course it has a miraculous cause. Miraculous,' he repeated quietly, 'or demonish. It's a sort of slow, black lightning.'

'But John, you yourself wrote that demons have no more substance than shadows cast by candles. You don't believe in demons.'

'Ah . . . suppose for a moment that demons exist. I feel somewhat haunted, Morris.'

'You're joking.'

I could see that he was not entirely joking.

'Don't bishops know how to deal with demons?' I asked him.

'Hmm. I should need to involve a colleague from within the Church. Word would inevitably leak out. Likewise, were I to start consulting eye specialists. Embarrassing, don't you see? Embarrassing to the Church! If I tried to arrange for the exorcism of a geniune – if troublesome – miracle, why, that would be worse. I should be attempting to cast God out of my life.'

'Time to wheel on the homeopathic vet, eh?'

'I could do worse. At least I can discuss the ins and outs of this with you. Mrs Mott's quite right on that score.'

As we talked, a certain suspicion began to dawn on me; a suspicion which I hardly dared put to John outright.

John had said that arsenic could cause toxic amblyopia.

Was it possible that Mrs Mott was slowly poisoning John? Since white is the colour of innocence, did her white meal that evening protest symbolically that she was innocent? But why should she protest innocence unless she knew her own guilt?

Why should Mrs Mott have encouraged John to seek my advice? Perhaps she did not admire me at all, and actually regarded me as a charlatan whose advice would lead John far astray and keep him away from doctors.

John depended upon Mrs Mott. He trusted her implicitly. Dared I cast any shadow of doubt upon their relationship? And what could the woman's motive possibly be? An inheritance – of a load of peculiar lighting apparatus? (The Palace certainly didn't belong to him!) Inheritance of royalties from his book? Those could hardly amount to a fortune.

Finally I decided to take the plunge.

To sugar the pill, I chuckled. 'Speaking of phosphorescence,' I said (though we hadn't been, for a while), 'in the old days phosphorus was often used as a poison because it's difficult to detect. Some phosphorus occurs naturally in the body. There's a famous case in which one intended victim was alerted when he noticed his bowl of soup glowing while he was carrying it to table along a dark corridor!'

'Hmm,' said John without more ado, 'so why should Mrs Mott wish to poison me?'

'I didn't mean to imply – '

'Oh yes you did. Tiny doses of an arsenic compound, eh? A little bite of rat-killer day by day. In rather more than a homeopathic dose! She has no earthly motive.'

'Maybe she has an unearthly one?'

'Explain.'

'Maybe she regards your book as, um, blasphemous. Maybe she believes you're in league with the Antichrist.'

'Mrs Mott? I hardly think so! Do you?'

I thought about the comfy, devoted, cheery soul in question; and shook my head.

That night as I lay on the verge of sleep in John's great oaken guest-bed, my mind wandered back to the story of the phosphorescent soup. A soup bowl aglow in a dark corridor . . .

> Is this a tureen which I see before me,
> The ladle towards my hand? Art thou lobster bisque,
> Vichyssoise, or plain beef broth with arsenic?

Art thou not, fatal bouillon, sensible
To tasting as to sight? Or art thou but
A potage of the mind?

I don't know quite why I decided to get up out of my warm bed to roam the November-chilly Bishop's Palace at midnight. Maybe I had some notion that in the pitch-dark kitchen I would spy some spice jar glowing phosphorescently, betraying the true poisonous nature of its contents. But get up I did, shuffling my slippers on by feel and belting my dressing gown about me, then proceeding to the door with hands outstetched.

I didn't use my pocket torch, nor had I opened the curtains. I knew that it was a dark, moonless night outside but I wanted my eyes to retain the sensitivity of a cat so that the tiniest dose of light might register.

I felt my way along the upstairs corridor, tiptoeing past John's room next to mine, though I had little reason to fear that my faint footfalls – or the noisier creaking of the boards – might disturb him. John had long since told me that he invariably slept the sleep of the dead. As soon as his head touched the pillow he became a log until dawn.

Still, the bathroom was in the opposite direction. How could I explain my nocturnal perambulation?

To cut the story of a long prowl short, I fumbled my way to the kitchen – then to all the other downstairs rooms, and even the chapel. Nowhere did I spy anything unusual.

The chapel was bitterly cold, but the chill I experienced was innocuous – winter was to blame. Unless a thermostat switched some heater on in the early morning John's half-hour of prayer must have been something of a penance. Supposedly there's another species of chill which runs down spines and makes dogs howl like banshees. Yet if it was devilish cold in John's chapel, I'm sure the Devil had no hand in hypothermia, no finger in frigidity.

I returned upstairs, only stubbing my toe once.

In the darkness of the upper corridor I miscalculated distances. I twisted a brass doorknob. It wasn't my own bedroom door that I opened – it was John's.

I realized my mistake at once because a ring of light illuminated the head of the bed, showing me John's face asleep beneath. He was wearing, of all things, a woolly nightcap with a big pompon which Mrs Mott must have knitted for him.

The ring of light was no wider than his head, over which it seemed to perch. Though my eyes were well accommodated to night vision, the light wasn't brilliant. But it clearly showed me John's slumbering countenance, and outlined the bed. Obviously the light was some reflection or refraction from outside, through the bedroom window. Perhaps of a powerful arc-lamp at the railway station?

I made my way to the window to check; but the heavy curtains were closed tight without a chink.

> I saw Eternity the other night
> Like a great Ring of pure and endless light . . .

There was no other glimmer in the room itself. No movement of mine dimmed or shadowed the ring of pearly light. Thoughts of Mrs Mott as purveyor of phosphorus soup flew out of the window (or would have done so, had the window offered any way in or out). I could pretend no longer. I *knew* what I was seeing.

Above John's head, as he slept, hung a halo.

A halo such as saints wear in paintings.

Not so bright, perhaps! Not a radiant glory. A modest halo, which wouldn't even be visible if other light competed. But a halo nonetheless.

John's head was snuggled in a fat pillow. The halo was tilted across his face. I stretched out a cautious finger to touch the apparition.

Perhaps this was foolhardy of me, but I suffered no consequences. I felt no buzz, no shock, no warmth. The thing couldn't be an odd form of ball lightning, or St Elmo's fire.

I swept my hand right through the halo, without effect. Then I shook John's shoulder.

'Wake up, old son! Wake up, will you?'

Eventually I roused him.

'House on fire? Burglars? What's the time?'

'No, no, no. None of that. Sit up.'

As he sat up, the halo shifted position so that it was poised above his nightcap.

'What's up, Morris? Where's my torch?' (John's bedroom was equipped with nineteenth-century carriage lamps.)

I gripped his wrist. 'No – no torch! Is there a mirror anywhere?'

'Inside the wardrobe.'

'Will you show me?'

Grumbling mildly, John got out of bed – the halo accompanying him – and soon he was pawing a wardrobe door open.

Now there were two haloes: one above John's head, and the other in the full-length mirror.

'Goodness, what's that light? I haven't got my glasses.'

'I'll fetch them. Where are they?'

'Table by the bed.'

I retrieved his spectacles and he put them on.

'Goodness!'

'Goodness indeed, John – by the looks of it! You're wearing a halo.'

He stepped to and fro. He swung his hand across his head. He pulled off his nightcap – as though I might have attached that ghostly glow as a joke.

'Oh dear me,' he said. 'My eyes aren't much use – but I

can see it. Dear me, I always thought there was something
frightfully priggish about haloes . . .'

'You must be becoming a saint, eh old son?'

'What, me? A saint? Don't be silly. Besides, saints never
had actual rings of light over their heads! That's just an
artistic convention. A way of picturing saints.'

'Maybe some saints had actual haloes – ones which
people could see? But not in recent history.'

'I think a halo would need to be brighter than mine, for
people to notice!'

'Maybe yours is just a baby halo. A young one.'

'Meaning that it'll grow stronger? As my eyes grow
dim? Let's light some lamps.'

My friend located his torch and went through the
rigmarole of getting carriage lamps to work. As the
illumination in the bedroom increased, so did his halo fade
away to a faint shimmer.

I sat on a chair; John perched on the bed.

'This is quite embarrassing,' he said. 'It's preposterous!
I can't possibly be a saint in the making. And what could
conceivably cause a halo?'

'*Grace*, perhaps, my Lord Bishop?'

'You don't believe that.'

'Any more than you believe it? I want to ask you, John:
did you write that book of yours to debunk radical
theology? Is the book a kind of holy offering – of
everything you cared deeply about – so that faith may be
sustained?'

'Gracious me, I don't think so. Morris, I've told you
that I feel an evil darkness spreading its shadow inside of
me. If I'm sprouting a halo, I assure you this is at the
expense of my soul! It isn't a spotlight to illuminate
saintliness.' He mused a while. 'How nice it would be to
imagine that it's some lamp of goodness. How nice to
visualize certain dim monasteries of the past as being
genuinely lit by sanctity – with a saint's head as a light

bulb! How lovely if cities of the future could be cold-lit by our own purity, should mankind perfect itself! Heaven would be radiant on account of its saints. Hell would be dingy-dark because of its sinners. That is emphatically *not* how I feel as this blindness eats up my vision.'

Eats up.

'Your halo is eating your eyesight . . . what could that mean? That the halo is some kind of organized energy? It needs energy to sustain itself; to grow . . .? Certain luminous deep-sea fish need to eat luminous plankton or else they stop glowing. And by glowing they attract their prey.'

'What are you trying to say, Morris?'

'Maybe this halo is some sort of creature – an animal not of blood and bone, but of energy. It's eating the photons that enter your eyes; or the electrical impulses in your optic nerves. That's why you're going blind. Your brain can sense it feeding inside you; consuming light, to produce light.'

'A parasite? Why should it generate a halo? Hmm, famous saints of the past haven't been noted for their blindness . . .'

'So haloes can't be the work of parasites, presumably.'

He shook his head in puzzlement. 'You mentioned luminous fish attracting prey. What *prey* would a saint attract to him? Why, the faithful. The credulous. Some sinners ripe for conversion. People who are religiously inclined. A halo might be God's fishing hook. It might be an angel that takes up residence, in order to angle for souls. And it drinks photons from the saint's eyes, to power the halo? I don't know, hagiographically, of many saints who had impaired vision!'

'Maybe there have only been a few true saints – whose haloes became legend? You're the next saint. The miracle for a godless age.'

'Are you *trying* to canonize me, Morris? You should be devil's advocate.'

'I'm only looking at the possibilities. Here's another one: maybe in the past there were more conduits to the divine light? The halo-angels didn't need to suck the vision from a saint. There were other sources of energy.'

'In that case why should I sense that my blindness is *evil*? Why should I feel such a lack of Grace?'

'I don't know.'

'When I become blind as a bat, does my halo glow with glory? Whose faith is being tested? The world's, or mine? Is this a test of faith at all – or is it the work of some vile parasitic creature from elsewhere, with its own motives? Is that what a miracle is: something you can't ever prove, but must take on trust, like God Himself? Even though you feel that you yourself are damned! Possessed!' He stretched out his hands towards me. 'If I beg you to cure me, Morris – God knows how! – do I damn myself? Should I let my halo strengthen and thus confirm the faith of millions of people – while I lose my own belief, sunk in my personal deep dark pit?'

'Maybe the thing will go away,' I said feebly. 'Maybe it'll fade, and your eyesight will improve.'

'Will you stay with me a few more days?'

'A week. Longer, if need be. Of course I will.'

He sighed. 'Thank you, Morris. Now you'd better go back to bed. And so shall I.' His bishop's authority suddenly blossomed. 'Be off with you, Morris! I shall extinguish the lanterns. I shan't toss and turn, or lie brooding.'

A week later I was still staying at the palace; and the halo was intensifying. I could see the ring of light above John's head in daylight or artificial lighting. My friend's eyesight had worsened drastically.

There was no question now of rushing him to an

optician's or to hospital. Moreover, John and I were in full agreement that Mrs Mott should be kept in the dark regarding the halo. I carried the meals she cooked to John's room on a tray, and cut up meat for him.

The Bishop was ill, incapacitated, and I was treating him – that was the story. He had a serious infection, though nothing dangerous or fatal. Mrs Mott only accepted the situation when John told her firmly, from the other side of his door, that this was so.

The business of the diocese was dealt with likewise. John's secretary took umbrage somewhat; he also wanted a 'genuine' doctor called to examine the Bishop. Through the wood of the door the Bishop overruled him loudly; and I witnessed an aspect of my friend which made me realize how he also had a tough streak – he hadn't become a bishop simply through a combination of good works and nepotism.

John's mind remained keen. The halo-creature which had infested my friend had no apparent ambition to speak through his lips, whisper words in his head, or influence his dreams.

But it brightened; how it brightened.

'Even when I become stone-blind,' John said to me, 'I'll not really be *blind*. It's just that all the light will be stolen to create my halo. And it won't be long till I'm stone-blind. Should we phone the television people, do you think? Tell them to rush here for a news conference? Should I display this miracle to the world? Should I say: *here* is God's lightning? It doesn't strike the transepts of cathedrals. It circles about my head calmly and brightly – while *I* dwell in a pit of mud for evermore, as if in Dante's *Inferno*.

'Should I say: behold the cold light of the future, of the next age of belief? I bear it as my cross – or rather, my circle, my ring of Peter, my *annulus angeli*. Yet I know that my angel is dark. It only glows by theft, by a vampirism of light. So how can it be from God? This has destroyed my faith in God as surely as it has destroyed my sight. If this thing is God's punishment, then maybe I should damn God! If it is His blessing: likewise! And if it's sent by the Devil, why then the world will never be perfected. We will never be enlightened.'

'Maybe,' I suggested, 'you need a spiritual adviser rather than a homeopathic vet?'

He shook his head brusquely; the halo remained steady. '*I* . . . must . . . decide. Only I know what it is like to be me at this time.'

And decide he did – in the most gruesome manner . . .

A distant cry clawed me out of sleep.

I flipped on my own bedside torch (absolute prerequisite in this palace where lighting systems varied from the latest to the least of technologies!). It was five thirty A.M. by my watch. The world was still deep in darkness. Had I heard an owl screech in the frosty castle ruins?

'Morris!'

My friend's voice came from far away.

I found him in the chapel. All the candles were lit. He knelt before the little altar. By him on the flagstone lay a bloodstained bread-knife. Blood ran down his cheeks – down a ghastly empty face. On the altar cloth, staring at the silver cross, perched his two eyeballs.

In moments of horror it's odd what petty details you notice. I noticed that John had used a bread-knife – with a sawtooth edge and a rounded end. The rounded end, to spring his eyeballs loose. The saw, to sever the optic nerves.

Maybe this wasn't such a petty detail. It proved how much forethought had gone into his mutilation of himself.

His blind, unblinking eyes stared moistly at the sign of Christ. Above his head in the light of so many candles the halo could hardly be seen.

'Is that you there, Morris?' His voice spoke pain.

'Yes.'

'Has the damned thing gone yet?'

'I think it's fading. Oh John, *John!*'

Fading, fading fast. By the time the ambulance arrived no halo was visible.

Needless to say I accompanied him to the hospital. By the time a doctor could assure me that John was resting comfortably, sedated, a detective inspector and two other officers had arrived at St Luke's anxious to speak to me. The ambulance men had radioed a report; the police had hurried to the Palace, arriving shortly before Mrs Mott. They had seen the bloody bread-knife and the eyes perched upon the altar. It must have looked like a sadistic crime performed by a madman, me.

Fortunately I hadn't touched the knife.

During the hours of questions until John recovered from sedation I learnt how the thought processes of the police resemble those of our more disgraceful tabloid newspapers. This should hardly have surprised me, since to a large extent both share the same contents. The Detective Inspector spent ages pursuing the notion that Bishop Ingolby and I, both bachelors, might have been homosexually involved since college days; thus the atrocity was the product of a vicious sexual quarrel, possibly with aspects of blackmail attached – the Bishop was a famous man now, was he not?

Even after John woke up and exonerated me the Detective Inspector was loath to discard his suspicions. After all, the Bishop might be trying to cover up for me; and for himself as well. My fingerprints weren't on the handle of the knife; only John's were present, and Mrs Mott's beneath. But I might have worn gloves.

Perhaps I oughtn't to blame the police. They must have

been well aware that I was lying – and later that John also was lying about a motive for the mutilation.

The one 'sure' fact relayed by Mrs Mott – namely that the Bishop feared he was going blind – seemed not so sure in view of John's doctor knowing nothing of this; nor the diocesan secretary either.

And in what mad emotional equation did fear of impending blindness lead to the wanton gouging out of one's eyes?

In a sense it was the gutter press which came to our rescue. Tipped off either by police or by ambulance men, newshounds descended on Porchester. To them the vital fact was that the eyes of John Ingolby – sceptical author of *Religion and the History of Lighting* – had been placed on the altar of God. What else could they be but an offering?

Thus the press added two and two together and made four. Whereas the real answer was some entirely irrational number. Or maybe a zero: the mysterious zero of the halo.

'Why did you really put your eyes on the altar, John?'

Two weeks had passed. John was back home in the palace, convalescing. He wouldn't remain at the Palace much longer; the Archbishop's personal assistant was pressing for John's resignation, rather urgently, on compassionate grounds.

By that hour Mrs Mott had departed. So had John's doctor who had called to inspect the eye sockets and change the dressings. We were alone in the palace together, John and I. How like the evening of my arrival; except that John wore a blindfold now. Except that we had eaten an ordinary dinner of brown beef, green cabbage, and golden roast potatoes.

'Why, John?'

'Well, what do you think? I've always been a tidy fellow. Where else should I have put them? Down on the floor? I didn't want anyone to stand on them and squash them!'

'That's the only reason? Tidiness?'

'I had to tidy up, Morris. I had to tidy up more than merely my eyes. You know that.'

'I suppose so . . . Will you accept artificial eyes? Glass, plastic, whatever?'

He laughed wryly. 'From artificial lighting – to artificial eyes! A logical progression, if an unenlightening one. Yes, I should think that glass eyes would be harmless enough. If not, they're a lot easier to get rid of! Just flush them down the toilet.'

'You're a brave soul, John. A true saint: a gentleman and a martyr – an unacknowledged one.'

'Let's hope I remain unacknowledged.'

Yes, he was a gentleman – of the old school of English gentlemen who produced many Anglican parsons and bishops in the past. In common with such he disliked hysteria, enthusiasm, and excess. He had performed that savage operation of optectomy (if that's the word) to root out a hysteria which was alien to him, but which might have spread outward in shock waves from his halo. He had carried this out in the cold light of dawn (almost), and certainly he had applied the cold light of reason – so that the future might be reasonable.

For sanity's sake he had denied himself any future glimpse of light, natural or artificial.

In my eyes this truly made him a saint. And a martyr too, even though he hadn't died. I alone knew this; yet how could I ever tell anybody?

John Ingolby had written a final, definitive, unpublishable chapter to his life's work – using not a pen but a bread-knife. Every time I sliced a loaf of bread in future I would feel that I was performing an act of anti-communion. A refusal to accept the unacceptable.

I felt that more than a mere bishop was on the point of

retirement in Porchester. So too was an enfeebled diluted God, whose last miracle had been rejected because it would harm the world, not help it. Just as it had harmed John.

'I'm donating my collection to Porchester Museum,' he told me. 'After I've moved out of here there'll be thoroughly modern lighting in every room.' He sounded as if he was choking.

'Are you all right, old friend?'

'I'm weeping, Morris. And I can't ever weep. Except inside.'

'Maybe God had nothing to do with any of this!' I spoke to encourage him. 'Maybe the halo-parasite was something else entirely. A visitor from elsewhere in the universe. A life-form we know nothing of. You felt it was evil, remember? It might have been natural – or devilish. Aren't angels supposed to announce themselves?'

'*I* felt it was evil,' he replied. '*I* did. Nobody else who saw my round, benevolent face with a lustrous halo perched above could possibly have imagined evil. They would only have seen the light of goodness shining forth. Mine was the evil, don't you see? *Don't you see?*' And tearlessly he wept.

Or at least I suppose he was tearless. He hadn't actually carved out his tear ducts. But no welling tears would leave his cheeks. Tears would drain into the empty sockets. I didn't press for details of how an eyeless man weeps.

I did my best to comfort him.

There was I, sitting in a convivially lit room; whereas he was sitting in darkness. Darkness, always. Forever haunted by the night which had overtaken him.

Just thirty months later the announcement has come, from Matsuya Biotechnic KK of Japan, of the development of artificial bionic eyes which can be plugged into the optic nerves.

Matsuya Biotechnic's de luxe model improves upon our

ordinary visual organs of muscle, jelly, and liquid amazingly. With tiny touch controls (hidden by the eyelid) these Japanese eyes can be adjusted to range into the infrared; to magnify telescopically; and to peer owl-like on the darkest night.

The world's armed forces are very interested; though there's one small snag. To use Matsuya Eyes first you need to have your own eyes amputated.

In the two years gone by I must have visited John almost a dozen times at his retirement cottage in a little village near Porchester, where Mrs Mott continued to care for him; and I knew how he was suffering.

Not pain – but anguish.

Not poverty – his book had sold massively in paperback and in foreign editions in the wake of his self-blinding – but claustrophobia of the spirit.

John had been fitted with false plastic eyeballs which were most convincing. The blue pupils were holographically etched so that the eyes looked twinklingly alive, more so at times than real eyes.

He phoned me a fortnight ago.

'I'm going to buy a pair of these new Matsuya eyes,' he told me. 'Assuming that their experts can summon up the nerve to fit them!' He laughed sharply. 'The optic nerve, I mean. Just so long as there's enough optic nerve still alive and kicking in my head. I can't take any more of this hellish darkness, Morris. The halo-creature must have died ages ago. Given up; gone home – whatever halo-creatures do when their host starves them out.'

We had spoken much about the 'halo-creature', John and I.

An angel? A demon? An extraterrestrial life-form? Or a creature from some other universe entirely – from some other mode of existence – which had strayed across the boundary from its reality into ours?

The creature wasn't necessarily intelligent. It might have

been no brighter, intellectually, than a fish of the abyss or a firefly.

Maybe it was a parasite upon some alien beings who had visited our world in secret; and it had escaped. Did it convey some advantage upon such hypothetical alien beings? Or was it just an inconvenience to them – a sort of common cold, a bug of the eyes? The evil which John had sensed might well have been the quality of alienness rather than some moral, metaphysical pang.

We had gradually settled on a naturalistic explanation, though without any actual notion of the natural history of the beast involved. Certainly a parasite which blinded its host and lit up a beacon above its head didn't seem very survival-minded. But maybe in this respect John was a South Sea Islander infected by European mumps or measles.

Or at least, *I* had settled upon this solution. John still spoke of hellish darkness.

Now technology would save him by banishing that darkness – just as improved artificial lighting had progressively banished spooks and spirits, devils and gods, lumen by lumen, century by century.

'I've been in touch with the Japanese trade people in London,' he said. 'Matsuya are going to fly a couple of their surgeons, and a pair of eyes, over the Pole. It's good publicity for their company. You could say I've been pulling strings. In ten days' time they can pull mine, inside my head, and see whether those still work. If all goes well, I should be home with my new eyes in a couple of weeks. *Jubilate!*'

All has indeed gone well.

John Ingolby can see again. He can see far better than ever he saw before in all his life. He can see better than almost all of the human race – unless they've had nature's optics removed and bionic eyes substituted.

The newly-revealed world comes as a revelation to him. My face, unseen these last two years, is a mystic vision. So too is Mrs Mott. Likewise her cottage garden of herbs and flowers.

Likewise the night-time which he can pierce with ease, seeing monochrome hills and trees and cows and hedges, the stars above drilling a thousand bright little lamp-holes.

Likewise the heat-image of the world at dawn with those same cows appearing as vivid red humps in the cool blue fields, leaving faint rosy footsteps behind them in the dew. A bird is a flaming meteor.

Such beauty redeems John's soul. His new eyes look less human than the plastic ones; they're silver-grey and at some angles seem like mirrors in his head. But that's of no account.

'John – '

It's the second night of my visit, and we have stepped outside to star-gaze. Mrs Mott has already retired early to bed.

'It's back, John.'

'Eh?'

'Your halo: it's showing faintly.'

'Don't joke, Morris.'

'I'm not joking. I can *see* it.'

He hurries closer to the cottage and peers in a curtained window-pane. Everything is much more visible to him. His reflection there confirms my word.

'Oh my God. So it wasn't living in my eyes and feeding on the photons. It was in my brain all the time. It's been lying dormant like a frozen virus. The light has brought it back to life. Oh my God. These Matsuya eyes are permanent. I can't pull them out when I feel like it . . .'

'And you can't switch them off?'

'Why should anybody want to switch their eyes off? When I go to bed, my eyelids do the job. An on-off button would be one control too many. It's early days yet for bionic eyes.'

He tells me how Matsuya Biotech KK boast that future bionic eyes will have computerized display functions activated by voice command, with memory chips located in a unit which might be surgically implanted behind the ear or in the jaw. Owners of Matsuya eyes will be able to call up statistics, run graphics across their field of view, access encyclopaedias.

Not for several years yet.

'John, this time I think we ought to tell people. You could begin by telling the Japanese.'

'No.'

'Why not? They'll be worried in case the halo's some fault of the Matsuya eyes. Or they might suppose you've stumbled on some hidden power of the mind which their eyes have triggered. The liberation of the third eye by their lenses! They'll have equipment for probing the halo. They might be able to look into your brain through the eyes.'

'No, Morris, the problem's the same as ever. Oh God, to have all the wonder of the world restored to me thrice over – then to have it polluted and thieved again! I'm no saint!' he snarls suddenly. 'I might have been a saintly codger in Porchester but I damn well stopped being one during these past two years.'

We go inside the cottage and drink brandy.

John gets drunk.

The halo isn't at all conspicuous when Mrs Mott serves us our breakfast of bacon and eggs. She notices nothing odd, but I can spy the faint shimmer.

The sky is blue, the sun is bright.

'Lovely spring morning,' observes John. 'Might cloud over later. We'll take a walk up Hinchcombe Hill.'

Hinchcombe Hill is a mile away along a lane then up

through a steep forest ride to a gorse-clad hilltop, which is deserted save for some Suffolk ewes. Suffolks are a chunky breed which lamb early, before Christmas; these ewes are already parted from their offspring.

It was cool walking up through the shade of the fir trees, but here on the hilltop it's as hot as a summer's day.

'Can you see our circular friend?'

'The sun's too bright,' I tell him.

'Good. Now, we all know that we shouldn't stare at a bright sun, don't we Morris? The sun can burn the cells of the retina. My retina is a machine. It's much more resilient. The flash from a hydrogen bomb might burn Matsuya eyes – but we all know that a nuclear flash is brighter than a *thousand* suns, don't we? So I ought to have lots of spare capacity even if I switch over to night-vision.'

'Don't do it, John.'

'I don't care if I harm these eyes. Not now.'

'You might damage your brain. The visual centres.'

'Where the beast dwells, eh? Unless it dwells in a separate universe, or in Heaven, and only has a peephole in my head.'

He sits down on a boulder facing the sun. 'You want feeding?' he cries out. 'I'll feed you!'

For some reason – habit, ritual, or insurance policy? – he crosses himself, then begins to stare fixedly at the sun. Loudly he hums the hymn tune, 'Angels from the Realms of Glory', over and over again monotonously.

Minutes pass.

'I can see it, John. It's glowing.'

Brighter, ever brighter.

Presently it's a full-fledged radiant halo; and still he stares into the sun.

He breaks off humming. 'Report, please!' he says crisply.

'I can't look directly at it any longer. It's getting too

fierce.' At least the halo's light is cold, otherwise John's head would surely start to cook.

'Not from my point of view! The day grows dim. The sun looks like a lemon in a mist.' *Ang-els! from! the Realms! of Glo-ry!*

I simply have to turn away. The ewes have all trekked off down the slope away from this second, miniature sun in their midst.

'I'm going blind fast, Morris. It's really gobbling light.'

'And pumping it out again!'

'I'll soon be back in darkness. But no matter.' *Ang-els! from!*

If only I had some tinted glass with me. I only dare risk a glance now and then.

Glance:

The halo isn't doughnut-shaped any longer. It's a sphere of furnace light just like a second head. Its after-image bobs above the fir trees as though a ball of lightning is loose.

The Realms! of Glo-ry!

I cast two shadows on the grass and gorse.

Glance:

'It's elongating upwards, John!'

A pillar of blinding silver radiance: it could light a whole street.

In the after-image a figure hovers over the trees, sliding from side to side: a body of sorts. It fades.

Glance:

Now the after-image is sharper. That isn't a human body. It's too slim, except where the chest swells out. The legs are too short, the arms too long and skinny. The head is like a bird's with a beak of a mouth.

Ang-els! from!

The after-image has wings, great trailing plumed wings.

It's the blazing angel who threw Adam and Eve out of Eden.

'There's a creature perching on your head, John! A tall
scraggy bird! It's like a man – but it isn't.'

Its claw feet are planted on John's skull as if his skull is
an egg which it is clutching.

Glance:

The after-image opens its beak.

'Hullo! Hullo! Hullo!' What a screechy, reedy voice.

John isn't humming any longer. The words are
screeched from *his* lips in the tones of a parrot or a mynah
bird.

'I hear you,' I shout.

I shade my eyes with both hands in a visor: John is
sitting as before gazing rigidly up at our sun.

'I come,' screams the bird of light. 'I announce myself!'

'Where do you come from?'

'I take!'

'Take what? Where to?'

'My prey! To my eyrie!'

John must be the creature's prey. I have to break his link
with the power of the sun! Sheltering my head from the
horrid pillar of light, I stumble at a crouch and buffet him
sideways off his rock. With my own eyes closed tight I
cast myself down beside him. Fumbling, I find his head
and seal my hands across his Matsuya eyes.

'Aiiieee!' shrieks the voice.

John's own voice calls out: 'Oh blessed visions! Realms
of glory! Celestial city of the angels! With the slimmest,
highest of towers all lit by cold light at night as though a
star has settled on every pinnacle – an angel perching on
each. White angels drifting through the pearly sky of day.
A meadowland below with little blue goat-elves all a-
grazing by the river of milk – '

'Don't heed it, John! Cast it out of your head.'

'My soul will go inside an angel's egg.'

'Refuse! The thing is trying to take your mind away
with it!'

'I'll be reborn – angelic.'

'They're birds of prey, John. Alien eagles, not angels.'

'No, they are celestial – ' His voice chokes off.

'Aiiieee! I triumph!'

John's body shudders then grows still.

Cautiously I open my eyes. The blinding light, the second sun, has gone. Only our own yellow sun beams on the gorse, the rocks, the grass; and on my friend's body.

I feel for his pulse; there's none. His heart has stopped. I don't know how to give the kiss of life but I still try to breathe animation back into him – in vain.

I sit by his sun-warmed corpse for a long while.

John thought that his mind would go into an angel's egg on that alien world, in that other reality.

Presumably he would hatch.

As what? As an angel, the equal of the other angel-birds?

Or as a prisoner, bringing honour to its captor? A slave? A sacrifice? A gift to the Lord of the Birds of Light?

I shall soon walk back down the hill, through the forest ride, along the lane alone. I shall have to say that the strain of the ascent caused a coronary and broke his heart. I shall say that his spirit has ascended to Heaven, where he is now at home.

I must hope that no one else saw the blinding light on Hinchcombe Hill, the radiance that raptured John away to an alien eyrie, leaving the abandoned clothing of his flesh behind.

Maybe John will be happy when he hatches, to the cold light of that elsewhere-city. And maybe there's no such city; maybe his last visions were lies, opiates pumped into his skull to paralyse his will . . .

A few ewes return, to stare at the two of us with mild curiosity.

When the Timegate Failed

We were carrying an alien passenger on that particular trip. It belonged to the race which had created the timegate. Its name was Mid Velvet Fastskip, and I was under orders to become intimate; to seduce it.

These orders ran contrary to every other rule as to how to behave aboard a starship. I didn't expect to retain the respect of my crew.

But I couldn't take anyone else into my confidence. Nor did I dare ignore those orders. One of my crew would be a covert security officer, briefed to see that I carried out my confidential mission. Which of my crew? I had no idea.

I could trust no one except myself; yet I had to win the trust, the 'love', of an alien. Because of this, no one would love me – least of all the woman whom I would need to exploit.

Nobody loved or trusted a starship, either. Not deep in our hearts, in our guts. Oh, we trusted the human-built stardrive to thrust us successfully from sunspace to sunspace. But how could any human being trust the timegate when we didn't understand it? That was why I needed to become the 'lover' of a creature whom no human being properly comprehended – and in two weeks flat. Obviously I would fail. It was the calibre of my failure which counted; what clues our scientists could deduce.

A certain Wittgenstein once said, 'If a lion could speak, we would not understand him.' Mid Velvet Fastskip and I both spoke Harrang, the artificial mediation language. But Harrang is essentially a functional language. Where emotion, metaphor, deep meaning are involved, around the periphery of language, one could only improvise hopefully.

'The timegate is a technical problem,' I'd been told. 'Harrang will suffice.'

I feared that this wouldn't be so. The timegate was invented by an alien psyche. It was envisioned out of alien moods and impulses which were surely opaque to humans. Otherwise human beings would have been able to invent the thing, surely? Or at least to unriddle it by now. I fancy that one's inventions and one's kind of consciousness are closer allied than is often imagined. We invented a star-drive; Mid Velvet's people failed to. Instead they invented something which we couldn't, and still can't, match.

Maybe I shouldn't make unduly heavy weather about the 'alienness' of aliens? When the chips were down, Mid Velvet might simply lie to me.

Ah no. Herein lay the cruel cunning of my masters back in Solspace. They claimed to have learned an essential feature of love among the aliens of Fastskip's species: the Truth Moment, the Sharing.

In Harrang, Mid Velvet's breed were known as 'Those Who Run Faster'. We called them the Tworfs for short, a derogatory-sounding name reminiscent of Wop or Chink or Dago. According to my masters all Tworfs were neuters. On their home planet the Tworfs parasited sexually upon large silky animals, semi-intelligent 'pets' which roamed wild, and which could even speak in a limited way. These beasts played the role of actual external sexual organs.

A Tworf would 'engage' a male animal by clinging to its back, sinking tendrils harmlessly into its nervous system. A certain amount of petting-courtship was apparently involved prior to this. Wooing songs. Wooing the animal was important, either ritually or biologically. Lots of foreplay, to attune Tworf to beast.

Once joined together, the symbiotic duo would chase after a female animal to mate with her. Spying a large parasite mounted on prospective mate, the female would flee furiously. The Tworf urged its mount to run faster. Catching up, the Tworf would en-trance the female. Vicarious copulation would take place, during the course of which the Tworf would pump a vast amount of information through the nervous system/sexual circuit of male beast, female beast, and Tworf. The Tworf would channel its whole being through the mating couple, and back into its neuter self. During this time the male animal would experience a heightened state of awareness. He would have access to the higher consciousness of the Tworf, which would be spewing out its intimate, secret person.

The simple male animals would chant simple myth-songs about their Tworf riders and these moments of illumination, of Godhood, which flooded them during mating – ungraspable after the event, yet able to be celebrated.

If the event was so desirable, why did the female animals flee, and need to be chased down? True, the females weren't themselves illuminated by the intercourse. Perhaps the chase, too, was a ritual matter. And perhaps racing caused hyperoxygenation or adrenalin release or some other necessary chemical, hormonal change. Perhaps!

After consummation the Tworf would split into two separate selves. It would give birth to a new self, a prismatic variation. Thus Tworfs reproduced.

Were the articulate male and female animals actually a second and third sex of the Tworf species? Morphologically different from the first, neuter sex, and mentally inferior? My masters rejected this idea. The bodily differences were too gross. Besides, if Tworfs and silky animals *were* of the same species, what hope was there of a human man and woman playing the role of 'beast with two backs' for the benefit of a randy neuter Tworf? A Tworf who would flood the human male with knowledge.

My masters wouldn't say how they had gained all this data about alien sex habits. No doubt security officers at the Earth mission of Tworfworld were the source.

Apparently timegates also had some indirect connexion with this bizarre practice. That was why we ought to have a timegate in proximity to the great experiment. Earth only had control of a limited number of timegates. Each one was a vital part of a starship. Hence the choice of myself as Casanova. As pervert, and violator of the safety rules, and violator of a crew member. I only hoped that the crew member in question, whom I must needs involve in the Truth Moment, might happen to be the secret security officer.

'Mid Velvet Fastskip?'

'Yes, Captain Nevin?'

'Do you have close friends back home?'

'Several.'

'What do close friends call you?'

'By my name.'

'By all of it? Or part? What name would a loving-animal know you by? What name would you whisper in his ear?'

'Mid is a position. Velvet is a texture. Fastskip is a way of motion.'

'I'm fascinated. May I invite you into my cabin to discuss such things?'

'Honoured, but puzzled.'

Let me describe Those Who Run Faster.

They're skinny bipeds who stand armpit-high to your average human male. Their feet are ostrich-claws which doubtless could eviscerate an enemy who tried to sneak up and leap on *their* backs. They have a tough, smooth, pearly hide. All down the front of the body tendrils peep from little follicle-holes, as if through a sieve. Excitement causes these tendrils to erect, and sprout forth. The tendrils are orange in colour so that the front of an excited Tworf would look like a rug stained with rusty blood. A Tworf's back is smoothly, flexibly ceramic.

A Tworf has two long, double-jointed arms, with four wormy digits apiece. In addition, two vestigial 'clutching arms' spring from the sides of the chest, and are usually clasped together as if in prayer. For hands, these minimal arms have suckery little pads.

A Tworf's head is a porcelain ellipsoid with big, wide-set violet eyes lacking obvious pupils, twin breathing slits, and a lipless mouth which opens and shuts like a rubber sphincter, dilating and sealing again. Inside are double rows of tiny teeth, set vertically not horizontally.

A Tworf breathes oxygen, and eats most foods.

Mid Velvet Fastskip – so I'd been told – was a sibling of the ruling clade of the northern hemisphere of Tworfworld. Its fields of expertise were alien hermeneutics – a fancy way of referring to the fact that it had acted as an interpreter for the human mission on Tworfworld, and for the two other alien missions there – plus 'time-dancing', plus oceanography.

Mid Velvet had travelled to Earth to study our oceans.

What the hell was 'time-dancing'? My masters back home – and their inheritors, their successors who would take over the reins of the Perpetual World State – dearly wished to know. 'Time-dancing' sounded relevant; thus the selection of this particular Tworf as target for seduction.

We shall disregard the other two intelligent, starfaring species, who were even more arcane than Those Who Run Faster. Both those exotic races ignored timegates. They could happily hibernate during the long decades of star travel. One of them dream-tranced; the other dissociated during a journey.

* * *

As I escorted Mid Velvet along the already dusty corridor towards my cabin, Jocelyn Chantal came out of her own cabin, through the polarized haze of the privacy-sheet.

Chantal: blond and tall and snub-nosed, sporting large frame spectacles which added a necessary extra dimension to her face, and gave her windows to peer at you through. Ship's Doctor. Political officer, too?

'Captain Nevin,' she said. A diagnosis rather than a greeting. 'And Mid Velvet Fastskip, I believe. Both together. In close proximity.'

On a starship one always kept a few paces from other persons if possible.

'I don't suppose I'll catch an alien disease,' I said.

'Of course not!' She sounded offended.

'If somebody falls sick, Chantal, you might need to touch them. Physically. In proximity.'

'Perils of the profession, Captain. One takes precautions.'

'So many precautions.'

Her eyes widened, aspiring to the size of her glasses. '*Every* precaution is vital to safeguard a starship.'

'Quite right. A starship's rather similar to the Perpetual State, don't you think, Chantal? Almost a mirror image! Nothing ever alters.'

Why did I speak so rashly? Out of sheer nervous anger at the role I was compelled to act out? Or in order to uncover the actual political officer, to target her for parasitical alien rape?

If I didn't comply with our masters' plan, I would be shot after long interrogation. The descendants of my blood would be expelled from citizenship.

'Star travel demands political continuity, Captain. Our place in the cosmos, ruled by the speed of light, requires long-term stability.'

'Hmm. So therefore all Earth's billions bow their heads

to a score of starships and a few far colonies. Cart before the horses? Baby and the bath-water?'

'What do you mean? We can't hibernate like our alien rivals.'

'We hibernate politically instead.'

'Political change means turmoil, which means war, which means eventual holocaust.'

'Yes, yes, I know. Come along, Mid Velvet Fastskip!'

I walked deliberately towards Jocelyn Chantal. She backed away from me, disappearing through her privacy-sheet. When I glanced back, she was looking out again, watching where we went.

At the start of the wide, dusty corridor Helen Kaminski was also observing intently. Capriciously I waved to my dark, trim Exec. And political officer? Another possible candidate.

Contemptuous, and deliberately provocative of public opinion – things could only go downhill from here on – I ushered the alien into the white mouth of the cabin with my own name, NEVIN, above the door.

'Cap – !'

The cry – from Chantal or Kaminski – was abruptly cut off as the privacy-sheet soaked up the sonics.

Now that I was inside my cabin, I could of course see clearly through the film of polarized air. I could look out through a doorframe with no door. You wouldn't wish to step out of your cabin blindly and risk colliding with somebody. I watched for a while. Kaminski walked into view shortly, keeping to the other side of the corridor. She loitered then strolled on. I drew the night-curtain briskly over the doorway.

Mid Velvet was studying the three digital clocks on my wall . . .

The first of these registered crew-time. The second showed ship-time – we were travelling at nearly the speed

of light. The third clock gave 'objective' time back home
on Earth.

Nine hours of objective time was equivalent to three
hours of ship-time, approximately. Please tip your hat to
Einstein and to the stardrive, product of human
engineering.

Three hours of ship-time was equivalent to one minute
as experienced by the crew. Now let's tip our hat to the
timegate invented by the Tworfs, a secret which we
drooled for.

Thanks to the timegate our trip would last two weeks,
for us. Twenty years would elapse on Earth. The ship
itself would age by almost seven years.

Before we met Those Who Run Faster, human crews
used to be cooped up in starships for years on end, for
decades. Those were journeys of exile, madness, hell.
Murder, tyranny, confinement. Not always; but all too
often.

Nowadays we traded sealed stardrives to the Tworfs.
The Tworfs supplied us with enigmatic timegates. One
for one.

We aboard the *Pegasus* were outward bound two days
from Solspace, crew-time, heading for our colony at
Twinstar Two (which also boasted interesting oceans).
Mid Velvet Fastskip would catch a Tworf vessel home
from T-Two eventually. It had already been absent from
its world for over a year, personal time. Long enough to
become randy? Several others of its species had been
present on Earth as visitors. However, Tworfs did not
make love to other Tworfs; and their articulate animals
lived in large herds, pining to death if isolated for very
long. You couldn't, wouldn't, take a whole herd of cattle
with you to another star system for the sake of an
occasional pint of milk. Analogy.

'Will you drink some wine, Mid Velvet Fastskip?'

'I will. Thank you.'

Would its tendrils thrust out of its mantle after a couple of glasses of Burgundy? Would its body flush with a ruddy hue? Would a glass too many increase the desire, but take away the performance?

How could there be desire between a Mid Velvet Fastskip of the Tworfs and a Captain Sam Nevin?

How could there be desire between a Tworf and an articulate animal with a silky, silvery fleece?

My own hair was blond, almost white, and I had let a blond beard grow.

'What is your most vivid memory of Earth's oceans?' I asked convivially.

'Turtles and gulls,' it replied.

'Not whales? Not the Marianas Abyss? Not coral reefs? Not swordfish and sharks?'

'Weeping turtles, never knowing their offspring, laying eggs ashore. New-hatched babies drawn by instinct, knowing no parent but Nature, scuttling over a desert to the cruel safety of the surf. Greedy gulls eating ninety out of every hundred.'

His fluency, and mine, surprised me.

'You are a poet, Mid Velvet Fastskip!'

Was this alien creature the Rachel Carson, the Lewis Thomas of his own race?

Why those particular images?

'Will you pass that memory on to your own offspring when you divide in half?'

'Terrible, beautiful memories,' it said, leaving me little the wiser.

'Do the loving beasts of your world only reproduce themselves because you stimulate them?'

'You are curious about us.'

'I find myself attracted . . . to the notion of a third partner involved in the act of love. A partner of a different and superior order. As though a god were to assist in copulation – inspiring, frenzying. It must seem so to the beasts. Perhaps.'

'You are a poet too, Captain Nevin. Poets tell lies by means of beauty.'

'Lies? I only seek the truth.'

'And they make those lies true.'

'Mid . . . May I call you something briefer than Mid Velvet Fastskip? A shorter name? Without offending you! You can call me Sam. That's my personal name.'

'You can call me Skip.'

'Skip. I will.'

'I shall call you Cap, from Captain. Our names join.'

Skip – short for Skipper, too! Skipper of a vessel. The pun existed in Harrang, the amalgam mediation language. I recalled how this alien was an interpreter.

I raised my glass. 'Here's health to Cap and Skip.'

Cap and Skip. Sharing names. Commencing our court-ship rites. I felt as though I, a lifelong heterosexual, had gone to a gay bar as an intellectual exercise, determined to offer my blond self to a man. Only, this was much stranger.

Skip and Cap: two buddies who would become inti-mate. Perhaps. And who would invite – chase, entrap, cajole – either Jocelyn Chantal or Helen Kaminski or engineer Sonya Wenzel to join in a lustful trio.

I had a flash-vision – or precognition – of myself capering nakedly along the corridor, ecstatic, drunken, ridden by alien Skip as if by a demonic god, bursting through the privacy-sheet into one cabin or another, my penis a paralyzing, entrancing sting, almost an ovipositor; and perhaps after all it wouldn't be a woman to whom Skip drove me. It might be one of the other men. Mark Bekker or Robert Hoffmann or Julian Takahashi.

What violent hatreds might erupt! The results could be as dire as any ghastly event aboard a long-trip ship from the old days, before the timegate. I might need the political officer to reveal himself (or herself) to protect me, to nurse the shattered crew to journey's end.

Maybe I wouldn't be in danger. Potential weapons of any sort were banned from *Pegasus*. We even ate with plastic spoons. We were strongly conditioned not to crowd each other, not to collide.

My cabin wasn't a particularly elegant boudoir in which to conduct an alien seduction. The walls were smooth and almost bare, with no irrelevant obtrusions. Entertainments were enclosed inside the walls; only a screen and speakers and the simplest of controls were visible. The whole floor was padded as a bed. Personal space must be kept extremely tidy. To encourage this, we possessed little to untidy a cabin with.

Already my home pad was slighty dusty. We were two days out from Earth but *Pegasus* was hundreds of days older. Before we arrived in twelve days' time, in eighteen years' time, dust would lie thick about the ship. It would be as though we dwelled in an ancient tomb.

How could so much dust collect out of thin air? Maybe the steady state theory of the universe was correct and matter was being created all the time, mostly in deep space, in the form of dust. Slowed in time as we were, dust seemed to gather with mysterious malevolence as though the ship's walls were sloughing dead cells of skin which must eventually gather so deeply as to stifle us.

In a sense dust was the main enemy. Dust alone visibly altered the anatomy of the ship. Nothing else about the ship could be allowed to change, to shift position.

At journey's end hoses would simply be attached to the snout of *Pegasus*, through the airlock at the front of Control. The whole vessel would be flooded like a sunken submarine, flushed clean, then dried and sterilized by blasts of burning air.

'Have some more wine, Skip?'

'Thank you.'

* * *

Yes, a starship is an unchanging environment. It's designed that way. No door ever opens or shuts in transit. As few objects as possible are movable: plastic spoons, cups, bowls. Clothes; we wear almost indestructible one-piece suits.

In the old days when journeys took half a lifetime, ships were littered with enough playthings and paraphernalia to occupy a whole cageful of monkeys happily half way to forever.

But any loose object can be misused, can cause an accident or be made into a weapon. And humans aren't monkeys. The same rich variety of adult toys and amusements and decoration, constantly seen for ten or twenty years, becomes invisible. After a decade and a half all those things may as well not be there. The crew would no longer admire them, care about them, even notice them. The ship may as well be empty and immutable, as *Pegasus* is. Apart from the dust.

Inner disciplines were more important than toys. Imaginative meditations. Indeed, what other kind of discipline could there be aboard a vessel exiled for fifteen or thirty years? Alas, those disciplines frequently degenerated; the crew became degenerates.

Tip your hat to the timegate, ship-mates!

One of the crew would need to become my mate, under Skip's influence . . .

I presumed that microphones and lenses the size of motes of dust recorded the monotony of daily life aboard *Pegasus*, though I doubted that the political officer herself (or himself) would have access to the electronic records; thus Earth could keep a check on her too (or him). Those records would be scanned by a high-speed computer programmed to take note of key words and tones of voice denoting hysteria, rage, pain. (Key words on this trip would include anything connected with timegates and

Tworfs.) That was how the terrible tale of some of those early, cursed, multidecade voyages had been decoded, even though the ageing remnants of the crew were themselves inarticulate or deep in hallucinations. Back before the timegate cut subjective trip time to a few weeks.

When nothing in the environment changes, it doesn't matter how quickly or slowly the crew members move about the ship, so long as they all move about at the same speed relative to one another. (Though we never *trusted* to this!)

Obviously we were utterly out of synch with mechanical systems for opening doors or emptying toilets or heating food. Before you could snatch a foil-pack of heated stew out of an oven the meal would have been cold for hours, ship-time. Cold nutritious slop was our chow.

Oh for a juicy steak, a Madras curry, steaming broth. But we could easily wait a couple of weeks for a decent meal.

At least I had some good vintage Burgundy to offer Skip. All our wine was vintage; once opened it had plenty of time to breathe.

Day Three, and it was time for me and Exec Kaminski and Navigator Bekker to check and triple-check our course, analyse the starbow, make any minor corrections. Since yesterday *Pegasus* had flown onward a hundred and fifty or so light days. Back on Earth a year and a half had gone by. Cosmic dust, gravity of neighbouring stars, the rotation of the galaxy, minute irregularities in the output of the stardrive could conspire to nudge us slightly off course. A starship slightly off course is soon a long way off. To correct significant deviations soon becomes fuel-consumptive and stressful of the stardrive.

The daily check was something of a ritual with definite

superstitious aspects. For Bekker, Kaminski, and I would step through the timegate one after another and be accelerated to ship-time; otherwise we could never handle the job. Then we three would return through the gate into the main body of the ship, and be decelerated once again. The rest of the crew would wait and watch. In some ways the event was like a prayer to a mysterious deity, one which had always proved benevolent so far, yet whose ways were inexplicable.

When I arrived in the bare dusty vestibule, Chantal, Takahashi, and Wenzel were already there. With backs to the curving wall, they kept their distance from one another.

Kaminski and Bekker were also waiting for me, near the red 'dike' ten centimetres high which surrounded the timegate.

'You're almost late, Captain!' Kaminski jerked a finger at the triple chronometer mounted overhead.

'Nonsense. Hoffmann isn't here yet.'

'He doesn't need to go into Control.'

Skip was absent too. A pity. It may have amused him to see the ignorant natives gathered around their idol, praying that the timegate would grant us a change of tempo, such as it had always granted; but not knowing, not knowing for sure. Amused him; and demeaned us. This might have helped my mission by making us seem like a bunch of . . . articulate animals. We weren't, at this moment, the technological masters of the stardrive. We were petitioners at an alien portal.

Beyond the red dike, duller with dust than yesterday, the oval hoop of the timegate cut a hole in the bulkhead enclosing a shimmer of air. Rainbow colours rippled faintly, as on a membrane of soapy water from which a child might blow a bubble. This membrane would let us step through it; unlike a bubble it wouldn't burst. Beyond the membrane I could see all the screens and instruments of Control, only slightly distorted.

'Here's Hoffmann now,' I said calmly.

What the witnesses saw when we stepped through the timegate, if they really concentrated, would be: a brief blur of activity within Control, the place full of flickering multiple images almost too swift to register. Then, ten seconds later, Kaminski and Bekker and I would re-emerge.

From our point of view the witnesses outside were frozen statues, snail-people.

We spent half an hour in Control. After a thorough analysis of the smeared images of suns in the starbow we trimmed course by a fraction of an arcsecond.

'They ought to install an oven in here,' I remarked. 'Then we could feast like the kings and queens of infinite space that we are. Or ought to be.'

'You can't have people flooding in and out of here whenever they're feeling peckish,' said Bekker indignantly. 'Think of the risk of collision! Slow-moving persons, fast-moving persons. It's frisky enough *us* using this doorway once a day.'

'We fear it, don't we? We treat it like an unexploded bomb. Or a glass mobile we're balancing on a fingertip over an abyss. We never dance with time, nonchalantly.'

'Our work's done,' said Kaminski. 'We ought to rejoin the others.'

'What's the hurry? They won't miss us. Just imagine . . . if we stepped back through the gate, and this time it didn't work.'

'Be quiet, Captain.'

'We would still be accelerated. They would stand there motionless. At first we would think it was a prank. "Hey you guys, don't joke. This isn't funny." Then we'd notice that they *are* moving, but very very slowly. "Okay, this is an order. Quit it." No response. We would have to write on the wall for them to read slowly. For the next seven years or so we three would have to live our lives at ship's time.'

'Captain. Please.'

'Except, in just a few months we would use all the food and drink. That's only a few hours from their point of view. They couldn't stop us raiding the larder time and again, gobbling our fill every few minutes. We'd have no choice. We'd buzz about them like a swarm of locusts. And when the cupboard was bare . . . would we eat Chantal and Wenzel, Hoffmann and Takahashi too? Would we tear our alien friend apart and eat him? Yes! Unless the Tworf knew how to dance with time. Unless he speeded up to escape from our hungry jaws – and showed us the art of dancing!'

'For God's sake,' Kaminski said.

For God's sake. Not for the sake of the Perpetual State. Maybe this proved nothing. Scratch a policeman and you find a priest. Priests are the policemen of the soul. Police are the priests of politics. Often both wear similar black uniforms. Kaminski might still be the security officer.

We went back through the timegate. We were reunited together in slow time. All was well.

'I shall tell you a poem of the origin of the timegate, Cap.'

'You will? Tell me, Skip. Tell me.'

'I shall tell lies by means of beauty. A substitute for a wooing song.' All down its front the orange tendrils twitched.

'Those Who Run Faster once suffered from a strange malady: of hyperkinesis. Hence our name! We were over-active, accelerated. Something had gone sadly wrong with our biological clocks. The clocks in our bodies, you know?'

'Yes, yes. Mitochondria, the little powerhouses of the cells. Circadian rhythms. The pineal eye.'

'Each successive generation of Those Who Run Faster was living at a quicker rate than the previous generation. We were maturing faster, moving faster, talking faster, discarding ourselves faster.'

'Discarding? Do you mean "dying"? Don't creatures who divide by fission live forever like amoebas?'

'We are more complicated than amoebas. Shall I digress?'

'Not yet. Go on, Skip. The Tworfs were speeding up.'

'We were burning ourselves out. The end of our race was predicted. In our case it was a race, and no mistake! But then our scientists pinned down the source of the trouble. A black hole of swelling mass was digesting our sun from within. This eating of our star caused a local anomaly in time.'

'This isn't a poem,' I cried with mounting excitement. 'It's a scientific explanation.'

'It is a song. Our hyperkinesis was an evolutionary adaptation to the fact that we must complete our history much earlier than Nature had expected. So we discovered how to retard ourselves, by use of timegates. The first timegates were spun out of our inmost being, our accelerated selves. As an earthly spider spins silk; as an earthly snail secretes a shell. The silk, the shell, was *time itself*. We ingeniously transferred time's extra momentum to the gates. Later, we automated the procedure. Our history continues.'

'But how did you accomplish this marvel?'

Hitherto Skip had been waggling his vestigial hands as he wove his narrative. Now he knit those suckers together across his bristling chest as much as to say, 'That's all. Story over.'

'But your sun must still be doomed!'

'Our whole species danced with time. We arrested the black hole. We cured our star.'

'Hang on a moment. If all of you were living faster, adapting at the same rate, what difference would the time anomaly have made to you?'

'A great difference. We Tworfs were adapting, because we were the most sensitive and highly evolved species. Our loving animals did not live any faster than before. Mounting them became frustrating and exhausting. Our wooing songs squeaked far too rapidly in their silky ears. Love took far too long.'

For the first time in our acquaintance Skip stretched out one of its long arms to touch me; to touch my virtually indestructible garment. Tentatively.

The next day Skip told me an entirely different story; though I suppose it complemented the first explanation.

'Yes, we are immortal,' it explained, 'unless killed by accident. Every time we mount a loving animal, and mate it and divide ourselves, we gain a new lease of life. However, as an earthly snake sloughs its skin, likewise we must lose something. What *we* have to discard is memories. We must cull our memories, or else our minds would overload with the enormity of the past. We couldn't function successfully in the present.'

'Ah, I see. You shed half of your memories into your offspring, into your double. That's what makes the pair of you different persons.'

'Yes and no. If we imprinted too much memory on our double it wouldn't have initiative and curiosity. Therefore, dancing, we secrete a jewel which contains that extra part of the past which we wish to discard. We excrete this, as an earthly bird excretes an egg. This jewel is memory. And memory is time. These jewels are essential to the functioning of the timegate.'

'You create a jewel each time you mate a loving animal?'

'We used to give the jewels to the animals afterwards. They wore the jewels as necklaces, of honour and worship. But they didn't understand the jewels properly. Now we use them scientifically.'

I barely curbed my excitement. 'You must be a very different person after mating, Skip. You must forget a lot that happened earlier on.'

'Do not your earthly poets refer to human orgasm as "the little death"? In a timeless moment, you forget yourself.'

I was spooning up some cold slop with my plastic utensil. Jocelyn Chantal positioned herself nearby.

'How are you feeling, Captain?'

'Okay.'

'How is our alien guest enjoying its voyage?'

'Is a voyage to be enjoyed – or endured? Perhaps neither! What does it really matter whereabouts we are in space and time, or what the quality of our circumstances is, so long as we survive without too much discomfort? And so long as we serve the Perpetual State? Thus we ensure the survival of humanity. Thus we guarantee its spread throughout the stars, that are so very far apart. Any means of enduring such a voyage is healthy. Impeccable.'

'Perhaps.'

'That's why we endure the timegate every day.'

'You endure it, Captain.' Chantal hesitated before adding, 'In company with Helen and Mark.'

'Everyone endures it, Chantal. Everyone.'

'Yes. We all do.'

'I think I'm starting to regard the timegate not with queasy dread, but in happy anticipation – as something vitalizing and inspiring. Each time I use it I die and am reborn. Almost as another person in another time. If we use the timegate often enough it may make us immortal. We shall journey thousands of light years all the way around the galaxy, instead of a measly ten or twenty light years from Earth. We ought to improve the cuisine, though. Does an immortal get bored with eating an infinity of meals? Mid Velvet Fastskip hasn't complained about the menu.'

'Is our alien guest immortal? How strange that an immortal race should bother to invent timegates.'

'Maybe they're immortal because they use timegates. *Post hoc ergo propter hoc.* Plus, their method of reproduction.' I oughtn't to be so frank with Chantal. My masters on Earth had sworn me to secrecy. Here was I on the verge of betraying my mission. I went on in lighter vein, 'What if they aren't immortal? Thanks to timegates they can dance their way right to the end of the universe within a single lifetime.'

Suppose you stepped through one timegate, to slow your life processes. Suppose you immediately stepped in the same direction through a second gate. Then a third! Decelerating and decelerating. The sun would zip through the sky. Day and night would strobe. The galaxy would revolve like a spinning top. The whole cosmos would expand to its utmost, pause, and collapse again. While you stood still.

'Certain time-dancers on our world are attempting this,' admitted Skip.

'You're a time-dancer too.'

'Those are slow dancers. I skip fast. None of those slow dancers have reached their fourth gate yet. They move so slowly, you see.'

'Oh.'

I had never visited Tworfworld. I was always on the same run from Earth to Twinstar Two. I tried to imagine Skip's planet.

The yellow prairies where herds of silky animals grazed and frolicked and chanted simple songs, and experienced fleeting ecstasies of high mentality and metamemory when ridden in love by Tworfs. The fanatical slow-dance Tworfs poised motionless between one gate and another. The single ocean on whose shores no turtles nested, above whose waves no gulls screamed hungrily. Lying sparkling on a silver beach, where Tworfs had ridden their mounts, mated, danced, and split, would be the jewels of time.

I visualized the Tworf cities of domes and minarets; the guarded embassies of the exotic races which could hibernate for years on end, at will; the spaceport from which Tworf vessels rose powered by human stardrives.

It was time for love; high time.

'Look at me, Skip. Behold me.'

I parted my indestructible garment down the frontal seam. I shucked if off like a snakeskin, newly moulted. I stroked my blond, near-white beard. I turned my back on Mid Velvet Fastskip.

'Touch me.'

Swiftly the alien mounted me. The long arms jointed themselves around my chest, locking together. The little arms burrowed under my armpits, suckering tight. Erect tendrils gently pierced my shoulders, spine, buttocks, nerves. Skip was nearly weightless; the least of burdens. My alien rider increased my strength, the bounce of my steps and the vigour of my body, my potency and sexuality. I had been impotent for years; not now. On the contrary!

It was as I foresaw. I was possessed by a daemon, by a living god. I rushed through my privacy-sheet into the corridor. There, I pawed the deck and champed like a thoroughbred stallion. I snorted. I whinnied wordlessly.

Just then Helen Kaminski appeared from around the far bend. She stared in amazement at her potent, eager Captain with the alien rider on his back, porcelain head peeping over human head. She broke into a run – not away from us but in the direction of her own doorless cabin, cloaked in its white privacy.

We raced to meet her. We ran faster. But she had less distance to cover. She vanished through the masked doorway. Forbidden!

Skip urged me through the privacy-sheet – through into the KAMINSKI cabin from which no sight nor sound could escape.

During consummation, as I flowed into my noisy mate, Skip flowed through myself into Helen Kaminski and back into my body through her raking fingernails.

I was filled with alien understandings and timely enlightenments such as I can no longer express.

Afterwards, Skip descended from me and danced for us. It whirled like a dervish till my eyes were dazed. It seemed to grow shorter, and spread out. As the wild dance slowed I could distinguish two short Tworfs whirling round together, disentangling from one another.

At last they separated and halted. Helen fled naked from her cabin. One Tworf bowed and presented me with a blue jewel that pulsed with inner radiance. The jewel was about the size of the iris of a human eye. This done, the Tworfs ran away like a couple of mischievous children or elves. I was left alone. My understanding dimmed, to that of an ordinary human being. My god had gone.

But I knew what I needed to do. Clutching my treasure, I set out for the timegate and Control.

I had lost my high, vital strength. Mark Bekker held me by one arm, actually touching me. Robert Hoffmann held my other arm. We were stalled in the vestibule. So near, yet so far.

I protested. 'I've learned the secret of the timegate.'

'There's no alien on board, Captain,' said Jocelyn Chantal. She too had intercepted me. She looked a lot older than previously.

'Quite right. There are *two*.'

'Two?'

'Mid Velvet Fastskip divided. They're probably hiding somewhere. The environment may seem unfamiliar.'

'There was *never* any alien on board. How could there be? We know of no aliens.'

'Those Who Run Faster gave us the timegate, Chantal.'

She sighed. 'There's no timegate, either. If only there was.'

'But look! There it is!' I attempted to point. Since my arms were pinioned I had to content myself with jerking my head in the direction of the red dike, and the shimmering oval gap beyond.

'I only see the entrance to Control,' Chantal said. 'Look at the calendar-clock above.'

I glanced up at the chronometer. Its digits were flowing too fast to read clearly.

'This is the fourteenth year of our *actual* voyage, Captain.'

'Free my hand, Bekker. Let me show you something.'

Bekker did so guardedly.

I opened my fist to display the time-jewel.

'Possibly there wasn't any alien,' I allowed. 'Yet now we have a timegate for sure! *This* has been created. This power-crystal.'

'It's one of those twelve-sided gaming dice that Helen uses, isn't it?' asked Bekker.

'Oh well, it might have been. Now it's altered. It was changed in the crucible of heightened consciousness! See how it glows. We need only link it in circuit with the stardrive. We'll fly through hyperspace, through hypertime. We'll arrive within days, not decades. I *know* this.'

Bekker asked incredulously, 'Are you seriously proposing that we open the drive unit up and insert this . . . object . . . into the matrix?'

'We could certainly give it a try,' said Hoffmann. 'Are

you quite positive that you achieved insight, Captain? A genuine altered state of consciousness?'

'Yes. Yes.'

Hoffmann released his hold. He stepped away from me. And I realized that *he* was the political officer of *Pegasus*. Pudgy, bald-headed Hoffman. Bland Hoffmann. Hoffmann was the secret supervisor of this journey of ours, which wasn't just a journey across light years of void but also a trip into powerful, parahuman dimensions of the mind.

'Are you as mad as he is?' Bekker asked softly. 'Jocelyn, don't you have any tranquillizers left?'

'After fourteen years?'

'Please give me that bauble,' begged Bekker. 'We've played along with this farce for too long. I absolutely refuse to countenance – '

Hoffmann hit Bekker on the jaw, decking him. Hoffmann's fist heaved some weight.

Unfortunately the time-jewel did not produce quite the desired effect. In fact the stardrive quit.

If only I could find where Those Who Run Faster are hiding, I could ask them why. I've glimpsed them a couple of times but they run faster than me.

We still travel onwards, nudging the speed of light as before. Unless we achieve another breakthrough such as mine I wonder how we will ever trim our course or slow down in time for our destination.

In the bad old days prior to the advent of the timegate it's well known that not all starships arrived safely at journey's end. Some vanished entirely and were never heard from.

No matter! Extraordinarily, Helen Kaminski is pregnant. Despite her age! Despite my mandatory vasectomy of fourteen years vintage! In such singular circumstances surely she will give birth to an unusual baby. A paranormal child, whom we will lovingly foster, who will show us the true way. Her baby will be semi-alien.

Even if Helen's pregnancy is hysterical she obviously hopes to give birth to something. She is conceiving an exotic salvation for us all. If no actual, physical infant is born when she arrives at term, whatever will occur? Something strange and wonderful and wise.

We only have another few months to wait.

The Great Atlantic Swimming Race

The longest distance ever swum by a human being was 1,826 miles down the Mississippi River. This was in the year 1930. However, the swimmer in question – Mr Fred P. Newton of Clinton, Oklahoma – wasn't exactly trying to set a speed record. 27-year-old Fred spent a total of 742 hours in the water, spread over the best part of six months. His average speed was just under 2½ miles per hour.

By contrast the longest continuous swim occurred in 1981. In that year 40-year-old Ricardo Hoffman swam 299 miles non-stop down the River Parana in Argentina. (There are no piranhas in the Parana.) Ricardo was in the water for 87½ hours. He averaged 3½ miles per hour.

However, both Fred and Ricardo were swimming down rivers. Oceans are obviously different kettles of fish.

The ocean record is claimed by Walter Poenisch, Sr. of the USA. In 1978 he swam 129 miles from Cuba to Florida in 34½ hours flat. 64-year-old Walter wore flippers, and swam in a shark cage.

Let's recall one other record: for the swim of longest duration. The women's record is held by Myrtle Huddleston. In 1931 in a salt-water pool on Coney Island she clocked up 87½ hours. The men's title belongs to Charles 'Zimmy' Zibbelman, who was legless, and who managed 168 hours in a pool in Honolulu in 1941, the year of Pearl Harbor.

Thus, by way of prologue to the greatest aquatic sports feat ever attempted: the sponsored swimming race across the Atlantic in 1990.

As deputy co-ordinator of this ambitious and heroic

project I intend to defend both the concept of the race and the way it was carried out. I address myself proudly to that Olympic pantheon of the ages which bestows laurels of fame on those who perform superhuman feats at whatever the cost. I also speak to that imaginary Court of History whose jury is the dead – killed by famine, by disaster, by disease, by war, by infamy. For as we all know the Atlantic swimming race aimed to raise funds for the victims of the ongoing drought in the unhappy countries bordering the Sahara.

The route: outward from aptly named Cape Race in Newfoundland, to any part of Europe.

The Labrador Cold Current should take competitors quickly south into the Gulf Stream. The Gulf Stream would nudge the swimmers along warmly in the general direction of Ireland.

The distance: roughly 2,450 miles.

Assuming an average speed of 2 miles per hour for 14 hours a day the swimmers ought to complete the course inside of three months. Apart from the first week or two, when thermal rubber suits would need to be worn, temperature should be no big problem.

Naturally there were other problems which it took a whole year of preliminary discussions to pinpoint.

Must the competitors spend all their time in the water? Must they feed in the water? Excrete in the water? If so, how? By swimming in the nude? Must they sleep in the water by using flotation collars or rubber ducks?

Here was where the 'maggot factor' emerged: a phrase coined by certain mealy-mouthed journalists.

A body which spends a long time submerged in water eventually takes on a puffy, leprous appearance; the skin grows sick. Add to this consequence of ninety days' immersion the 'zero gravity effect' – and when the swollen swimmers reached their goal they might only manage to crawl ashore like bloated worms, hardly a pleasant spectacle.

Obviously each of the competitors would have to sleep on board a support vessel; and since the swimmers might be spread out over many sea-miles each would need a separate support vessel, with an impartial scrutineer on board to ensure that each vessel held its station exactly overnight – something easy to check with satellite navigation systems.

Then there was the vexed question of whether to use flippers. Walter Poenisch, Sr had used flippers. Why shouldn't all the competitors use an identical size and design of flipper? Indeed flippers might be the only way to keep the race within the confines of three months. Swimmers might encounter storms. Icebergs might bear down on them, compelling detours. If the race stretched out longer than three months, autumn would begin to creep towards winter, and the Atlantic would become death.

On the other hand, what if another legless 'Zimmy' Zibbelman were to enter the race?

And how about the use of snorkels? Over such a long period constant buffeting by waves might cause tissue or brain damage. Why not swim the whole course with one's face underwater like a fish?

Ah! This would cause sensory deprivation (which might become a problem anyway). Hallucinations and madness could result. Swimmers might end up believing they were cod and haddock.

In 1989 a great conference was convened in Monrovia, Liberia; a Third World venue being chosen to underline the philanthropic purpose of the race. The conference lasted for a month, and all interested parties attended: the Olympic Federation, swimming organizations, Ministry of Sport delegates from numerous countries, and representatives of multinational sponsors such as Hoffmann-LaRoche, Union Carbide, Nestlés, and Philip Morris, Inc.

Gradually the final details were thrashed out:

A maximum of one hundred competitors. A support vessel for each, with TV facilities for interviewing the aquanauts while out of the water. Sonar search in case of stray sharks. Rules for encounters with icebergs and jellyfish. Commerical and naval shipping to steer well clear of all competitors. A supertanker to be hired as a supply and hospital facility, its huge flat deck to be used as pad for a fleet of ten helicopters, equipped for aerial filming. And much else – not forgetting the international parimutuel gambling system for betting on the daily progress of the competitors.

The date for the start of the race: July 1st, 1990, exactly one year to the day after the winding up of the Monrovia Conference. This would allow adequate time for preparations, selection of competitors, and training.

Despite its romantic Arthurian name Newfoundland's Avalon Peninsula – culminating in Cape Race – is usually a dour, windswept place.

Yet on July 1st, 1990, it would have required the paintbrush of a Raoul Dufy to do justice to the offshore scene: the mile-long barrage of rafts and pontoons with the hundred support vessels moored to it, each fluttering a flag blazoned with the symbol of its aquachampion; the mile of tents and marquees gay as a medieval joust; the dragonflies of helicopters buzzing about overhead; the bright red and yellow dirigible balloon with the starting cannon jutting from the snout of its gondola.

In the style of a sports commentator let me introduce those swimmers who were to prove most prominent during the subsequent weeks . . .

But no. Wait.

In Newfoundland the uniqueness – the individual or national genius – of these special men and women was still disguised by their wetsuits (identical but for the dayglo numbers printed across the shoulders).

So let us fire that cannon. Let us speed our hundred swimmers on their way. Let us jumpcut many days hence to that morning when the leading support vessels had all quit the Labrador Cold Current for the Gulf Stream, and when our aquachampions first appeared on deck at dawn to be televised to the world no longer clad in black rubber but only in their native skins (well greased), their waddling penguin-feet, and their swimming costumes.

Let me introduce the dandy of the swimmers, Monsieur Jean-Pierre Bouvard with his slim twiddly waxed moustaches and his long tricolour *maillot* as worn at Deauville circa 1890.

And tough, suave, imperturbable Captain the Honourable Jim Turville-Hamilton, gentleman athlete and officer in Britain's Special Air Services, whose pinstripe trunks were embroidered with rolled umbrellas.

And the 'Zen swimmer', Toshiro Tanaka, tattooed with a kamikaze headband, his ears amputated to improve the stream-lining of his body.

And the 'Marxist-Leninist swimmer' from little Albania, Comrade Zug, who wore microfilm editions of selected works of Stalin and *The Collected Speeches of Enver Hoxha* stapled to his brow. Through an interpreter Comrade Zug announced himself forever at war with the revisionist USSR swimmer, lovely Anastasia Dimitrova, and the neo-capitalist Chinese swimming ace, Qi Bingbo.

Then there was the 'Jesus-Walks-on-Water swimmer', dazzlingly beautiful pentathlon champion Sally-Ann Johnson, ex-centrefold and avowed virgin, in whose cleavage was taped a microfilm Bible. Sponsored by the Christian Majority Church, she swam for the glory of the Lord.

And who could fail to mention Leila Fouad of the Fundamentalist Islamic Jamhuriya, whose body grease was stained pitch-black as a substitute for chador and yashmak? Her every passage between camouflaging Atlantic and her tent aboard the support vessel must be hidden behind seven veils. Five times a day the call to prayer blared out from a loudspeaker at the mast-head, and Leila floated motionless for a minute, ducking her head in the direction of Mecca.

In all a total of ninety-six swimmers reached the Gulf Stream but it is these eight champions that we should concentrate upon: Fouad, Johnson, Qi, Dimitrova, Zug, Tanaka, Turville-Hamilton, and Bouvard. (Oh yes, and perhaps we should add the name of René Armand of Geneva for different reasons.)

Let us hasten forward six weeks. Our champions are well in the lead. Fifty other swimmers are strung out over many miles of Atlantic waters.

By now forty-odd others have dropped out, prey to fatigue, hallucination, anomie, despair, and in one case insanity. There have been three deaths: from drowning, from a stroke, and surprisingly from hypothermia. Another swimmer vanished inexplicably.

Most of the surviving competitors are on course, though not all. A New Zealander has veered south into the lower Gulf Stream. Eventually the North-Equatorial Current will carry him back round into the Caribbean, if he persists. A Dane did not swim deep enough into the Gulf Stream; its northern branch is bearing him remorselessly towards Greenland.

Excerpts from interviews:

LEILA FOUAD: 'I am carrying water across the desert. No, that is wrong. I am carrying water *to* the desert. To the great Sahara desert where men die of drought. Every mile I swim is another mile of water for parched throats. I am a Bedu: I pitch my tent every night on a different wave, but the stars are the same!'

QI: 'Mao swam the Yellow River. A mountain is shifted by a thousand hands. The ocean succumbs to a million strokes.'

DIMITROVA: 'Hope, energy, glory of the future, hands across the water. If I were a ballerina I would dance across the wavetops. They are as wide as the steppes. I am a troika racing towards joy.'

JOHNSON: 'Praise the Lord for my muscles, praise McDonald's for the goodly protein. If I weren't a virgin I'd feel just like Samson with his hair cut off. I tell you all, each wave's a new stripe on the flag of freedom. Each beat of my heart is a prayer.'

TURVILLE-HAMILTON: 'One doesn't wish to blow one's own trumpet, but one does rather feel like Captain Scott or Sir Edmund Hillary.'

BOUVARD: 'La question natatoire est, au fond, une question phénoménologique où l'on s'adresse à notre univers fluide contemporain.'

TANAKA: 'A particle: me. A wave: it.
            Together: existence.
            Death or splendour.'

ZUG: 'Death to the swimming dogs.'

The number of deaths from the Saharan drought over the past decade was estimated at anywhere between fifteen and thirty million people. Since the race was first mooted, up to that moment in mid Gulf Stream, perhaps another three hundred thousand souls had succumbed: ten per cent interest, you might say, on the debt of drought.

But this wasn't the largest number which the media were currently bandying about. Gambling upon the progress of our champions had reached fever pitch. The total sums involved were huge; and of course five per cent of all moneys staked on swimmers was to be reserved for the Sahara Fund.

Indeed it's no exaggeration to say that daily betting on

the race was coming to rival the world stock and currency markets in the amount of cash changing hands – and because of the emotive, nationalistic, ideological implications of rapid progress or otherwise on the part of Sally-Ann or Toshiro or Anastasia (plus the intervention of speculators), the race was beginning to cause major fluctuations in the value of national currencies.

Thus it came about that repeated cramp and fever on the part of René Armand, sponsored by major Swiss banking interests, caused the Swiss Franc itself to avalanche; and unfortunately the whole of the Sahara Fund was held in Swiss Francs, once thought as impregnable as the north face of the Eiger. Half of the accumulated fund melted like snow in a sunny valley. But we did not dare shift it too hurriedly.

Day sixty-five: an unpleasant incident. Comrade Zug caught up with Anastasia Dimitrova and assaulted her in the water. Before her support vessel could intervene, 'Gentleman Jim' – who was only a short distance ahead – heeded her cries, chivalrously *turning back* to assist the Russian.

It later transpired that Jim Turville-Hamilton's father had been involved in the incompetent post-World War Two British plot to destabilize Zug's newly Communist homeland. Albion had tried to shaft Albania.

Immediately there was talk of disqualification: Jim demanding Zug's, Zug demanding Jim's and Anastasia's, Anastasia demanding Zug's. Comparisons were made with the alleged tripping of American race champion Mary Decker during the '84 Olympics by ex-South African politics student Zola Budd, following which great protests against apartheid erupted across America; these might have been more serious still if Mary Decker had been black.

However, despite all the time we had spent preparing

for a host of contingencies (culminating in the Monrovia Conference) amazingly we had drawn up no rules about competitors indecently assaulting one another in the midst of the extraterritorial ocean.

Zug swam on, in the lead.

Jim and Anastasia swam hand in hand for a while, to the disgust of Sally-Ann Johnson.

Monsieur Bouvard referred to 'un crime passionel politique'.

Leila Fouad took to wearing huge black goggles.

Day seventy: Captain Turville-Hamilton announced his engagement in the water to Anastasia Dimitrova; and the British Pound sagged from 50c to 35c. Speculators started to speculate about a possible future *negative value* for the Pound, whereby one Pound Sterling would be valued at (say) minus five US cents. Britain's long-reigning Conservative government declared itself unperturbed. Here was an economic tool at last for cancelling out the national debt. The US government might care to apply it one day to their trillion dollar budget deficit.

Day seventy-three: Comrade Zug assaulted Leila Fouad who had overtaken him, by swimming close and snatching off her black-glass goggles while she was praying. A brief, one-sided nuclear exchange took place between the Fundamentalist Islamic Jamhuriya and Zug's homeland, following which Comrade Zug was the only surviving native Albanian. Undeterred, Zug declared (through an interpreter) that just as long as one member of the true Albanian Communist Party remained alive, Lenin, Stalin, and Enver Hoxha were in safe hands.

Day eighty: perhaps due to side effects from the amputation of his ears (his sense of direction being upset by parasites?) Toshiro Tanaka began to swim in circles.

TANAKA: 'Seas, a sphere of water
In space; no land.
Straight line is through, not across!'

The next day Tanaka dived like a sleek seal; and did not come up again.

The Yen also dived. Unfortunately the Sahara Fund had at last been transferred, secretly, out of Swiss Francs into Yen.

However, Zen priests claimed that Tanaka had surfaced in the Sea of Japan. The Yen rallied slightly, then sank.

Since all major currencies were now fluctuating wildly in response to the strokes of the swimmers, what remained of the Fund (to date) was hastily transferred by an increasingly eccentric chief accountant into a basket of minor currencies. Money for the Third World ought to be banked in the Third World, he explained. Hence his sudden new allegiance to the Vietnamese Dong, the Colombian Peso (unfortunately, a civil war broke out in Colombia), the Turkish Lira (hyperinflation instantly set in), and the Malawian Banda (a military coup followed).

Day eighty-five: an Irish seagull alighted briefly, like the dove from the Ark, upon the head of Sally-Ann Johnson.

Day ninety: Qi Bing-bo stepped ashore in Ballyconneely Bay, Connemara, and criticized himself.

Comrade Zug arrived second, an hour later, soon to disappear mysteriously into the ranks of the IRA.

Arriving offshore, Sally-Ann Johnson declared that since Connemara appeared not to be American territory she would not set one toe upon it. She turned and headed out to sea again, to swim home. A US nuclear 'stealth' submarine finally surfaced, and deterred her.

Leila Fouad also refused to tread that soil – of infidels, soaked with alcohol.

Monsieur Bouvard stood upon the *plage* of County Clare, drank champagne, smoked a Gauloise, and quoted Descartes. ('I swim, therefore I am.')

Captain Turville-Hamilton gallantly carried his Soviet fiancée ashore over rocks. (See the feature movie subsequently made about the young couple, the darlings of the world, starring Anastasia and an American actor closely resembling Turville-Hamilton with whom she later ran away, before returning homesick to Russia: *Chariots of Water*.)

Alas, it was then discovered that besides lodging the depleted Fund in eccentric currencies, the chief accountant had embezzled large sums; and disappeared without trace.

When the residue was withdrawn with difficulty from Ho Chi Minh City, Bogota, Ankara, and Lilongwe, and all outstanding bills were paid, and some prizes awarded, it transpired that no money whatever remained.

This should not discourage us! The principle was correct. We need to think even more ambitiously. We need to think bigger.

If the Atlantic can be swum successfully, why not the wider yet warmer Pacific?

This is what I propose to raise adequate aid to save the peoples of the Sahara: the Great Pacific Swimming Race! The drought in Africa continues. The Sahara expands year by year. We have ample time on our side to organize this even more challenging international competition. I can already see the route in my mind's eye: either from Baja California via the Northern Equatorial Current to the Philippines (only 8,700 miles), or else from Punta Pariñas in Peru by way of the Southern Equatorial Current to New Guinea (about 9,200 miles). The shorter route would take round about 310 days, which does not seem wholly unreasonable – it's well within the confines of a single year.

Obviously shark cages will need to be used. These should be specially designed so that they're huge, giving each swimmer a sense of perfect freedom and space. How silly to swim the wide Pacific inside a little cage! I foresee giant cages twice the length and breadth of an Olympic swimming pool, and a hundred yards high (in case of giant waves), jutting ahead from the bows of each support vessel. Oil-rig technology is quite capable of manufacturing and fitting these.

Over a period of 300-plus days the field of competitors is likely to spread out rather more than in the Atlantic. Even the leading swimmers might be half a day or a whole day apart from each other. Might this lessen the keen interest of the world audience? I very much doubt it!

I have a dream. Why should the whole waistline of the world not one day be circumnavigated by swimmers?

The Wire Around the War

Today as usual hundreds of buses from all over the country are converging upon these fields and narrow lanes. A marshal waves our own bus on to a parking place at the head of a long line of other buses decorated with peace posters. After three hours of travel we can disembark and stretch our legs beside golden cornfields ablaze with poppies.

An invasion of poppies! Maybe the poppies are a nuisance to the farmer, but they're a beautiful nuisance.

As journeys go, ours has been quite short. Further up the lane I spot a small party of Africans in tribal robes. Beyond them, some Buddhist monks in saffron cloth.

But wherever in the world we marchers come from, you might say that the longest journey begins right now – with the walk to the wire. Beyond which, space undergoes a change. From which, not everyone returns.

'Alicia! You forgot your sandwiches!'

It's Mark, swinging my rainbow-ribboned knapsack. Mark's a physicist, so he understands a little of events beyond the wire.

'Oh . . . I was just going to have a pee. Hang on a moment, will you?'

Actually, till this moment I hadn't thought of emptying my bladder; though it's a sensible idea. There's a little copse of quivering aspens behind the bus, which other marchers are using for the purpose.

By the time I rejoin Mark, Sandra and Jack have unfurled our banner with its white dove swooping across a sky-blue background, a broken rifle clutched in one claw like a snapped twig.

Fronted by the banner, the thirty of us set off up the lane past all the buses which arrived before. Several times we detour on to the verge to let a new bus nose its way through. Away across the cornfields we can see another long line of buses parking on another lane.

From here to the wire is a good two miles, and the lane is crowded. Soon I find myself munching a tuna sandwich. I don't quite recollect deciding I was hungry, or diving my hand into my knapsack. It's almost as though I want the sandwich out of the way. Well, it's easier to carry food in your tummy than slung over your shoulder!

The others start to sing. *We Have Overcome* . . .

A marshal cycles by, tinkling his bell in accompaniment.

'How many here today?' calls Mark.

'We reckon thirty thousand.'

'Will we even get *close* to the wire?' I ask.

The marshal laughs. 'Oh yes. You'll touch it. Everyone will. That's the whole point, isn't it?' He cycles on.

Our party overtakes a young fellow pushing a wheelchair in which an old, wrinkled, joyful woman sits with a thick brown rug over her knees even though the weather's warm. As our banner-bearers bunch together to pass by, our linen dove hunches its wings and dives for a moment like a hawk. How the old woman smiles and claps her hands at our song. And joins in, quaveringly.

We in turn are overtaken by a striding churchman in grey flannel suit and purple singlet with dogcollar. Maybe's he's a bishop. He wears his pectoral cross slung upside-down.

'Look, Mark!'

What a host of marchers stream ahead; and how slowly we make our way. But right across the very next field – of oats – I can see arc-lights, towers, and a long barrier shimmering with rainbow colours, lancing out occasional flashes where razor-wire twists sunlight.

An ugly black helicopter is lumbering up from close

behind the wire. From very close. It looks like a flying bathtub with rotors at both ends; and it must be big enough to carry an armoured car inside it. All we hear, even so, is the distant clang of bells and clash of tambourines and shrill of whistles sounded to ward it off.

'That's a Chinook,' says Mark.

The chopper only reaches a height of fifty feet before it banks over on its side and heads away inward – shrinking ever so fast. Within a few seconds it's no more than a tiny smut of soot.

I find I'm finishing off my second sandwich of salami and tomato.

And here we are, right next to the wire.

Mark and I, and thousands of others in a line two or three deep stretching away into the distance.

Behind us, ripe oats.

Ahead, death and destruction, all the engines and personnel of doom.

First of all there are coiled bales of ordinary barbed wire, shoulder-high, impaled upon steel stakes. Then there's a twelve-foot-high barbed wire fence topped with tangles of razor-wire which could slice gloves, boots, and flesh into shreds. Finally there's an inner fence which is just as high. We all reach to touch the outermost wire at least once.

Beyond the triple barrier are runways, fuel trucks, F-111 fighter-bombers, giant Galaxy cargo jets, and sunken silos. Missile transporters trundle slowly about. Radar dishes swivel. Military police speed about in jeeps. Choppers poke their snouts through the air with lazy menace like questing sharks.

Obviously this area is an American base. But is it in Britain or Sicily or Turkey, or in America itself? Who knows in which country the original is sited?

At first glance the base looks jam-packed with hardware and personnel. But this is something of an optical illusion: 'a compression effect', as Mark calls it. Also, the size of objects diminishes rapidly. A Galaxy jet a bit further away looks no bigger than a gnat.

Here in the real world outside the wire, a mile is a mile. Inside, distances obey a 'negative exponential curve' – which means that whole bases and battlefields get compressed into a strip of space which we, from here, would only take to be a few yards wide. A few feet. A few inches. Deep in the interior a nuclear explosion would throw up a mushroom cloud no bigger than an actual field mushroom sprouting from horse dung in a pasture.

As we head slowly around the wire the American base shimmers into a Soviet base with different uniforms, different planes, different rockets pointing at the sky. Maybe this next base is located in East Germany or in Mongolia. But here it is, as well. Here is its double, its 'analogue', busily functioning away – while somewhere else the original base hunches frozen and inert, wrapped in Sleeping Beauty slumber. Nothing moves in those quiet places of the Earth where no one goes. All the deathly activity has been translated inside the 'event horizon' of the wire – into the circles of hell within.

'See: American and Russian and all other war bases are connected topologically,' says Mark. 'They share the same linked space.'

'And we keep them glued together inside, don't we? It's the pressure of our presence that pens them in. And the bells we ring. And the songs we sing.'

'And something else too, Alicia.'

'Yes. Something else.'

Within: steel and concrete, tanks and warheads. Without: oats and corn and poppies and happiness.

There's a long queue at the first of the telescopes.

'Shall we wait?' he asks.

'Yes, Mark. I want to see.'

Sandra and Jack and the banner move onward.

In fact it's only a quarter of an hour till I get my turn at the eyepiece. Through it, I spy depth within depth, airbase within airbase, camp within camp, death within death, as far as the lens can pierce.

'Could those soldiers ever burst out through the wire?'

'Not while we're here, Alicia. Not while *he's* here.'

Not while he's here. Our god-child. Our devil-child. Our prince of peace.

I say child. Yet what is childish about our prince – apart from his age? Apart from the fact that he was originally wheeled here in a stroller through chocolate mud four years ago – when there was only a single war base newly built behind the wire. When he was only two years old.

Now all the war bases of the world are here, securely fenced in.

His mother was an ordinary peace protester, Sarah Gardner. Recently divorced. A social worker. He was a toddler, Tommy Gardner. And he reached out from his stroller and grasped the wire.

A Christ child was born in Bethlehem. The years rolled by and the world witnessed the Crusades and the Holy Inquisition and the torture and burning of witches and heretics, and pogroms and infernos and holocausts, and a hundred wars of religion, and the manufacture of fifty thousand nuclear warheads to defend the faithful from atheism.

Perhaps it *had* to be the devil's turn to be born as man, to save the world. Maybe only the devil could be bothered or concerned enough. Maybe only the devil understood evil and madness and stupidity well enough. Not God but Satan. Not Allah but Iblis.

Yet not without some sacrifice. Last time, the Christ child sacrificed himself to save mankind. This time, it's up to us to make the sacrifice ourselves.

Willingly. Oh so willingly.

We continue on along the outside of the wire for a further mile. Two miles.

'There he is!'

Up on a stout wooden platform just above the heads of the crowd sits our devil-child, our hope, our bliss. Who was once the toddler Tommy Gardner. Who is now altered utterly.

At that particular point the barbed bales are piled high so that the platform thrusts right into them. Steps lead up to it. Ten minutes more, and we're near them.

One of Tommy's great ogre hands brushes the sharp barbs as you might stroke a cat. His other clawed hand is open and empty.

He's horned and bloated and huge – the size of a young elephant. His great violet eyes blink monotonously at the wire. The eyes of an octopus? His mouth is a giant horny beak.

He's a gross fat Buddha mated with Beelzebub. He's a beast-human. He's the greatest ugliness in the world; and yet he has an eerie grandeur. So therefore the dais around him is thickly strewn with flowers: with poppies, musky white lilies, spikes of pink lupin.

He starts to nod his inhuman head. His empty hand begins to flex open and shut.

And a yellow-robed monk mounts the steps to the platform, his palms together in blessing. His skull is shaved bald, though his face is young; he can't be much more than twenty.

The monk bows his head. Our Tommy grasps him gently round the waist. Tommy's claw-hand completely encloses the young man's midriff. For a while the crowd falls silent, and the silence spreads. No gongs beat, no whistles blow. Then our devil-child hoists the monk aloft. The beak gapes; Tommy pops the offering in. Gulps; and swallows.

And the crowd breathes out a sigh like wind rustling through wheat. Tambourines clash, and bells clang – as rainbow light blushes along the wire.

'How soon till he feeds again?'

Mark shrugs. 'An hour or two. Could be three. It varies.'

'Next time he feeds, *I'll* be the one.'

There: I've said it. At last I have allowed the thought to surface.

Mark gapes. 'What?'

'Next time – '

'But . . . Alicia, you can't be serious!'

'Why shouldn't I feed myself to him, if I wish? And if he wants me? Someone has to feed him willingly. Do you think it's too vile a payment for peace? One life every few hours – so that untold millions of people can survive? And fields and forests and beasts and birds?'

'Of course not. Of course,' answers Mark in confusion.

Our prince of peace has hardly ever spoken. But in the beginning he told us why he must take us to him one by one, absorbing our flesh into his flesh. The power of his mind maintains the prison of the wire, but he needs to channel the energy of our own souls into it.

And why not indeed? In the old days we who campaigned for peace sacrificed our comfort, our freedom, sometimes even our lives. And sometimes we made headway for a while. Then the momentum of war would sweep onward. Nowadays our sacrifice is always of life itself – as regards the person who makes the sacrifice. But this sacrifice is completely effective.

'When did you decide?' asks Mark.

'Now. Earlier. I'm not sure.'

'But there'll be other people here who are eager to . . . Willing to, anyway!'

'*I'm* the person who feels willing. Me, here, right now. Maybe no one else is willing just at this moment. But I am. And because I am, in another few hours somebody else will be willing.' I even laugh. 'That somebody else doesn't need to be you, Mark. Don't think of it! You carry on considering the physics of this thing. The topology of space inside the wire, okay? Maybe you'll make some wonderful, vital discovery – just in case our prince ever grows tired, or goes away. That's your path. Mine is up these steps.'

I ease my way closer, with Mark at my shoulder.

'Be happy,' I tell him. 'Don't feel sad. Don't feel guilty. Think about connectedness.'

'I thought *we* were connected. You and I.'

'Yes we are. And we'll always stay connected, forever after.'

'You'll be dead.'

'Better little me, than millions burned in a fireball.'

There's really nothing more to say. Any other talk would now be trivial. So we stand together inside our own silence, Mark and I, while around us songs are sung, and gongs go *bong*, and bells clang and tinkle.

An hour passes, then most of another hour.

Till once again our prince begins to nod his head and to grope with his empty hand.

Mark stays below when I ascend the steps, on to the rafts of poppies and crunchy lupins.

Tommy is so close to me now. So large, so monstrous. His body smells oddly of fish-oil, though the dominant smell is the musk of lilies. I'm afraid yet not afraid. Maybe my fear is my courage.

He notices me. His violet eyes regard me. Not exactly with compassion but rather with a deep, calm, soothing vacancy. Within him is all the violence in the world, which he annuls and neuters.

I wonder: within the boundary of the wire, is time the same as it is for us? Is consciousness the same? Some of those soldiers who are trapped in the collapsed geometry of that zone perhaps never wished to be soldiers; perhaps hated being soldiers. Do they grieve that an incomprehensible hell has closed about them? Or do they simply go about their military business in a species of trance, repeating the same activities day after day, unaware that everything has altered? I don't know. Perhaps I soon will know.

Tommy's free hand moves towards me. His grip is so light, yet so unrelenting. He lifts me upward, headfirst to his gaping beak. I see a red cave, a dark throbbing tunnel opening downward.

And I don't die.

I flash with brightness. Rainbow colours wash my senses. I taste gold and silver and steel. I am extended. I am the wire; the wire is me.

I sense the presence of my prince in the way a wave senses the whole ocean. I sense the thousands of souls preceding mine – the young monk and all the others – as a fish senses the other fish swimming in a vast shoal. Or as a bird senses the rest of its flock. Bird or fish are only one little individual mind. Yet at the same time each is the whole of the flock. How else could a shoal all dart in the same direction at once? How else could a flock swoop or soar?

Together we are the circuit of the wire. I'm at once a little part of it, yet nevertheless all of it.

I'm at peace; yet it's a peace which pulses like a beating heart, a peace like the breeze upon a mountain top, a peace like the rolling, powerful sea.

War is compressed within me like a tumour which is frozen, like a cancer paralysed. Or like an oyster's pearl.

Tommy lets us glimpse the future reflected in this pearl. Or perhaps, timelessly, the future has already happened – so that we sense events which have occurred already outside the wire, or are occurring even now.

Within fifty years the first alien beings are joining us in the wire. They have come to Earth, or else human beings have reached the stars; I'm not sure which. Maybe Mark found a way to connect Earthspace to Starspace. At first these aliens arrive out of curiosity; then presently as pilgrims. I believe Tommy is the size of a blue whale by now. Yet his hands still reach out, one to strum the wire, the other to accept the visitors who offer themselves to him.

And our flock, our shoal, always grows.

And the wire gleams bright.

When Idaho Dived

'Gather round, elders, wives and juniors! Gather round, brothers and sisters of the tribe! Listen to the tale of how I piloted the sand submarine named Idaho down to the deep cave of treasure and bones.

'So you have heard it all before? Well, you will hear it once more . . .'

In the century following the end of the world, when skies were always grey, when plants grew flimsily, when birds fell from the air, when even the rattlesnake lost the voice in his tail, when wild dogs were our food, and we were theirs, the last tribe of the family of man made its way out into this desert land. For all the rest of the earth had become a deadly desert, but here, where the dunes roll and the salt-pans glisten, was merely desert pure and simple: clean desert as it had always been.

Sores sprouted on our bodies, and strange thoughts moved into our minds: strong dreams and nightmares. The sicker we became and the thinner with hunger, and the more we glowed in the dark with fever-heat such as only the rattlesnake was able to perceive in earlier times, the more so did the minds of some of us children grow fierce with new senses; and of all I was the fiercest, though my legs were rickety and my chest was patched with red spiders' webs.

In those days, children pointed the way to safe pools and edible roots, pulling their puzzled ailing elders by the hands. And I pointed farthest of all, deep into the desert, which seemed a wild and foolish way to walk; but it was clear and clean to me.

The journey was too late for all but one of the grown-ups of the last tribe of people; but we children knew which of those who fell were safe to eat, and which parts of which ones: the liver of one, the brain of another, the heart of a third. What parts we did not eat fell to the lot of the mongrel packs on our heels; and many hounds died of what they ate, or became enfeebled and could not follow us onward.

Only seven of us arrived here: six children, and young Gabriel's Grandad whose eyes had melted many years before when a sun suddenly rose in the north. Gabriel's Grandad never seemed to know how to die – as though this was a skill he had lost along with his eyesight.

And so we came at last to this dry valley in the very heart of the belly of the desert, where we found to our joy this metal village where in later years you were bred from our loins and now dwell.

What a person knows with full familiarity, a person cannot see with the eyes of fresh perception; so I will say how our home seemed to us when we first arrived; and how it sounded to the ears of Gabriel's Grandad.

Side by side along the valley floor stood seven mighty cylinders, all jet-black, with winged towers on top of each to enter by. These are our long-houses now.

When we told their shape and size and structure to Gabriel's Grandad, he answered madly that they were called submarines; that they were made to swim beneath the seven seas – a sea being a pool of salty water as wide and as deep as the sky.

You've never seen such a thing as a sea, my tribe. No more have I. So what were these mighty vessels, which Gabriel's Grandad said were made for swimming beneath the seven seas, doing here standing in a line in middle-desert? Had the great winds of the end of the world, of which our parents had talked, picked those submarines out

of the pool called the Pacific and carried them here and set
them all down so neatly together?

'Not so!' wheezed Grandad. He recollected – so he
claimed – that submarines had been buried in this empty
desert many long years ago, to get rid of them safely
without harm to fish or water. They were 'active', he said,
and their activity could rot a man's testicles. The great
winds of the end of the world must have uncovered them
all, so that the seven submarines appeared like a village
planted on the valley floor. Or perhaps other winds since
had done the work, funnelling down and scooping out our
valley.

We advanced. By piling up sand in a ramp for several
hours, then using blind Grandad as our ladder, we were
able to scramble up on top of one of the submarines and
gain access by way of the 'cunning tower', the clever high
entrance door. We descended and explored the crowded
darkness within, which wasn't as dark to our eyes as it
might have been to our dead parents' eyes; besides,
mushrooms and fungi glowed on furniture and tubes and
walls.

We found shelter. We found food: those fungi and
mushrooms. We found water. We had found our new
homes.

We traced the word-shapes that our ancestors once used,
and which we discovered within this submarine and the
others, upon Grandad's palm; and he told us the names of
our new long-houses: names such as Kentucky and Idaho.

But Grandad wasn't able to tell us a great deal. It was as
though those words told him what he had forgotten,
namely how to die; and he did so soon after. So we ate his
best parts.

Yet Grandad's best parts did not last long, nor for that
matter did the fungi and mushrooms growing in our seven
fine sanctuaries. We ate our way through the lot; and
hungered again, and our minds grew fierce.

It came to me, in this glowing state of being, that Grandad had been mad these many long years, and that what he had said about the origin of these 'submarines' was nonsense. He was of the old days; he had no vision. It was obvious to me that these great hulls had *dived*, for they were of the right shape to thrust themselves sinuously through other matter with as little hindrance as could be. But though our ancestors were crazy and caused the end of the world, no one could have been crazy enough to carry these vast hulks for the weeks and weeks (or even years) it would have taken to bring them here, just to pile sand over them. Nor could any possible wind have borne them all the way from the Pacific Pool. Therefore the submarines must have dived right here, down through the sands of the desert; and here was their real home and harbour. Rocks jut out of the desert, but the great pools of sand in between might sink as deep as the core of the world.

And why should these vessels dive down through this part of the desert if there was not something rich and rare beneath to seek?

Grandad had mumbled at times concerning the caves that men had dug during the last days before the end of the world, before the false suns burned and the wild winds blew and the sky became grey for years: caves filled with meat and drink, with forever-food and fresh water. The people of old must have dived to such caves in these submarines, down through the sand and the earth to the deep safe places.

And maybe our ancestors weren't all dead! Maybe we weren't the only remaining tribe of man! Maybe deep below our feet lived men and women who could be our new parents or servants, or new brothers and sisters.

Could a submarine take us down below the ground to the caves of our ancestors?

Oh that was a wild and glowing time, a hungry time, a

yearning time, a time of bright visions and fierce wishes; especially for me.

And as I sat there alone within Idaho, starving, I conceived – not as you conceive, brothers and sisters, sons and daughters; but I conceived within my mind. I conceived a power such as never before nor ever since has been conceived.

I went to the room in the midst of Idaho where there are seats to sit in and many handles and little jutting metal fingers to push and pull and twist. I sat me down. The power burgeoned within me. I grasped handles. I snapped the metal fingers up and down. And Idaho awoke.

I know you do not fully credit this, my juniors. I know that you whisper behind my back that this is simply a 'myth' of how we came to be as rich and prosperous and populous as we are today; and how many do I count of us here today, crowded into this mighty steel hall of the self-same Idaho? This hall, which Grandad named the 'missile compartment'? Nigh on two hundred souls! Oh I know that your voices buzz behind my back; for I hear them buzz, saying that all our forever-food and other riches were already stored here in Idaho and its six companions when we children first arrived. But I tell you: it was not so! It was just as I say!

Idaho awoke under my hands. Idaho moved. Idaho tilted and dived, down through the sand, down through the earth.

After a while Idaho levelled off, and travelled. I know not for how long. Time had stopped.

Eventually Idaho also stopped. Its metal heart quit thumping, its lungs ceased to pant softly, its blood no longer pounded.

I climbed up through the cunning tower and discovered that Idaho was at rest in a huge stone chamber many times its size, where lights burned brightly. The mouths of several well-lit tunnels led away, but Idaho was too huge to have entered the chamber by any of these mouths. Yet behind Idaho the chamber wall was flawless – apart from ancient marks of cutting and chiselling. Nevertheless Idaho had slipped through.

Many things were stored in that first chamber; and many more things in other chambers, to which the tunnels led. There were enormous stocks of sealed forever-food, boxes of fine garments, stores of seed, barrels and bottles of drink, tools, knives and axes, neat bundles of stitched bound paper covered with meaningless word-shapes, enigmatic devices of all shapes and sizes wrought in metal and glass.

I found many skeletons, too, the bones of our ancestors lying about on the floors. But though many still had leathern skin and muscle-string and hair attached, these bones did not whisper anything to me.

A month and more I must have spent in filling Idaho with the plunder of these chambers, enough to last us many lifetimes. I sensed that my small band of sisters and brothers would not starve in the meantime, however long I took; for did I not say that time stood still? Yet while I worked I also feasted and slept and put on weight.

Finally I retired back into that room in the midst of Idaho and felt for the power again; and the power duly came to me.

Idaho carried me and my cargo back. Idaho rose and surfaced once more here in our desert as though it had never been away.

My brothers and sisters fed; they drank. A tiny lump of forever-food fills the belly wonderfully, does it not? Presently we increased and multiplied.

And that is how it was, when Idaho dived.

So you have heard all this before? And you wonder why, if this was so, the power has never come to me a second time and Idaho has never dived again?

Listen, elders, wives and juniors, sisters and brothers of the tribe! I am old; and until now there was no need for the power. Yet I feel that the power is near me once more. I feel it waiting for my hand to grasp it.

I tell you that there is nowhere else in this world for us to live except here amidst these sands. Yet now that the all-grey skies of yesteryear have cleared, the sun beats hot upon us by day, the moon shines cold by night. Every day it is too cold and too hot. And I know that two hundred mouths, even the little mouths of our golden babes held in your arms as you hear me, will gobble many lifetimes of forever-food before many more years pass by. What then, my tribe, what then?

Do you challenge me to dive Idaho down again underneath the earth to the same chambers of plenty? Do I hear that?

The power, oh my tribe, may only be used once in one direction.

But it can be used again – in another direction!

Consider the sun by day, the moon by night! Those are *places* afloat in the sky, of fire and of ice. Consider the thousand smaller twinkling lights in the black sky, which first showed themselves to us when the sky-blanket fell into threads!

The power tells me that we must go to one of those lights in the sky! Idaho will take us all up there, to fields of green and to bubbling streams, to plains of skipping game-beasts and pools of fat fishes. It will take us all to a new living-place, as once it took me to the caves of treasure and bones; and it will take us timelessly.

Do not doubt! For here you are all gathered together; and did you not know that the cunning tower is closed? Nothing will leave by it now, not even a breath of air, till I say it is safe.

Now I shall go to the room of handles and metal fingers, to steer us to a star.

Let me through! Do you not feel the floor beneath our feet begin to tilt? Upward, yes a little upward!

Let me through, I say!

Why are you all staring at me so? Why are you hemming me in so tightly? What is this harm you mean me? What folly is this, what madness?

I repeat: the power is upon me! This is the time! Can you not feel Idaho quivering to rise? Do you not wish to tell your babes' babes the tale of how Idaho *flew* – to a star in the sky?

You are fools, fools. Alas, my tribe, you are fools.

And now you will eat my brain and my heart and my liver. But first of all you will eat my tongue, which spoke to you, saying all these things.

On the Dream Channel Panel

I had always regarded myself as a vivid dreamer, but even I was amazed when my dreams were interrupted by the advertisements.

I was climbing by rope-ladder up the outside of a lighthouse to catch an airship due to depart from the top – all in my dream, of course – when the scene suddenly blanked out and cans of food were dancing round me to jolly musical accompaniment, mainly percussion.

The labels showed some peculiar fruit or vegetable, which at first I took to be maize but then decided looked more like a hairy banana; and a moment later the tops of the cans ripped off of their own accord, and the contents emptied out, *steaming*, on to floating plates – so those must have been self-heating cans, only no one had put self-heating cans on the market just yet. Stripped of their hairy yellow skins, the insides of the 'fruits' seemed more like frankfurters.

A choir of disembodied voices sang out gaily, '*Pop a can of kallopies!*' And there was I back on the rope-ladder again. The dream continued . . .

'Have you ever heard of a tropical fruit called a *kallopie*?' I asked Phyllis when I got to school the next morning. Phyllis teaches Geography.

'You can get all sorts of imports at the Third World Food Centre,' she said. 'Okra, yams, breadfruit. Maybe you can get whatever it is there.'

'But have you ever heard of them?'

'No,' she admitted. 'What are they? Where are they from?'

Not from the Third World, I thought; just from the world of my dreams. But since when did dreams have commercial breaks in them?

I pursued this line of thought. It so happened that the commercial TV networks had been blacked out by strikes for the past week; and while I hardly regarded myself as the kind of TV addict likely to suffer from withdrawal symptoms, maybe without knowing it *I was*. Were we not all conditioned, to a greater or less degree, by advertising? Wasn't it a sad fact that commercials were often better made than the programmes? Hence my subconscious felt obliged to offer a substitute . . .

Admittedly this was a far-out hypothesis, but it led on to the thought that if *I*, a fairly selective viewer, was hallucinating advertisements in my dreams, how much more so must many of the school kids (TV addicts all of them) be feeling the strain?

My second class that day was Current Affairs; so I decided that we would discuss the role of the mass media. Who knows, maybe I was the first adult to notice this quaint phenomenon, of advertising-dreams?

After a while I asked the class, 'Do any of you ever *dream* about watching TV? For instance, how about last night? Think back!'

Alas, no one could recall anything. Still, that wasn't at all unusual. So I set my class a simple project: to keep pencil and paper by their beds and note down the first thought in their minds when they woke up. For this is an infallible way of remembering dreams. However absurd or random, and eminently forgettable, that first thought might seem to be, nevertheless once capture and fix it, and like a string of silk scarves emerging by magic from a conjuror's sleeve, in its wake dream after dream would spill forth from amnesia into the light of day.

* * *

My own dreams were broken into again that night. As I lay abed in my little bachelor flat, enjoying some wonderfully Byzantine spy story of my unconscious mind's devising, suddenly there came a commercial for *koozels* – which were apparently a crunchy snack wondrous to the taste buds.

The next morning I was supposed to be teaching that same class the history of the French Revolution; but I checked up on the assignment first.

About half of the class had done as I'd asked, probably because of the novelty value; so I put it to them, 'Did any of you have a dream interrupted by some sort of advertisement – like a commercial on TV?'

And the jailbait of the group, sexy fifteen-year-old Mitzi Hayes stuck her hand up. She alone.

'A voice was trying to sell me something crunchy and delicious.'

'Called what, Mitzi?'

'A noodle.'

General hilarity erupted; the rest of the class were sure she was japing me.

'Think, Mitzi.'

'No, a *koozel*: that's what it was!'

'Anyone else?'

'No one else.'

So I quickly switched over to the topic of Robespierre, determined to avoid the teacher's trap of asking young Mitzi, when school was out, to a coffee bar to discuss her sleeping activities . . .

What I did instead was place a small ad in the local newspaper: '*Koozels or kallopies? Anyone who dreams of these please reply Box 17 in confidence.*' And for good measure, digging deeper into my pocket, I placed similar small ads in four national newspapers.

Within a week I had eleven replies. Remarkably, most

were from Appleby itself; and none was from further away than twenty miles.

So the twelve of us – discreetly excluding Mitzi – got together at my flat one evening the following week.

We were a retired dentist, an antiquarian bookseller, a ladies' hairdresser, a butcher, a hamburger cook, a shop assistant, a secretary, an unemployed plumber, a garage mechanic, a middle-aged lady medium, a postman, and a teacher (myself). So we constituted ourselves the 'Dream Channel Panel', with myself as Chairman, and tried to puzzle out what the explanation was, and who we could complain to.

Max Edmunds was our dentist; and in his opinion some scientific laboratory in this very average – and thus ideal – town of Appleby had been funded by big advertising money to build a prototye dream-transmitter which could interfere with the brain waves of sleeping people and insert messages. He pointed to the restricted radius of replies I'd received, as evidence of a local source. At present only mock advertisements for imaginary products were being broadcast as tests; but soon it would be the real – and dangerously invasive – thing.

To date, by the way, another half a dozen products had paraded themselves before us in our nightly fantasies, besides repetitions of kallopies and koozels; and these had all been exotic and implausible foodstuffs: such as *kalakiko*, a powder which when sprinkled on a slice of bread promptly sprouted luscious brown mushrooms; *humbish*, an oily liquid which seemingly congealed a pint of water into lobster in aspic; and *ampathuse*, sparkling golden wine in self-chilling flasks . . . But why go on? The TV dispute was over by now; the dream-advertising wasn't.

Mary Gallagher, our medium, had originally been of the opinion that the commercials were mischievous spirit messages 'from the other side'. But when Elsie Levin, our cook at the new McDonalds's in town, suggested, 'Perhaps it isn't *really* advertising? Perhaps it's a Government thing? Maybe it's an experiment in mind-control!' Mary threw the fat in the fire by saying, 'And maybe one of *us* is actually one of *them*? If it's people, not spirits, who are doing it – why then, they could have read your small ads as easily as we could, Mr Peck.'

It took the best part of the next half-hour to try to prove our bona fides to each other; and it was Glenda Scott, our hairdresser, who finally hauled us back on course.

'Maybe there isn't any dream-transmitter,' she said. 'Not in Appleby, anyway – not in *our* world. What if there's another world alongside ours: one where the people really do eat such things? What if they know how to broadcast dreams as entertainment – with commercials on the different dream-channels? And somehow we've picked these up. One of our hair-driers used to pick up radio paging at the hospital. "Doctor Muhammed to Emergency!"'

Max Edmunds nodded. 'A tooth filling sometimes picks up radio shows.'

Glenda beamed at this confirmation. 'So we're intercepting dream broadcasts from the other world. But not,' she added for the benefit of Mary, '*your* "other world".'

'So where is it?' asked Tom Pimm, our butcher. 'I don't see it.'

'Of course not. How could you? You're awake, and in our world.'

Max snapped his fingers. 'Ah. You might have a point there! It's a well-known fact that if you keep somebody awake for long enough, they'll start hallucinating. People have to dream, and if they can't get any sleep to do it in, they'll do it wide awake. Might I suggest that one of us volunteer to stay awake for several days – while the rest of us form a rota to *keep* him awake? To see what happens.'

Jon Rhys Jones, our unemployed plumber, raised his hand. 'I suppose I'd better be the volunteer. Got nothing better to do, have I? And the wife's away visiting her mother.'

'Over to you, Brian,' Max said to me, as Chairman. 'We'll only need one person on duty to start with, but after the first couple of days we'd better have several in attendance.'

I took a vote on the proposal; but we were in general agreement, so I drew up a rota then and there.

'Room's swimming,' mumbled Jon, five days later, as Glenda and Rog (our postman) marched him to and fro across the lounge in his house. 'Can't stand up.'

So they steered him to the sofa, where Max checked his pulse; then Glenda sat beside him, and periodically slapped him on the cheek like a glamorous interrogator, varying this by pinching and shaking him.

It was late Saturday night. Besides Glenda, Rog and Max, I was there, and Mary Gallagher and Tom Pimm. Empty lager cans lay about on the carpet, though we weren't allowing our volunteer to consume any alcohol in case this helped him to pass out. The TV was on, and in the kitchen a radio was playing pop music. All to keep us lively. At twelve o'clock the night-shift was due to arrive.

And all week long the dream-commercials had continued to besiege us – though not Jon – most recently with outstanding claims for *sklesh*, a jar of violet paste to be spread on kallopies, as a relish.

It was eleven-thirty when it happened.

Suddenly part of the ceiling glowed – and it was as if a cornucopia opened. Or as if a jackpot had paid off in actual fruits. From nowhere, cans and jars and tins and phials fell through, bouncing on the carpet. One can hit Mary on the toe, and she squealed. We all retreated to the walls for a while, dragging Jon with us.

In fact the shower of produce probably lasted for less than a minute, but by then the middle of the room was ankle-deep in kallopies and sklesh, kalakiko and humbish and other things – enough to fill half a dozen hampers. As soon as the shower ceased Max rushed forward, grabbed up a can of kallopies and popped it open. Immediately, with a little cry, he set it down again and blew on his fingers. Then he hastened to the kitchen and returned with plates and forks. Soon we were all picnicking on the sizzling sausage-fruits – all except for poor Jon, who had staggered back to the sofa and fallen fast asleep. Goodness, kallopies on their own tasted delicious enough; but spread with sklesh they were bliss.

'Have to give it to them,' admitted Tom Pimm, kissing his fingers. 'First rate. Beats any sausage I've ever made.'

And Glenda winked at Mary. 'Our first delivery from the other world, eh?'

The doorbell rang just then. The night-shift had arrived, in time to join in the feast. But there was plenty left over afterwards.

The rota was a time-consuming business, though, and as for volunteering to be the one who stayed awake, only a few of us could spare several days at a stretch. The bookseller Don Thwaite was next; then Glenda who took a week's leave from the salon; then Mary Gallagher. By this time we had a fair stack of foodstuffs in my flat, where we had decided to centralize everything and hold all subsequent 'wakes', with me keeping strict inventory. But we were all feeling frayed and exhausted when the whole of the Dream Channel Panel met on that fourth weekend for a stocktaking. Besides, there were several domestic crises brewing, due to all the hours that some members of the panel were absenting themselves mysteriously from home. Though the dream-commercials still continued, teasing us with even more fabulous luxuries.

Mary stifled a yawn. 'Surely there must be a better way! I'm quite black and blue from my stint.'

'But how else can we get the stuff to materialize?' asked Rog.

Mary looked around our circle; most of us were seated on the floor. 'Twelve of us,' she mused. 'If only there were thirteen.'

'That's unlucky,' objected Elsie.

'Why thirteen?' Tom asked.

'The number of a coven,' said Don Thwaite. 'That's what you're driving at, isn't it?' He chuckled fastidiously. 'However, I don't happen to be a witch.'

'And neither am I!' snapped Mary, indignant. 'A medium is no witch.'

'She might have been,' said Max, 'in the Middle Ages.'

'As far as I'm concerned,' said Don, 'a medium isn't anything at all. Mary certainly didn't conjure up the food; and it isn't made of ectoplasm. I doubt if it comes from Fairyland – *or* the Inferno.'

'All I'm saying,' said Mary, 'is that we tried one strange idea already – Mr Edmunds' notion – and it worked. But that doesn't mean it's the only way, or the best. There must be *something* about the number thirteen . . .'

I hesitated; and then confessed. 'Actually, there *are* thirteen of us. There's a girl at my school who's been picking up the commercials too.'

'Well, why didn't you *say*?' demanded Tom Pimm. 'Good grief, if there's any easier way to get our hands on the stuff!'

'I thought she was too young to be involved.'

'How old is she?'

'Fifteen.'

'Just the age,' said Don Thwaite wisely, 'when children are supposed to produce poltergeist effects. Thanks to all the strains of adolescence, and the sexual volcano stoking up . . .'

'Well, you'd better involve her now,' declared Tom.

'And so say all of us.' Rog, who had dark rings under his eyes, nodded.

'But I can't do that! I'm her teacher. How can I possibly invite a girl pupil along to what'll look like a coven?'

'Quite easily,' said Glenda, juggling with a jar of sklesh. 'She'll be flattered.'

'I refuse. It's too risky.'

However, the Dream Channel Panel voted me down.

'This is Mitzi,' said I, leading her into my crowded flat the following Saturday.

I had kept my invitation as low-key as I could, while still asking her to tell no one; and had stressed that it was to meet friends of mine who were interested in her dreams. But Mitzi turned up at the door wearing a brief skirt and cheesecloth blouse, with her hair done in a pert ponytail and perfume subtly applied.

Whatever disappointment may have overcome her when she discovered the Dream Channel Panel in full session promptly vanished as soon as she tasted kallopies with sklesh and crunched some koozels – while I explained what had been happening during the past few weeks.

'So what do I do?' she asked us, posing in the centre of the room.

'Ah now, that's just it, isn't it?' said Mary. 'In my opinion we all ought to join hands and close our eyes.'

'If she's supposed to be some sort of virgin witch,' said Rog, eyeing Mitzi hopefully, 'don't we need an altar – a table'll do – and candlesticks and a hen? And shouldn't she take her clothes off?'

'That'll do,' said I sternly. 'We'll try Mary's suggestion. And we'll all chant "Pop a can of kallopies", and the rest of the songs.'

Soon, feeling faintly absurd as though we had been translated back to childhood to games of Ring-o-Rosies, we were all shuffling round in a circle singing jingles. This

was hardly the picture of a coven of warlock shoplifters.
But before long something tribal and primitive seemed to
grip us and wash away our embarrassment; and we really
swung into the spirit of it . . .

And part of the ceiling glowed.

No kallopies or koozels rained down, though.

Instead, what I can only call a 'ladder of light'
descended. Its side-rails and spokes were fluorescent tubes,
but minus the glass.

'Oh,' gasped Elsie Levin. 'Oh.'

For a moment this seemed the best comment that any
of us could make; but then Mary said, '*Thirteen* rungs:
count them.'

We did, and she was right.

'What is it, then: Jacob's Ladder?' asked Jon Rhys Jones
in wonder.

'I don't notice many angels ascending and descending,'
said Don Thwaite.

'Since nothing's coming down,' Tom Pimm suggested,
'how about one of us nipping up to see?'

All eyes turned to him. But he shuffled evasively.

'Bit on the heavy side, aren't I? Looks fragile to me.'
With a professional glance he weighed Mitzi up. 'The
girl's the lightest.'

'And it *is* my ladder, isn't it?' Heedless of whether the
light might burn or electrocute her, she gripped hold.
Quickly she climbed up, pausing once to smooth her skirt,
not that this hid much, and vanished through the glow.

A minute later her hand reached back for balance and
her face peered through. She regarded us upside-down.

'Hey, there's a real feast waiting! Come on, the lot of
you.' Back out of sight she popped.

'I don't know about *all* of us,' mused Jon Rhys Jones. 'I
read this book about mysterious disappearances, see . . .

and, well, maybe one of us ought to hang on down below. If Tom's bothered about his weight . . .'

However, a hungry look had come over Tom Pimm's countenance. So in the end, it was our shop assistant Sandra – a shy creature – and Bob the mechanic who stayed below.

As Chairman, I was the first to follow Mitzi up. A moment later I was emerging through a similar glow in the floor of a simple open-air building: a circle of white columns supporting a cupola. Steps led on to a greens-ward, with woodland a few hundred yards distant. Twin fountains were spouting and plashing back into alabaster basins. Bird-song filled the air, though I didn't notice any birds. What I did observe was a whirling kaleidoscope of colours midway between the fountains. At first I took this to be simply rainbows in the spray-drift, since the sun was shining brightly; but really the kaleidoscope was far too busy and vivid. The air smelled of lilies and honeysuckle, though I couldn't see any flowers either, only neat lawn.

Other seductive aromas floated from a long alfresco table spread with gourmet goodies – which Mitzi was already sampling.

As were we all, before long.

'But where are we?' wondered Glenda as she nibbled a wafer spread with humbish.

Tom Pimm grandly waved an open flask of ampathuse, and was perhaps about to offer an opinion . . . when a chime sounded through the glade. About a hundred yards away the air began to glow, and an Aladdin's palace – somewhere between the Taj Mahal and a Chinese pagoda – emerged from nowhere into solid substance, like a Polar-oid picture developing. A band of people wearing skimpy tunics flocked out of it, barefoot, and headed gleefully for our rotunda and the waiting feast. Noticing us, they straggled to a halt.

Only one man and one young woman continued. She was the image of the young Brigitte Bardot; he was Cary Grant in his middle years.

As for the others: Omar Sharif, Greta Garbo, Sophia Loren, all looking their very best . . . I gave up.

'Golly!' cried Mitzi. She was the only one of us dressed like them. Which must have been why Bardot addressed her first.

'How here?'

'We climbed up this ladder out of Mr Peck's flat – ' began Mitzi.

'Flat?'

'Fixed homes in heaps,' commented Cary Grant. 'Twentieth, twenty-first. Favourite era. Must be ex past-time. Weirdest.'

'There was this glow on the ceiling. And it's in there too.' Mitzi pointed at the rotunda.

Bardot skipped away and mounted the steps. Meanwhile I began explaining to Cary Grant about our dreams of kallopies and koozels; but Bardot returned before I'd quite done.

'True. Looked down. Surprise for two below!'

'Do you people have to talk like crossword-puzzle clues?' grumbled Don Thwaite.

'Cross word?' Bardot looked mildly puzzled. 'No, no anger. Psychophysical weak spot detected. Maybe excessive reality alteration?'

Cary Grant nudged her. 'Time travellers lured by Dreamfood. Great endorsement!'

'I don't know whether I'm dreaming or awake,' said Mitzi.

Cary Grant touched the palm of his hand to her forehead, as if to feel whether she was fevered.

'Frustration level seven,' he told Bardot. 'Desire level twelve! Fantasy level ten. Figures!'

'A hole in time,' said Bardot. 'Troublesome.'

'Nonsense. Harmless. Imagine summoning great pre-Dream humans. From era of sleep and hard reality. Spearshaker, for instance. "Imagination bodies forth the forms of things unknown, turns them to shapes, gives to airy nothing a local habitation," eh? Erase memory afterwards. Safe.'

'Remind you: cannot erase subconscious memory. Besides, more likely summon black–dreamers than white. Wizards, witches, wildfolk. Recall: number thirteen.'

'Just what *has* the number thirteen got to do with all this?' I interrupted them.

'Easy,' said Bardot. 'Thirteen–sided resonance crystals implanted here,' and she touched her own forehead. 'Helps us tap the Power. Of Reality Flow. Energy into matter; matter into energy. Whole universe oscillates in and out of reality at every moment, as though all is but a dream in the cosmic mind. So catch it on the hop; alter bits as you wish. Change self-form. Cook up dreamfood, as could never be otherwise. Whole thing highly commercial, of course. Big Comp-brain co-ordinates all minds through crystals. Dream-patterns patented and licensed. Otherwise anarchy.'

'Do you mean you can change reality at will? You can make imaginary things real?'

Bardot nodded. 'World is all a dream. Science of it thus . . .'

And she explained, but I couldn't understand a word of her explanation. She was just getting on to the economics of it all – mental market forces, psychophysical supply and demand – when Cary Grant took pity. He clapped me on the shoulder.

'Eat, drink, be merry.' He waved to the rest of the people who had turned themselves into film stars of our era.

'Hang on,' Max Edmunds said, 'if this is a world of

dreams made real, then what does the world *really* look
like?'

'Underneath? Under layer on layer of dream? Like
geological deposits pressing down?' Cary Grant shrugged.
'Who knows? Maybe it's a fossil. Dead stone.'

But already Garbo and company were flooding past to
the banquet, and tugging us along with them.

Tom Pimm slapped his belly.

'Full up,' he announced tipsily.

'Time for Aphros, then,' said Bardot.

'Afters? I couldn't eat another crumb.'

'*Aphros*. Aphrodisiacs.' She whistled a sequence of
notes, and out of the busy kaleidoscope between the
fountains, clouds of heady vapour began to spray.

I must draw a discreet cloak over what took place on the
greensward next. Suffice it to say that we were quite
weary by the time those future people escorted us back
inside the rotunda, to the glow.

Escorted? *Marched* us, almost.

'What century is this, anyway?' Max Edmunds thought
to ask as they were popping him down the hole; but
Bardot only patted him on the head and thrust him out of
sight.

Tom Pimm licked his lips. 'Do you always finish your
meals like that?' Bardot winked, and down he went too.

Next was Mitzi, but Cary Grant felt her forehead first.
'Frustration level zero. Desire level one,' he told Bardot.

She laughed. 'Better go last. Hole might close early.'

One by one we were hastily popped through the glow.
Down in my flat it turned out that Bob and shy Sandra
were hurriedly pulling on their clothes in some embarrassment, with their backs turned. Aphro-gas must have
drifted through . . .

Last of all came Mitzi. As her feet touched the carpet

the ladder began to fade, and the ceiling darkened over. Soon there was only painted plaster above.

Tom Pimm rubbed his hands. 'Right! Next Saturday, everyone?'

But during the next week I dreamed nothing memorable, and on the Saturday I found that this was true of the others too.

The thirteen of us still linked hands, danced round the room and sang jingles. But no glow appeared. No food fell. No ladder descended. In the end we had to give up.

'It's Mitzi's fault,' declared Mary Gallagher. 'She should have stayed pure. A virgin. It's like Mr Edmunds said a while back . . . What did they call her up there? A sexus, was it?'

'A nexus. A connecting force.' Max Edmunds nodded authoritatively. 'It's all a question of adolescent libido and psychic energy. She was the paranormal channel into our dreams, and to the future Dream-world. She was the sexual volcano – and now she's blown off steam.'

'And whose fault is *that*?' Tom rounded on me accusingly. 'I saw you and her, after the meal.'

I defended myself. Hotly. Not least because a week had gone by and normal behaviour ruled again. 'Don't blame me! Bardot arranged that deliberately – to fix the weak spot.'

'And now we'll never eat as well again. All thanks to you. None of the rest of us would have touched Mitzi.' Tom flushed with moral indignation.

'*You* were too busy with Greta Garbo,' I pointed out. But I appeared to be in a weak position. For Glenda spoke out vindictively.

'What was all that about "desire level twelve" beforehand, and "desire level one" afterwards? What a mess you must have made of it. But what can one expect from a professional bachelor? You probably turned the poor girl off for life.'

I turned to Mitzi, but she was staring away out of the window. I'd been wondering why she was wearing a shapeless sweater and old jeans; but surely that couldn't have anything to do with it.

'We'd better divvy up the takings,' said Tom, just as though he was the Chairman; and no one disagreed. So he headed for my larder, to rifle it.

'Couldn't we,' said I, 'try a different approach?'

Jon Rhys Jones fairly glared at me. 'It's all over, boy, don't you see?' I particularly resented the 'boy'.

But it wasn't all over.

Two months later Mitzi discovered that she was pregnant. She didn't tell me, though. The first I knew of it was when two police officers called. Because, of course, Mitzi was under the legal age for sexual relations. There was even a vague hint of unwillingness on her part. A whiff of rape rather than seduction. But I think this was just the police trying to get me to confess to something more serious, which might look better on their records.

Naturally, I explained the events leading up to this awkward outcome; and referred the two officers to Glenda, Don, Max and the others for confirmation. By this date, alas, I hadn't any dreamfood left and had tossed the empties away. But I assured the officers that various cans, tubes and flasks would be buried in the garbage in-fill outside town. They might even still be lying on the surface. A search ought to turn them up . . .

'So,' said officer number one, ignoring this helpful advice as he scribbled in his notebook, 'you freely admit that you had sexual intercourse with Mitzi Hayes here in your flat.'

'No, no; up there.' I pointed.

'On the *ceiling*? Like a fly?'

'Above.'

'In the *loft*?'

'No, in the future . . . And it spoiled everything.'

'I'll say it did,' agreed number two sourly.

Still, they were quite formal and polite, merely arresting me and promising to corroborate my story with the others – and with Mitzi, who apparently had said nothing of the sort when they interviewed her. Well, that was understandable.

I also referred them for good measure to the small ads I'd placed a few months earlier. Why do such a thing, if this wasn't all gospel truth? They promised to check that out too.

Would you believe it, *not one* of the former members of the Dream Channel Panel backed my story up? A few conceded that they knew me casually by sight; the others swore blind that they had never met me in their lives.

While I was out on bail pending prosecution for sexual offences against a minor – and out of my job too, pending the outcome – Jon Rhys Jones slipped round furtively to my flat one night.

'We're awful sorry, boy,' was the gist of what he had to say. 'You know how it is with us who have families to think about. And family businesses, such as butcher's shops. I mean, getting ourselves involved in an orgy! Good thing young Mitzi had the sense to confide in a man of experience like Tom . . .'

So that was it.

The really ironic thing was that I might have got off with a few months in jail, or even a suspended sentence. But not in view of what I'd said. This ensured that I was referred for a psychiatric report.

I had read about cases like mine before. Somebody commits a trivial offence, and next thing the poor sod is detained indefinitely at the pleasure of the overworked psychiatrists of our prison service. Because he's considered 'mad' he can spend five years inside. Or ten.

Hastily swallowing my pride, I swore that I'd been lying.

And no one believed me.

Because of the newspaper ads. Which was particularly galling, as I need never have mentioned those.

Except that I had to, to explain how the Dream Channel Panel got together.

Except that it never did, according to the others – whose names I must have picked out of the phone book or a street directory, they supposed.

There was one small consolation in all this. I wasn't considered a violent sort of looney. So I wasn't sent to a high-security lockup for the criminally insane miles from nowhere on some windswept moor. Instead I was despatched to a permissive prison for mild cases, where we inmates could weave baskets and grow cabbages for the Governor, and perform other useful intelligent forms of therapy.

It's been six months now, and as feared my case hasn't come up for review.

Prison food is ghastly, after you've tasted sklesh on kallopies. Boiled cabbage, mashed potatoes, stringy stew: it's enough to drive any self-respecting gourmet round the bend.

But I'm making progress.

Because we're considered low risk in my group, the male nurses sometimes leave us in the workshop unsupervised. And I seize the opportunity to tell my fellow inmates tales of the dreamfood of the future. Not forgetting the orgy that followed.

And then I choose twelve disciples to dance round with me in a circle, singing:

'Can't refuse
'Ampathuse!'

And:

'We wish
'Humbish!'

There's no Mitzi here, of course. Women are kept apart from us. But consider: three of my group are under twenty. Morris, Martin and Paul. Morris is in here for exposing himself to little girls. Martin is a Peeping Tom. Paul stole ladies' underwear off washing lines. In their own way they're volcanoes of sexuality, and bound to be virgins too.

And all our dreams are troubled, now that I've persuaded my disciples to spit out their nightly doses of largactil and chlorpromazine, as soon as the nurses' backs are turned.

Troubled; though not quite yet by advertisements for kallopies and koozels. But if I plug away at my own propaganda, and if the prison kitchen keeps on dishing up such soggy cabbage, it's inevitable.

Consider: Frustration level ten. Desire level ten. Fantasy level ten!

We nearly did it this afternoon, too.

Thirteen of us were dancing round the workshop floor amidst neglected baskets. Morris was sweating with more than mere exertion. Paul was positively drooling. Martin looked goggle-eyed.

And a little circle upon the ceiling glowed. It wasn't only a patch of sunlight. It was The Glow.

'Keep it up!' I cried. 'Pop a can of kallopies! Pop a can, pop a can! What do we wish? Humbish!'

At this point my lookout at the keyhole, Sparky Jones, an alcoholic, spotted male nurse Turner approaching at speed down the corridor. So, alas, we had to break ranks. The glow promptly faded out.

But tomorrow we'll do it. Or the week after. Now that the Dream Channel Panel is back in session again.

Food of the future, how I yearn for you!

The People on the Precipice

One evening Smear climbed down to our ledge and told us a story about people who lived in a two-dimensional world.

He had made the story up, of course. To amuse and enlighten. (This could have been Smear's motto.)

'Just suppose,' he said, as the daylight dimmed, 'that a whole world is as flat as a leaf! And suppose that creatures live within that leaf, who themselves are perfectly flat. Imagine that this narrow ledge here simply carries on' – he chopped his hand out into empty space – 'in that direction forever! Imagine that it is a simple, infinite surface with nothing above it and nothing below it. And with no precipice to jut out from.'

Bounce giggled at this idea so much that she almost fell out of her bower of vine-rope.

Tumbler, our chief – who had no sense of humour – said, 'Preposterous! What would hold your ledge up? How would we ever get over the lip, to harvest sweet fungi below?'

'I'm asking you to imagine a different kind of world. A plane – with no "below" or "above". With no "up" or "down". The inhabitants are flat, too.'

'But how can they grip anything? They'll all slide away, and slide forever.'

'No they won't. You see, they don't live *upon* the flat surface. They're *part* of the surface.'

'You'll do me an injury!' squealed Bounce.

'So how do they make love?' enquired Fallen. 'How can they squeeze on to one another?'

'Aha,' and Smear winked at her, 'now you're asking.'

'Tell us!' cried Bounce.

But Tumbler interrupted. 'I hear that young Clingfast from three ledges down fell off yesterday. That was his mother's fault for giving him such an unlucky name. "Bounce" is a risky name, too, in my opinion.'

This remark annoyed Bounce. 'Just you try to invade my bower, Tumbler, and *you'll* get bounced – right off the cliff. That'll teach you what my name's all about.'

'Can I please tell my story?' asked Smear.

And so he did.

He regaled us with the hilarious adventures of Ma and Pa Flat in their flatworld; and what preposterous antics those were, to be sure! Still, his story seemed to have a couple of sly morals buried in it. Compared with the imaginary flat-people we were fortunate indeed – being gifted with all sorts of mobility denied to Ma and Pa Flat. In other words, things might be a lot worse. But also, Ma and Pa at least tried to make the very best of a bad job – did we always do likewise?

By the time Smear finished it was black dark, and we had long since tightened our tethers for the night. Obviously Smear would be spending the time of darkness on our ledge.

Soon after, I heard suspicious scraping sounds, suggesting that Smear was recklessly edging his way along to reach Bounce's bower. (He had positioned himself close to her.) Subsequent smothered giggles and gasps indicated that he had succeeded: a surmise proven true in the morning when light brightened and we saw Bounce and Smear clinging together asleep in her harness of vines.

Smear quickly roused himself and departed upward, his horny toes in all the proper cracks, his left hand holding a guidevine, his right hand reaching up in approved style for well-remembered, reliable holds. You could never wholly trust guidevines with your total weight. They might snap or rip their roots free. Then you would be taking the long trip down through empty air.

We breakfasted on the leftovers from yesterday's harvest of berries and lichen, rockworms and beetles.

The pearly void was bright; the day was warm. Below, the precipice descended forever. Above, it rose forever. To left and right, it stretched out unendingly. Occasionally, thin silver water-licks oozed from the rock, dribbling down till the droplets bounced into space. Here and there were still some surviving pastures of moss and fungus and fleshier plants; though by now our appetites had stripped most decent rock-fields bare, adding to the area of naturally occurring barrens. Soon we would all have to migrate – just as we had already migrated at least a hundred times since I was born. A planning conference was slated for today high up on Badbelay's ledge. Tumbler as our chief would attend.

As our tribe clung to the rockface considering which way to forage, a scream from above made us tighten our holds. We tried to flatten ourselves completely – just like Smear's mythical beings. A young lad plunged past, an arm's length away. I could have reached out to touch him, if I was foolish enough.

'Butterfingers!' shrieked Fallen in sympathy. The lad probably never heard her.

The falling body diminished until it was a mere speck deep below.

Bounce surprised us by saying, 'Next time we migrate we ought to head upwards and *keep on* migrating upwards for a whole lifetime, to see what happens.'

'That'll be one of friend Smear's fancy ideas, I suppose?' Tumbler spat contemptuously into space. 'What a strain *that* would be, and what peril, compared with migrating sideways. My dear Bounce, it's all very well to climb up a few ledges, and down a few ledges. Indeed this keeps all our muscles in trim. But to climb one way only? Faugh! Do you imagine our grandchildren would reach a *top*? Or a *bottom*, suppose we migrated downwards? And what would be at this imaginary bottom? Bones and rubbish and shit, floating in foul water, I shouldn't be surprised!'

'I didn't mention any bottom.'

'And what would be at this top of yours? Not that it exists! I'll tell you: a place where our muscles would weaken through disuse so that we could no longer harvest the precipice. We'd starve within a generation. Our present way of life is perfect.'

'Clinging on by your fingertips all life long is perfect?' she retorted. 'There might be a huge flat space up at the top – with oodles of really big plants all over, because they wouldn't have to worry about their weight ripping them away.'

'What's wrong with hanging on by one's fingertips, pray?'

'A certain tendency to *fall*,' she said. 'Especially when you get old and sick and mad and exhausted.'

I spoke up, since something had been worrying me for a while. 'When we migrated here, it seemed to me that this particular patch of precipice hereabouts was . . . well, strangely familiar. When we arrived I felt as if I'd been here before – when I was only a child. All the cracks and finger-grips were somehow known to me.'

'That,' said Tumbler, 'is purely because of the expertise you develop at clinging on after twenty or thirty years.'

'So why do experienced adults ever fall off?'

'They get tired and ill and crazy,' said Bounce. 'Everyone does, in the end, after a lifetime of clinging on.'

'We always migrate leftward,' I pointed out.

'Obviously! Who on earth would migrate back to a patch which had been stripped the time before?'

'What if,' I asked, 'the sum total of our migrations has brought us back to the very same place where we were years ago? What if our precipice isn't a straight wall but a vast . . . um . . .'

'A vast cylinder,' said Bounce.

Tumbler pointed impatiently to the right where the view was more barren. 'Look: if that isn't straight – !'

'Maybe it only seems straight,' said Splatty unexpectedly, 'because it's so enormous. Maybe it bends ever so slightly? We can't actually see the bend, but after tens of years of travel . . . If so, what's the sense in migrating?'

'To find food, slippy-thumb! To survive! Suppose we do come back to the same patch eventually – so what? The pastures have fleshed out again.'

'It's hardly *progress*,' said Bounce.

'Progress? Cylinders? Bends? Have you people gone nuts? Are you planning to let go and dive into the abyss? This is all Smear's fault. Listen: we hang on by the skin of our teeth. We make daily forays up and down for food. When we've scalped a patch we migrate sideways. That's life.'

Even Topple joined in. 'It's life. That's true. But is it *living*?'

'Damn it, it's as good a life as any! In fact I can't imagine any other. How about you?'

Topple shook his head. 'I've been clinging on for a lifetime. What else do I know?'

'And you'll die clinging on. Or rather, you'll die pretty soon after you *stop* clinging on. Now, today I'm climbing up to the Chief-of-Chiefs for that conference. Bounce will guard our ledge and keep the kids tied up. Loosepiton' – that's me – 'will escort me upwards.'

'Why me, Boss?'

'Perhaps you would like to plead your notion that we're climbing round in a circle. That ought to raise some laughs.' (Aye, and likely damage Smear's advocacy of migrating upwards . . .)

'The rest of you will forage. Splatty and Fallen and

Plunge can head far to the left, and chart the distant cracks while they're about it. Slip and Flop can forage to the right for what's left of the familiar pickings. Gather well, my tribe! We need to store some supplies in case we have to cross wide barrens.' To me he said, 'Come on, Loosepiton. Best foot upwards!'

And he began to ascend the sheer precipice, toehold by toehold.

'On what wide surface shall we store our huge harvest, oh Chief?' Bounce called after him. He ignored her.

When Tumbler and I paused on Smear's Ledge for a quick rest we learned that Chief Smear had already preceded us upwards. Apparently Smear had done a lot of shinning about, visiting other ledges and telling merry stories, recently.

'He's campaigning to change our lives,' I remarked to Tumbler.

However, our chief seemed more annoyed with Bounce. 'That woman's a fool,' he groused. 'A vertical cliff puts constraints on the amount we can store. Of course it does. That stands to reason. So this limits the amount we can sensibly harvest. Consider the alternative! If we could tear up everything and pile it all on some vast ledge we'd exhaust our resources much more rapidly. What's more, we'd overeat. We'd grow fat and clumsy and far too heavy to haul ourselves up and down.'

We climbed onward together.

Another body fell past us; a woman's. She held her arms wide out on either side of her, as down she flew.

'Diver,' puffed Tumbler. 'Deliberate dive.'

'Dive of despair.'

'What's there to be desperate about, eh Loosepiton? Beautiful weather today. Soft breezes. No slippery stone.' He plucked a crimson rock-worm loose with a 'plop' and popped it into his mouth.

Not long after, some excrement hit him on the shoulder. Excrement usually falls well clear of the wall but some freak contour must have directed otherwise. Without comment Tumbler wiped himself clean on a nearby danglevine.

We passed six more ledges, rested and ate a meal courtesy of the tribe clinging to the seventh, then climbed past fifteen more. We reached Chief-of-Chiefs Badbelay's ledge in the early afternoon.

The ledge was already crowded with a line of chiefs – and in the middle Smear was chanting out another of his stories about bizarre worlds. In this case: about people with suckers like a gripworm's on their feet who lived on a huge ball afloat in a void. Smear was leaning quite far back to call his words past the intervening bodies.

'Shit in your eye,' Tumbler greeted him grumpily as we two forced a space for ourselves on the ledge.

'Aha,' responded Smear, 'but up here, where would that crap fall from? Either another tribe of tribes clings immeasurably high above us – or else not. If not, why not? Why do no strangers ever fall from above? Because no strangers live higher up! Yet if our precipice extends upwards infinitely, surely other people must dwell somewhere higher up. *Ergo* – '

'Unless those other people have migrated further along than us!' broke in Tumbler. 'Unless they're further to the left – or to the right, for that matter.'

'The reason,' Smear continued suavely, 'is that our precipice isn't infinitely high. It has a top.'

'The real reason,' growled Badbelay, 'may simply be that we are the *only* people. All that exists is the precipice, and us.'

'Maybe we're the only people on the precipice itself. But maybe hundreds of tribes live on top – and every now and then they gaze down and have a good laugh at us.'

'Why should anyone laugh at us? Are we not courageous

and ingenious, persevering and efficient, compassionate and clever?'

'Undoubtedly,' Smear replied, 'but perhaps if we were fools, liars, cheats, thieves, and slovens we would have slid down to the bottom years ago instead of trying to cling on here; and we would have been living in rich pastures.'

'So now it's the *bottom* that's our goal, is it?' challenged Tumbler, 'Kindly make your mind up!'

'I spoke by way of illustration. Obviously, with all our fine qualities, it is ever upward that we ought to aspire. We may reach the top within a single lifetime.'

'Then what do we do?' asked another chief. 'Sprawl and sleep?'

The argument went on all afternoon.

Eventually Badbelay gave his judgement. We would all migrate in ten days' time – diagonally. Leftwards, as was traditional; but also upwards, as Smear had urged.

'If we do find lush pastures leftward and upward,' explained Badbelay, 'we can always steepen our angle of ascent. But if we run into difficulties we can angle back down again on to the time-approved route.'

Some chiefs applauded the wisdom of this compromise. Others – particularly Tumbler – voiced discontent. Smear looked disappointed at first but then perked up.

That night we slept in vine-harnesses on Badbelay's ledge; and in the morning we all climbed back down again.

A couple of days later Smear paid another visit to our ledge – with apprehension written on his face.

The rest of our tribe had already fanned out across the precipice, a-gathering. I myself was about to depart.

'Tumbler! Loosepiton! Have you looked out across the void lately?'

'Why should we waste our time looking at nothing?' demanded Tumbler with a scowl.

Smear pointed. 'Because there's *something*.'

To be sure, far away in the pearly emptiness there did seem to me to be some sort of enormous shadow.

Tumbler rubbed his eyes then shrugged. 'I can't see anything.'

I cleared my throat. 'There *is* something, Chief. It's very vague and far away.'

'Rubbish! Nonsense! There's never been anything there. How can there be something?'

Tumbler, I realized, must be short-sighted.

Smear must have arrived at a similar diagnosis. However, he didn't try to score any points off Tumbler. He just said diplomatically to me, 'Just in case, let's keep watch, Loosepiton – you and I, hmm?'

I nodded agreement.

Whatever it was seemed to thicken day by day. At first the phenomenon was thin, then it grew firmer, denser. No one else glanced in the empty direction – until the very morning when we were due to migrate.

Then at last some fellow's voice cried out, 'Look into the void! Look, everyone!'

Presently other voices were confirming what the man had noticed. For a while minor pandemonium reigned, though Tumbler still insisted: 'Fantasy! Smear has been spreading rumours. Smear has stirred this up!' Which was the very opposite of the truth.

Bounce clung to me. 'What is it?' Now that her attention had been directed, she could see the thing clearly; though as yet none of us could make out any details. All I could be sure of, was that something enormous existed out in the void beyond the empty air; and that something was changing day by day in a way which made it more noticeable.

'I've no idea, dear Bounce.'

'Migrate!' ordered Tumbler. 'Commence the migration!'

And so we began to migrate, leftward and upward; as did the tribes above us, and the tribes above them.

Over the course of the next ten days the business of finding novel fingerholds and toeholds occupied a huge amount of our attention. Besides, we had our kids to shepherd, or to carry if they were still babies. Consequently there wasn't much opportunity for staring out into the void. Splatty made the mistake of doing so while we were traversing unfamiliar rock. He forgot himself, lost his poise, and fell.

On the tenth evening Smear climbed down to our camping ledge.

'Don't you recognize what it is by now, Loosepiton?' he asked.

'There *might* be some kind of dark cloud out there,' allowed Tumbler, peeved that Smear was addressing me.

'It isn't any cloud, old chief – nor any sort of weird weather. Look keenly, Loosepiton. That's another precipice.'

I perceived . . . a faintly wrinkled vertical plane. Like a great sheet of grey skin.

'It's another precipice just like ours; and it's moving slowly towards our precipice day by day. It's closing in on us. As though it ain't bad enough clinging on by our fingertips all life long . . .!' Smear crooked a knee around a vine for stability and held his hands apart then brought them slowly together and ground them, palm to palm, crushingly.

The wrinkles in that sheet of skin out there were ledges. Without any doubt. The hairs on the skin were vines. My heart sank.

'We oughtn't to have migrated in this direction,' declared Tumbler. He was simply being obtuse.

Smear gently corrected him. 'We aren't migrating into an angle between two walls. Oh no. That other precipice faces us flat on. And it began to move towards us before we ever started our migration. Or perhaps *our* precipice began to move towards it. The result is the same.'

'We'll be squashed between the two.' I groaned.

To have survived bravely for so many years of hanging on by our fingernails! We had never railed excessively against our circumstances. Sometimes certain individuals took the dive of despair. But children were born and raised. Life asserted itself. We had hung on.

All so that we could meet a second precipice head-on – a mobile precipice – and be crushed!

This seemed a little unfair. A little – yes – hateful and soul-twisting.

Days passed by. We had settled on our new cliff pastures. We explored the cracks and ledges. We wove vines. We foraged. We ate worms and beetles.

All the while the approaching precipice became more clearly discernible as just that: another infinite precipice, limitlessly high and deep, limitlessly wide.

As the gap narrowed pearly daylight began to dim dangerously.

Smear had conceived a close affinity for me. 'Maybe it's just a reflection,' I said to him one day.

'If that's the case, then we should see ourselves clinging on over there. I see no one. If I could bend my arm back far enough to throw a chunk of stone, my missile would hit solid rock and bounce off.'

Several people from upper ledges took the dive of despair. A few parents even cast their children down; and that is real despair.

Yet consider the difference between taking the dive –

and being slowly crushed to death between two walls of stone. Which would you prefer? Maybe those individuals who dived died peacefully from suffocation on the way down. Or maybe they did reach a bottom and were instantly destroyed, before they knew it, by impact.

The remaining daylight was appallingly dim by now. The other precipice with its cracks and ledges and vines was only a few bodies' lengths away. In another day or two it might be possible to leap over and cling on – though that hardly spelled any avenue of escape.

I paid a visit to Smear.

'Friend,' I said, 'some of those ledges over there are going to fit into spaces where we don't have ledges. But others won't. Others will touch our own ledges.'

'So?'

'So maybe there'll be a little gap left between the two precipices. A gap as big as a human body.'

'Leaving us uncrushed – but locked inside rock?'

'We'll have to wait and see.'

'See?' he cried. 'With no light to see by? Yet I suppose,' he added bitterly, 'it *will* be a different sort of world. For a while.'

Different. Yes.

Yesterday – though 'days' are now irrelevant – the two precipices met.

All light had disappeared but with my hand I could feel the inexorable pressure of the other rocky wall pushing forward – until from above, from below, from left and right there came a grating, groaning, crackling noise; then silence for a while.

Nobody had screamed. Everybody had waited quietly for the end. And as I had begun to suspect some days earlier, the end – the absolute end – did not come.

I was still alive on a ledge in utter darkness, sandwiched between one wall and the other.

Voices began to call out: voices which echoed strangely and hollowly down the gap of space that remained.

Yes, we survive.

There's even a little light now. Fungi and lichen have begun to glow. Maybe they always did glow faintly; and only now have our deprived eyes grown sensitive enough to detect their output.

We can still travel about – along a ledge to the end, then by way of cracks up or down to the end of another ledge. We scarcely see where we're going, and have to guess our way through the routes of this vertical stone maze. Also, it's still possible to fall down a gap, which would cause terrible injuries.

Yet in a sense travel is also easier nowadays. We can brace ourselves between both walls and shuffle upward or downward or left or right by 'chimneying'.

Perhaps I should mention a disadvantage which has actually stimulated travel. Excrement can't tumble away now into the void. Stools strike one wall or the other.

What's more, the collision of the two walls destroyed a lot of vines; nor can lush foliage thrive in the ensuing darkness.

Consequently we are ascending steadily, just as Smear once recommended.

Instead of living one above the other, our tribes are now strung out in a long line; and all of us climb slowly upward, foraging as we go, eating all the available lichen and fungi, worms and beetles. Now we're permanently migrating.

Are we moving towards somewhere? Towards Smear's mythical top? Maybe.

And maybe that place is infinitely far away.

The new kids who are born to us on the move will enter

a world utterly different from the world of my own childhood. A vertical world confined between two irregular walls. A world of near-total gloom.

They will live in a narrow gap which extends sideways forever, drops downward forever, and rises forever.

How will Bounce's child (who is also either mine or Smear's) ever conceive of the old world which we will describe: that world where one precipice alone opened forever upon the vastness of empty, bright space? Will he (or she) think of it as a paradise which might yet exist again some time in the future if the two walls ever move apart? Or will the child be unable even to understand such a concept?

Sometimes I dream of the old world of open air and light, and of clinging to the cliff. Then I awaken to darkness, to the faint glow of a few fungi, to the confinement of the walls.

The other day Smear said to me, 'We didn't know how well off we were, did we, Loosepiton? But at least we survive, and climb. And maybe, just maybe, *right now* we're well off – compared with some future state of the world which will limit us even more severely!'

'How could we be more limited?' I asked in surprise. 'What new disaster could occur?'

'Maybe this gap will shrink to become a single upright chimney! Maybe *that'll* happen next.'

'Life forbid! It hasn't happened yet.'

'Not yet.'

Meanwhile we climb upward. And upward.

Amazingly Smear still tells his peculiar tales about imaginary worlds; and tells them with gusto.

Skin Day, and After

Nance stirred and yawned.

'What day is it, Benny?'

What a little-girl question! I don't mean that my Nance *looked* anything like a little girl as she lay sprawled in the sheets with her red hair setting the pillow afire. But it was a seven- or eight-year-old's kind of question. You know, when they've been counting the days till their birthday or some treat? They know what day it is, all right, but they need to be told just to put the icing on the cake.

I stooped over her and whispered, 'It's Skin Day, Nance.'

And she opened her eyes wide and sat straight up.

'Watch out – we'd better get moving! I'm going to wear my sealskin bra and my leopard-skin pillbox hat. And, oh, the ocelot stole! And of course that neat little lambskin muff. And the tail, the tail! The Bengal tiger tail, springing out behind me!' She flexed her fingers, feline fashion.

'Hey, no hurry. No one'll be on the streets yet. Let's fix some De-caff and boil an Urf.' I hurried off to the kitchen area, flipping on the TV en route, and spooned a good helping of De-caff into the pot, then popped a couple of Urfs in a pan on the back burner.

Actually I was beginning to prefer Urfs to real eggs, even though I was a registered Carnivore myself. I'd been getting dissatisfied with the Bootleggs we bought now and then. Too many real eggs had those gluey jelly bits in them that stuck to your teeth, and the yolks were generally paler and smaller than the synthetic sort. Since an egg wasn't really meat, I didn't see that any particular principle was involved; an egg, a philosopher might have said, is not a chicken. Still, a Carnivore had to watch out for his frontiers being eroded, so I did still fork out a dollar each for a Bootlegg occasionally. If no eggs got laid, after all, where would the chickens come from?

But anyway, it was Urfs for breakfast this particular Skin Day morning. Nance never did put her name down as a Carnivore, so I didn't feel as though I were short-changing her. She would join me in a steak, to be companionable; but always she would want hers well done, not rare and bloody the way it ought to be. Personally I was a Carnivore, and Smoker, and Anti-Kids, and Anti-Nuke, the max you could sign up for. Nance was only Skins, and Save the Rain Forests (I suppose because jaguars breed there) and Smoker (too), but she seemed happy enough with her trio. We got on well together, especially on Smoking Day.

Anyway, Nance was in the shower by now, where I could hear her stinging herself all pink and fresh so that she could really revel in the touch of those animal skins.

And the pre-News commercials were on.

'Cherchez le Obster! Five-star flavour. Five-star texture. But nobody boiled it alive! Nobody made it scream! Remember: le Obster!'

This annoyed me quite a bit: all these snippets of bastard French that the synth-food biz was laying on us. What was it last week? *Burf*: the latest false beef. It sounded like somebody belching. We weren't all *that* close to the Quebec border. I guess the manufacturers thought this added a swanky touch of gastronomy.

I was wondering whether to cancel my Anti-Kid registration and sign up as an Anglo-Saxon Supremacist instead. Then I could shoot up to Montreal on a day trip and wander round insulting everyone by speaking English. But presumably half of Canada would be doing that on the day, so I just wouldn't stand out in the crowd. And that wasn't the point of special days at all, at least not to my way of thinking.

Anyway, the pot of De-Caff boiled just then, and so did the Urfs. I fixed some toast and cut it into fingers to dip with, the way Nance liked it. 'Soldiers', she called them. She'd been Anti-Military before she switched to Save the Rain Forests, and she enjoyed biting soldiers' heads off. I took our breakfast through to the other room just as the News was starting – and as Nance emerged from the shower wrapped in her towel.

'Hi there, citizens. This is Cal Garrison, and today's Skin Day, so just you watch out for all those Palaeolithic types wearing their cavemen clothes – '

Nance pouted. 'What a nerve. He's got no *concept* of elegance. Just look how he's dressed: T-shirt and jeans.'

'Yes, Folks, it isn't exactly Nature-Hating Day, but it's the next best thing – for those who can afford it. And as I see it, only the stinking rich can doll up in animal skins – '

'That just isn't true,' she said. 'Why, that ocelot stole I picked up was an absolute – '

'I mean, any citizen can go trample the flowers in a park – '

'He's just trying to whip up feeling,' I pointed out mildly, 'so the day'll really shine.'

' – all the cruel exploiters of lovely furry animals, who think God's creatures are put on earth for us to *adorn* ourselves. All the rare tigers in the forests of the night and the noble Polar bears and cuddly seal pups and hoppity bunny rabbits – '

'I just love furry animals,' said Nance, stroking her hands luxuriously down her thighs in anticipation.

'I love animals, too,' I said. 'I love eating them.'

'Well, citizens, let's have some footage from yesterday before we turn to the murky old international scene, eh? And what was yesterday? It was Wino Day, with all the drunks and lushes out abusing sober people – '

We didn't pay a lot of attention to the film footage, since we were busy with our Urfs.

'. . . and the good old Social Tension Rating is computed down to 400 overnight – '

'Hey,' said Nance, 'it hasn't been that low since Anti-Nigra Day.'

I pushed my empty Urf aside and made the familiar motion of a couple of parted fingers to my lips. Nance nodded, so I fetched the pack of cigarettes; you could hardly read the brand name any longer for the health warnings. I stuck a token in the wall slot to switch off the apartment's smoke alarms for the next fifteen minutes, and we lit up. There were only another four cigarettes left in the pack, so we wouldn't be lighting another couple. Sure, we had half a carton each stashed away, but we were hoping to save three packs each for Smoking Day. At twenty dollars a pack – and that was with the tax deductions for registered Smokers – you tended to go easy.

Nance puffed hers right down to the filter, crushed this out, and rose dramatically.

'Now,' she announced, and marched to her wardrobe, dropping her towel negligently on the floor behind her. I picked it up and hung it on a chair back. This was all part of the ritual.

Of course, most of the days we weren't registered for we didn't bother about too much. Not to the extent of going out of our way to do anything.

Some we did. Veg Day, for instance, when all the Vegetarians picnicked on the grass in the park (like Herbivores, right), and bust into decent licensed Carnivore restaurants demanding algae soup and nut cutlets. We'd hoot and jeer then.

And Doggy Day, too, when all the proud owners let their pets off the leash to defecate anywhere. Nance always worked herself into a froth about that. She would run up to dog owners whose Fido had just dropped a load in the playpit in the park and scream in their faces, 'Do you realize a child's hands could touch that, and it'd *go blind*?' That was her favourite gambit. Usually they'd scream back that this was nothing compared to what they did on Anti-Kid Day. A lot that worried Nance, with me being Anti-Kid myself. But generally she got a good verbal fight going, and that made the doggy-walkers happy, too, as they thought they were offending her. All very therapeutic.

But days like Gerry Day we sort of ignored; and a lot of old folks often stayed indoors, too, though you did get the odd pack of militant grandmas and grandpas tripping you with their walking sticks and hauling youngsters out of the seats on the bus, and such.

And Yid Day, too. Why should I bother sticking on a swastika badge and chanting 'Judenraus!' till I was hoarse outside some kosher butcher's window, so that he could rush outside brandishing his Star of David at me, bellowing, 'Oy Vey!'?

And I felt that some of the days were a bit, well, puny; though I guess those who registered for them, and those whom they rubbed up the wrong way, felt otherwise. Obesity Day, Sci-Fi Day. Who cared?

Nance looked stunning in her mink jacket, leopard-skin hat and real leather skirt and boots. She'd decided against the lambskin muff in favour of the kidskin gloves, trimmed with zebra; and against the ocelot stole in favour of a gorgeous red fox-fur draped round her shoulders with the head (with black glass button eyes) hanging down one side and the bushy tail the other. It really blended with her hair. She'd scrapped the idea of the tiger tail, too. In her right hand she swung a crocodile-skin bag. Perfection. She was dandy.

I wore my ordinary denims, of course.

And out we went: along to the elevator, down to the lobby with its jungle of Swiss cheese plants, and through the auto-security checkout into the street. Clancy Avenue, actually. You know, six blocks north of Jefferson Park, and the zoo, ten blocks west of downtown.

'Where'll we go, then, Nance?'

'You *know*, Benny.'

'Zoo?'

She nodded intently.

Of course. As usual. The zoo. Where better to parade her costume? People who loved animals – *au naturel*, as the Macrobiotics mob say – would be flocking to the zoo, ready to take offence.

Still, first we had to get there. And certain adventures happened en route. (Damn all this French. Long live the English language, pure and unpolluted.)

First we hailed a cab, but that didn't work out. The first couple of drivers pulled over and foul-mouthed Nance, then zoomed off, burning rubber and leaving us in a cloud of fumes; which takes some doing with exhaust-emission filters fitted, but they managed it. Though not before Nance treated them to some choice invective of her own.

So we set off to walk the six blocks. Next thing, as we were passing a Gay Veganburger bar, out popped a shaven-headed Buddhist monk in saffron robes and rope sandals. He was thumping a little drum; and like an Ancient Mariner, he homed in. He stank of patchouli.

'I pray for their souls,' he wailed, tagging along with us, 'that they are at peace.'

'Whose souls? Ours?' said I. Some people tended to talk about you in the third person if they didn't want any direct interpersonal interaction but still felt bound to make an observation.

'The souls of all the slaughtered beasts.' And he chanted on, in Sanskrit or Tibetan or something, noisily banging that drum near our ears.

'You can bet they're at peace,' shouted Nance. 'Which is more that I can say of anyone in your vicinity, you clown! What are you, the answer to dandruff?'

I frowned. This wasn't quite high-class stuff, such as I expected of Nance. I think the monk had thrown her a bit; and that wouldn't do at all.

'Om, om, om, on,' he droned composedly, accompanying us.

Oh, yes, I got it now. The monk was laying his own public nuisance on us even though it wasn't Hare Krishna Day. He was latching on to us. And he was upstaging Nance. But she couldn't really say so, not herself. So I said it for her.

'Push off, buster. You're poaching. I'll file a complaint. I will, too! You'll be deregistered.'

That got rid of him, but not as satisfactorily as if Nance had lipped him off herself. She looked a mite resentful, but cheered up when a doggy-walker steered her couple of leashed, muzzled poodles in our path, and at the same time a doting mother swung her twin buggy of brats to block us. Of course the first woman was impeded not only by her poodles but also by her sack: containing canine excrement shovel, plastic bags, and sterilizing spray cans – and the mother by a bag of veg unbalancing the buggy. So they would be a pushover.

At the sight of Nance's furs and leather, the doggy-walker went white-lipped.

'You . . . demon woman!' she shrilled. 'God bless all living creatures.' As though Nance had sacrificed that fox to Satan and drunk the animal's blood.

'Well, these ones are *dead* – '

But Nance hardly had a chance to get in with her riposte when both poodles leaped up at the buggy and slobbered through their muzzles all over the toddlers.

'Toxicara virus!' the incensed mother cried in horror,

like some plague victim ringing her bell and shouting, 'Unclean!'

'Oh, I'm so sorry!' exclaimed the doggy-walker. Quickly she whipped a spray can out of her sack. 'Close your eyes, little darlings,' she cooed, and promptly squirted their faces and hands. And of course the brats began to scream. Immediately Nance announced loudly to all and sundry, 'Just listen to that noise! It's bursting my eardrums. I declare, it must be ninety decibels.' The mother naturally had to clap a hand (two hands actually) over their little mouths; and their faces went bright red – and with both her hands off, the buggy tipped backward, spilling artichokes and chicory along the sidewalk. Excitedly the poodles began leaping again. Oh, it was precious. Laughing triumphantly and flicking her fox fur about, Nance steered deftly between this Scylla and Charybdis.

And then after that – but you don't want me gabbing on about every little encounter on the way. You want to hear about the zoo. That's where you'd expect the real collisions on a day like this. The real catharsis, as the old Greeks used to say. The true satisfaction: to know you were doing your bit toward a sane society.

That's the whole point of it, after all. Think of society as a roomful of balloons. They're all trying to inflate at the same time in a finite space. So each balloon is trying to squash its neighbours flat. And of course if one balloon expands *too* much, it goes pop. That's messy. It costs, to clean up. But balloons like to expand; it's their nature. So what do you do? You build in special days for certain *classes* of balloon to expand, and special days for other classes to be squeezed. Usually both at the same time. And the psych-pollsters watch over it all with their Social Tension Ratings. Simple.

That's called an analogy.

Though maybe it isn't the right one.

Anyway . . . the zoo.

We arrived at the gates, and got in with only a few hisses and whistles. No one was actively picketing; not at the gates.

'Polar bears, Nance?'

'No, *cats*. The Big Cats.'

There were quite a few Monitor Cops about, as you'd expect on Skin Day at a venue where some fine skins are in residence (as yet still filled with bodies); and one of these promptly made a beeline for us. I thought this was distinctly fussy of him, but then he was obviously a rookie – fresh-faced and young.

'Morning, Ma'am. May I see your registration card?'

'Hey,' I said, 'do you think she'd be all dolled up like this if she weren't kosher?'

The rookie eyed me. 'You got your days mixed up?'

'It's OK, Benny.' Nance pulled her card from the crocodile bag.

The rookie scrutinized it for quite a while, as if he had some literacy problem, while we fretted and chafed at the bit. Finally he handed it back, and stared contemptuously up and down Nance's attire from head to foot. You've heard of people's lips curling? Never seen it before, myself; but his lip curled. He said nothing; but still I wasn't taking *that*.

'Hey, you got something personal about skins? Because if so, you oughtn't to be on duty today.'

At this the rookie's Adam's apple bobbed a few times as though he had something stuck in his craw.

'C'mon, Nance.' And we walked off. Past the spider monkeys and along by the cockatoos. I couldn't decide whether the encounter was a plus or not.

'Feather boas,' murmured Nance, slightly distressed – though off at a tangent to the probable cause. 'Bird of paradise hats . . .'

I chuckled. 'And a morpho butterfly pinned in your

buttonhole? Those don't go with fox and mink and leather.'

'Suppose not.'

'Nance, you're fabulous today. That guy wasn't offing your taste.'

'You sure?'

'Cross my heart. Let's get along' – and I nudged her – 'to the catwalk.' And we both burst out laughing, and linked arms and stepped out down Penguin Terrace.

Down by the tiger compound, there was an Animal Lib picket, because naturally it was their day, too, in a way. In an inverted 'squeeze' way. A couple of placards waved lamely, protesting at how all the beasts were imprisoned; and as part of the act, they had a home-made bamboo cage with a guy in it dressed in a business suit, looking puzzled and occasionally shaking the bamboo bars, though not too strenuously in case they fell apart. HOW WOULD YOU LIKE IT? read a sign on top. But it was all lacklustre, till Nance swanked up. Then they really gave tongue.

A fat young woman with greasy hair waddled forth. She jabbed a chubby finger at Nance's fox fur.

'I wanna buy that,' she said furiously, brandishing a few moth-eaten dollar bills. 'I wanna buy it and *burn* it.'

'Do you, now?' said Nance. 'With so much insulation, you feel *cold*? You got the wrong day, baby: you want Obesity Day.'

'You must think you're pretty ugly yourself, lady,' a thin man called out, 'needing to drape yourself in that lot before you dare show your face.'

'Go play with a tiger, Androcles,' retorted Nance.

'I ought to have worn the tail,' she whispered.

'I got a real Bengal tiger's tail at home,' she proclaimed aloud. 'Shot it myself, on Safari. Trouble was, I used an elephant gun by mistake so I blew the skin to pieces. But I kept the tail. And the cubs. I had one of them stuffed, and

I used the other as a nightdress case.' (All lies, of course. The closest Nance had been to India was a restaurant.) 'That's real cuddly in bed.'

'Bitch!' screamed the fat woman.

This was all shaping up quite well, and I noticed a Monitor idling near by, nodding his head as if racking up points while keeping a note that there wasn't any fouls, such as actual assault and violence. We'd gathered ourselves a sizeable audience, too.

But just then . . . all eyes sort of drifted away from Nance.

For this incredible dude came strolling along.

A leopard: he was a leopard! By which I don't mean that he was wearing leopard-skin *clothes*. Oh, no, he was wearing an actual leopard – or at least it looked that way. But maybe it was two leopards cunningly joined together. I didn't think, even if you stretched it, a single leopard could fit so tall a man (though maybe I was wrong). And was he tall. Six six, like a basketball ace. And black. He wore that leopard as if it were his own skin. He had clawed pads on his feet; and his hands were clawed paws. And the head! His own head was squeezed inside the leopard head, which was split open with the upper row of teeth creasing his brow and the lower row his chin. And a leopard tail jutted out ramrod-stiff behind him.

'Ohmygosh,' said Nance.

The ace flexed his claws and snarled, showing his own ivories within that larger frame of leopard teeth, like a mouth within a mouth.

I could see a zipper up the front of the leopard, but that didn't diminish anything.

'Hi there,' he said to Nance, acknowledging a fellow skin buff, while the Animal Libbers generally cowered away, appalled beyond appal (to put it poetically). He poised on the balls of his padded feet, leaning slightly forward.

'Skins and Smokes,' he said.

'Smokes and Rain Forests,' she replied.

'Wow-ee!' exclaimed this dude. 'Jaguars and Jivaro.'

'Shrunken heads and orchids!'

'El Dorado and anacondas!'

'Lianas and hummingbirds!'

'I didn't know that any leopards came from South America,' I butted in.

But they ignored me, enchanted. They didn't care. Or maybe this dude just hadn't been able to lay hands on a jaguar or two. Or maybe this was his ancestral tribal costume from Africa, though he really hankered to roam rain forests, not savannas . . .

'Piranhas and rubber trees,' he said.

'Sloths and amethysts!' And Nance reached to stroke his fur. Most sensuously. Now I knew that it was her day; but even so.

'Hey,' said I.

Right then the Animal Libbers rallied. 'Slaying and flaying!' they began raving. 'Blood and bludgeoning! Slaughtering and torturing!' And the guy in the business suit capered and gibbered behind the bamboo bars.

'Let's split,' suggested the leopard dude to Nance.

She winked, 'Macaws and chewing gum, eh?'

'Tapir and bananas.' He draped a leopard's paw across her shoulder.

'Hey!' I repeated, over the din. And Nance just looked at me as if I were a stranger.

No, not quite a stranger. Not yet. 'Amazon swordtails *and* – ?' she inquired.

I racked my brains. But I couldn't think. I couldn't talk this mystic language.

'And?' she prompted.

I shook my head. Then had second thoughts. 'And Inca gold?'

'Oh, *man*,' said the leopard derisively. 'We've had El

Dorado.' And he drew Nance away with him. And away Nance went.

Since, of course I (in my denims) was nothing to take offence at, the hubbub subsided. Forlorn, I stood in a pool of silence, watching that spotted beast with the long stiff tail lead my lady off, the two of them still exchanging phrases in secret code. Like a pair of spies who had come together at long last and successfully matched the torn halves of a dollar bill.

So that's the story of how I lost my Nance on Skin Day.

For a time I thought of registering as Skins myself, to try to win her back. But frankly, I couldn't see myself in furs. Anyway, it wasn't really the Skins that had lost her to me. It was the Rain Forests. And no again: it wasn't really even the Rain Forests.

It was that dialogue they had fallen into so snappily – just like two halves of the same person who had been hunting for each other ever since the world began.

And I wasn't Nance's other half. He was. She had known this immediately. Instinctively.

It's as if by slicing up the year into special days of obsession, for the social good, people, too, have been sliced up in the process. Sliced up, shortly to be recombined. Like DNA. (That's an analogy.) The slicing-up time is coming to an end; the time of recombination is just around the corner.

The day before yesterday, I spied an encounter in the street that sent a shiver down my spine.

Between a young Puerto Rican lad and a middle-aged middle-class white woman. (It was Abortion Day, by the way.) He stepped right in her path and said, 'Peyote and peace pipes.'

And she replied, 'Teepees and tomahawks.'

'Buffalo and adobes!'

'Sitting Bull and moccasins!'

'Wampum and totem poles!'

And they strolled on together arm in arm, sweet as you please.

Then yesterday (which was Porn Day) I noted a skinny girl in biker gear rush up to a crew-cut military type and hail him with, 'Legions and aqueducts!'

To which he replied, quick as can be, 'Orgies and togas.'

So that's the way it is. Or will be within another few months. The whole country is shaking itself out, and folding itself a different way.

And somewhere out there my soulmate is longing for me. And I for her, or him.

It could be you. Couldn't it?

Just let me try you out. Please.

'Chartreuse and truffles?'

'Bardot and guillotines?'

'Bonbons and tricolors?'

I'm waiting.

Windows

'Where do Windows come from, Danny?'

'That's easy. They come from Mars.'

'Mars is where the Venturer expedition found them. Where do you suppose they originally came from?'

'Can I have a Window for my birthday, Dad?'

'If you can tell me –'

'Unfair! Nobody knows.'

'Take a guess.'

'Maybe Martians made them.'

'What Martians, Danny?'

'Maybe Windows *are* Martians!'

'So how did they make baby Martians?'

'You break off one Window and stick it in the ground on its own. A second Window grows from one of the edges; at, er, forty-five degrees. Then a third Window grows from the second – which makes a triad. A triad of Windows is like a big prism that's hollow.'

'What then?'

'Nothing – till you pull a Window loose and start again.'

'So for Windows to multiply, you need some busybody to interfere.'

'Like bees pollinating flowers.'

'Not exactly. You need a creature that's curious and greedy and has hands.'

'Or has tentacles. Or claws. Maybe the ancient Martians were –'

' – octopus – crabs?'

'That's silly!'

'Windows don't make much sense either, Danny – unless they were specially planted on Mars for us to find.'

'Maybe they just grew naturally out of the Martian soil, like big crystals?'

'And till a few years ago there were just six triads. Now there are millions standing around on Earth, and we're multiplying them, all the time.'

'Gardeners split plants and spread them everywhere.'

'These things aren't plants. We don't know what they are.'

'If you think they're invaders, Dad, that's paranoid. Windows can't do a thing without us. My science teacher says that's why they can't be von Neumann machines.'

'Can't be what?'

'Machines that reproduce themselves. Named after John von Neumann, the computer wizard. Suppose a race of aliens wants to spread through the universe. The easiest way to do it is to send von Neumann machines to the nearest star systems. These machines mine the asteroids and build more of themselves. Some stay put; most travel on to the next nearest stars. The machines which stay either explore the solar system they're in and send messages back to their makers; or else they have DNA blueprints of their makers with them – so they build a crèche and recreate their makers and teach them. But Windows just stand around. Can we have one, Dad?'

'No, we can't have one. It would turn into three.'

This is a capsule of a hundred such conversations which Danny and I had before my resistance finally weakened. Our government in its wisdom had decided that any private individuals could own Windows just so long as they bought a Window licence – and so long as they were older than eighteen, as if owning a Window was equivalent to driving a car or buying alcohol. It's true that the licence system let the government monitor how many Windows there were in the country, and whereabouts – rogue ones excluded! Adding an age limit, as if to protect impressionable youngsters, provided an additional excuse; which was a load of nonsense, since kids had ample opportunity to goggle at Windows – Windows were all over the place. I'm sure the main idea was to raise revenue. Back in the eighteenth century or so the British government had taxed ordinary glass windows. Witness bricked-up frames in various old buildings. Here was window-tax revived in a new guise.

Mark you, *I* didn't mind. I was able to hold out against Danny's pleas for years.

Of course, in the beginning Windows were very expensive: rare marvels from Mars. After six or seven years you could hardly go anywhere without passing a Window; so much had they been multiplied – and their cost reduced – by people's eager hands. I don't suppose you would have seen too many Windows in Outer Mongolia or New Guinea. But most other places on Earth boasted a crop of Windows; privately, publicly, corporately, whichever.

'When I grow up, Daddy, I want to be a Window cleaner!' That was Danny, at age eight. That was the year that his mother Ruth died in a road accident. At that stage Danny had only seen one actual Window, though other examples had been on television. And Danny intuited that if ordinary windows in people's homes needed to be cleaned, why so too would Windows from Mars.

In a sense he was right. During the early years some smart businessmen made a killing by pretending that you needed special skills and chemicals to clean Martian Windows. Nowadays owners just sluiced them down with a garden hose. Windows didn't scratch or grow dull. Nor were they notably fragile, though a brick thrown with enough vigour would put paid to one, obliterating the view.

The view . . .

I remember, as if it was yesterday, that first real view

Danny and I had through a Martian Window when he was eight.

The Window in question – which was still as costly as a Rolls Royce – was on display in Harrods near the Food Hall. We had to queue for quarter of an hour to get near.

The thing was like a sheet of plate glass the size of a house door, with a bottom that broadened to support it. The base was set in a bed of soil, and already a second, half-formed Window – blank as yet – was growing from one of the edges, taking its substance from the soil, presumably by osmosis, and perhaps even from the air, which was rich with aromas of roast coffee-beans and venison pies and cheeses.

The view through the Window wasn't of the Food Hall beyond but of a moonscape – of craters and boulders, jet-black shadows and a glaring white dusty plain with a bright spatter of stars above. The view was entirely real. You could have stepped through into that lunar landscape – except that nobody could walk through Windows.

The moon was definitely not our own moon. For there were two suns in the sky. One was small, a blinding blue. The other, a fat red orb.

Small hand in large hand, Danny and I gradually worked our way through the crowd round to the other side of the Window. From there, the view was different. The backside showed a meadow of viridian mosses fringed by groves of tree-like ferns whose fronds wafted in a breeze. Lemon daylight; fleecy clouds overhead. Fat furry insects resembling enormous bees flew by.

A window upon an alien world – with alien life on it.

As Windows multiplied over the next few years we found out the range – and limitation – of views on offer.

A good many Windows showed lifeless worlds or moons. Others showed worlds with vegetation and living creatures. Never did any of the creatures appear to be of advanced intelligence. Never did we spy any sort of civilization; nor even the ruins of one.

(Did some Windows show civilized alien beings? And had those particular Windows quickly been sequestered by governments? This hardly seemed likely. New views appeared all the time at random in newly grown Windows. No such secret could have been kept.)

A proportion of Windows showed us views of Earth, and of human beings. Empty landscapes could be pinned down to somewhere in Canada or China, Argentina or Australia. Scenes with people were more immediately locatable: an Italian vineyard, a Japanese railway station.

Conceivably we hadn't yet arrived at a view of an alien civilization. Maybe the first view of such would turn up after fifty million Windows, or a hundred million or more. Was this the inducement? The bait, to persuade us to make more and more Windows?

People continued to pull triads apart and set up each part separately to multiply in turn.

'All right, Danny, we'll buy one.'

By now the second manned expedition had been to Mars and returned home. Venturer Two had found no new clusters of Windows, nor anything else to set the Earth on fire. True, they hadn't been over the whole of Mars with a fine-tooth comb, yet maybe there was nothing more to discover on our brother planet beyond rocks and grit and wasteland. Perhaps there would one day be a permanent human base on Mars. And perhaps not.

'Where shall we put it, Dad?'

'By the patio. We'll kick those woody roses out of their bed. But let's stick with the resulting triad, eh? Let's not divide it.'

'Then you can't see the views from *inside*.'

'Oh yes you can. Try climbing a ladder.'

Scientific studies of Windows had been unrevealing, to

say the least. We knew nothing about their internal structure while they were whole and showing a view. On the other hand they could be crushed or melted – which destroyed that structure – and their chemistry analysed. Windows were mostly silicon, plus other common elements. Evidently they were able to transmute raw material into the compounds they needed, in the right proportions. Which made them extremely remarkable objects; so remarkable that science was baffled.

Up to the time that Ruth died, I'd been a designer for a home furnishings manufacturer. (Ruth was killed by a truck which jack-knifed across the pavement she was walking along.)

I started out in kitchens then moved into bathrooms. It was me who designed the Whale-of-a-Bath, in the shape of a sperm whale (though smaller!). And the crocodile bath, and the hippo bath. Not to mention the nymph's grotto shower-cubicle. After Ruth's death, with Danny to bring up, I free-lanced from home. I designed totem-taps with animal heads – or with human heads, such as Hitler's or Yoko Ono's. I designed toilets in the form of animals was gaping mouths; you sat on the lips, and afterwards shut the tongue. I designed wash-basins with holographic nudes capering in the bowl. These all proved rather fashionable with people who had too much money. Why had no one thought of these styles before? Because no one had needed them – until I designed them. I could always be relied on to come up with a fresh capricious oddity.

Some day a book might be devoted to my weird designs. If I were writing the preface I'd suggest that as a designer I was anticipating something which hadn't yet occurred: namely the exploitation of genetically-engineered animal flesh and fur to serve human comfort – beds which massaged and warmed you, chairs that adjusted to your shape, toilets that ate your waste.

Perhaps I felt so ambiguous about Windows because I suspected that somehow they must be exploiting *us*. Plus the fact that they designed themselves.

One side of our new Window showed – by day – a street market which was bustling and obviously Arab; and by night a mostly deserted street. The backside view was of a changeless golden desert. The sun moved ever so slowly across the sky; the day might last a year.

We held a 'Window warming' party.

Amidst our other guests Danny invited his first ever girlfriend, Thea – short for Dorothea – who was a plump, abrasive sixteen-year-old with red hair. I invited my own more sophisticated lady-friend of the moment, Denise. Denist was thirty, an ash-blonde divorcee with a snub nose, neat figure, and ironic teasing eyes. She and I had been to bed a total of three times in as many months. Twice, she had been sweet. Once, she had been savage. Denise radiated several frequencies of empathy and friendliness, along with another wavelength which I didn't trust at all: a sort of slyly destructive, ego-puncturing, selfish cruelty. During a deeper prolonged relationship I guessed that this latter might well tune out the nicer frequencies. Right now, though, it still added a sparkle of danger which I found stimulating. She kept me on my toes. (If I married her, she might dance me to death in red-hot shoes.)

The centrepiece of the party wasn't really the new Window. People had seen plenty of Windows in the past ten years. The centrepiece was one of the Mars astronauts from the second expedition, Donna-Jean Scott, geology specialist.

D-J was a petite black woman from New Orleans, who was fast becoming rich on account of TV fees, book serial rights, consultancies and product endorsements. On board Venturer Two there had been a crew of seven men and four women. One of D-J's media coups had been when she revealed how this ratio was arrived at – by a Californian psychologist-astrologer who ran a Center for Emotional Numerology.

I had inveigled her to the party through Sam Jakobs, London boss of a multinational for whom I'd designed a personalized bestial bathroom. D-J was currently promoting a new Antarctic tourist resort which Sam's outfit had just opened as a sideline. Antarctica and Mars were much alike in a couple of respects. Both were barren, and bloody cold. Need I say that black skin showed up excellently against white ice; or that if filmed through red filters snow-fields looked just like Martian dunes ought to look?

My motives in luring Donna-Jean Scott to the party were several. One: to please Danny, and enhance him in the eyes of Thea. Two: to control Thea's adolescent brashness – someone of D-J's stature (or rather, fame) ought to abash and stem any uncouth rudeness. Three: to signal to Denise that I could swing celebrities. Last but not least: having eventually succumbed to Window ownership I wanted a warranty, a reassurance.

It was a sunny evening. A barbecue sizzled, busy broiling kebabs and bratwurst. A lute player in medieval costume – nice touch, this – sang ballads. A couple of hired waiters circulated bearing glasses of chilled Hock and warmer Burgundy. D-J obligingly admired the busy Arab market, then the alien desert.

'Is that Mars?' Thea asked her, jerking a thumb at the sands.

'No, Honey, it's the wrong colour.'

'Maybe it's a bit of Mars you missed,' said Denise. 'It was just over the next dune, but your boots were full of sand so you hiked back to the ship.'

'We rode buggies,' D-J corrected her. 'And if you have sand in your boots you're already dead.'

'How nice, if there were pyramids and camels,' Denise

continued idly. 'How boring Mars must be. Apart from the Windows.'

Thus rubbing home the point that the Windows had been discovered by the first expedition?

'Boredom, Honey, is in a person's soul. And on a place like Mars, boredom *kills*.'

'Is it as bad as that?' Denise sounded innocent.

'What I mean is: if you don't pay attention *all* of the time – '

I intervened. 'Donna-Jean, you visited the site of the first Windows; right?'

'We paid a call. There were still six triads, same as ever. You'll recall how the first team shipped two triads home intact. But first they dismantled one, which grew two replacements. Look, this Window of yours is budding already.'

So it was.

'Could the Earth ever fill up chock-full of Windows?' asked Thea.

D-J laughed. 'Not while human consumers are involved. No way. There had to be a natural saturation level, same as for any other product. You ought to regard this kind of craze ecologically. A niche fills up after a while, same as in nature. Demand tails off.'

Danny spoke up. 'Do you suppose aliens could be watching *us* through the Windows? And that's their real purpose?'

'I'd doubt that, Daniel. How would the information get to these aliens?'

'By faster-than-light particles – which we can't detect.'

'And which no one has ever proved to exist.' D-J shook her head and raised her glass of Burgundy. 'Here's to your new Window and its twin offspring. May those show something really neat.'

'Windows are just like fruit machines,' remarked

Denise. 'Don't you think? We keep on playing and playing in the hope we'll hit a jackpot.'

An image popped into my mind of toilets designed like fruit machines, with a flush handle to operate them. What had old Freud said about money? That money was like faeces? That hoarding cash – amassing wealth – was a harking back to infantile anal retention?

If I designed fruit-machine toilets these might have a deep subconscious appeal to wealthy purchasers . . .

Or would my patrons feel haunted by an inexplicable fear of bankruptcy and develop constipation?

The idea needed thinking through.

It took a week for Window number two to grow. As soon as it reached full size the views appeared. One was of a glacier which might have been on Earth or on a planet half-way across the galaxy. No way to tell; sun and moon looked much the same. The other was of a savannah which certainly wasn't on Earth. Its grass was grazed by stilt-like creatures resembling grey flamingos with the heads of gazelles. Occasionally the creatures all raced away, perhaps to escape some slinking predator; or maybe they just raced for exercise.

Danny spent a good while staring at these views as though he personally owned that savannah and the glacier.

'Two cherries,' was what Denise said to me when she called round.

'Hmm?'

'Two cherries on the fruit machine. Lowest pay-off.' She put an arm around my waist and hugged me lovingly. Perhaps for exercise.

By now I'd decided in one part of me that most of my creative life had been spent uselessly and farcically – even though another part of me was still busy churning out fresh ideas, such as fruit-machine toilets.

Windows seemed to offer a perverse reflection of my own activities. Endlessly they generated fresh perspectives upon far-out places . . . which weren't really worth visiting. Even if we could reach them; which we couldn't.

The only really attractive views were those of Earth.

Was this the true purpose of Windows? To disenchant us? To serve up a superfluity of empty alien scenes — plus a percentage of earthly sights, where at least something worthwhile was happening?

Could Windows be a compassionate, if enigmatic legacy from some superior alien culture which had been on the point of tossing in the towel, or perhaps emigrating to the next galaxy, or achieving nirvana? Aimed to tip us the wink so that we shouldn't waste our time in futile pursuits?

I believed myself to be somewhat of a trend-setter in styles. Was this mood of mine one which would presently infect the whole Earth, as Windows multiplied and always showed us meaningless places?

Ah. But let us consider the malicious-conspiracy explanation. Could Windows have been planted on Mars so that we would find them and lose heart? In actuality the universe was full of faery worlds and wonders, revels and adventures, cities and spires. But after a million Windows we'd never believe it.

Perhaps I was simply growing old. Danny appeared to prefer the empty alien scenes to those of the Arab market. Those seemed to appeal to him more. And to Thea, likewise. Maybe that was because they pictured as landscape the essential emptiness of adolescence, the kind of hormonal elegiac sadness which causes bad poetry to be written.

Our second Window began growing a third to complete the triad.

The final Window switched its view on during an afternoon while I was alone at home. I stepped out on to the patio to inspect.

And I was looking upon a windswept moonlit tundra. A quartet of little moons scattered light. A bright constellation dominated the sky. I immediately thought of it as 'the Ape'. The Ape was scratching for fleas, of lesser stars. Maybe our own sun was one of its fleas; probably not.

How charmingly bizarre, on a sunny afternoon, to stand gazing into alien night. Oh yes, how charming. Here was a window upon my own darkness.

Though if that tundra's sun rose after our own sun had set, how illuminating this view would be! We needn't use our electric patio lantern any more at night. We would save a few pennies courtesy of an alien star.

When Danny arrived home half an hour later, with Thea in tow, they really admired the moonlit tundra and the grinning itchy ape presiding overhead, bandy-legged, arms tucked in armpits.

Then Danny asked me, 'What's on the inside?'

'Yes, what does the other side show?' demanded Thea.

I shrugged.

'You haven't *looked*, Dad?'

'I thought I'd leave it,' I lied, 'for you two.'

From our outhouse Danny fetched a tall pair of steps.

'Bring a ladder too,' urged Thea. 'I want to climb down inside. We can both climb down inside, Dan.'

A ladder, plus two bodies, crammed into the triangle between three surfaces the size of doors?

'That'll be a tight squeeze,' I said.

'It'll be *fun*. It won't seem cramped,' she insisted.

'That's up to you.'

So Danny went to fetch our light aluminium ladder.

Would they kiss and stroke each other, there in the space between three worlds?

I had just visualized — and rejected — the notion of adapting a triad of Windows into a shower cabinet. For who would want to enter or leave a shower by way of a ladder?

This led on to the thought that to date no one had actually tried to incorporate Windows into houses. Well, you could hardly stick one in a window-frame in place of plain glass; not when one sprouted three. But maybe there *was* some domestic use for Windows?

Or would this be on the same level as turning elephants' feet into umbrella stands?

Fashion articles and décor manufactured from dead animals – zebras, crocodiles, tigers – were definitely *out*. Disapproved of. Yet the ancient desire of the human hunter to decorate his cave with trophies had to find some outlet. Thus my success with bestial baths and toilets (made of plastic).

It was at this point that I heard the familiar triumphal growl of arrival of Denise's Turbo. After pulling up at the end of a journey Denise always raced the engine fiercely once before switching off. As though the car was a child with a cold and she was officiously blowing its nose for it.

I let her in and without enquiring fixed her a customary Campari and soda, and myself a Scotch. Out of the corner of my eye, through the open French windows, I noticed Danny squirming around on top of the steps. Our ladder jutted out from inside the triad. A red head was disappearing from sight.

Why did people drink Campari? It tasted like dentifrice to me. The proper place for Campari and soda, in my opinion, was in a dentist's surgery as a medicated mouth-rinse (alcoholic, to calm the nerves).

Denise and I clinked glasses.

'Cheers.'

'*Salute.*'

I was definitely sinking into a deep depression – just as Danny was descending into a tight wedge of alien worlds. Everything seemed fouled and worthless.

Perhaps the ultimately depressing feature was the impossibility of actually stepping through any of those

Windows – even if the destinations weren't worth visiting. Thus they were a double taunt. Suddenly I hated Windows, though perhaps it was only myself I was hating.

A scream cut the afternoon like a knife slicing flesh.

I ran outside, pursued by Denise. That had *not* been the kind of squeal caused by standing on someone's toes.

'Danny!' I cried.

'Thea!' shouted Denise. She must have noticed red hair vanish too. But why had she called Thea's name? Was that because I had neglected to? No doubt!

Danny was scrambling out of the top of the triad, on to the steps. 'Dad! Help, Dad!' He nearly knocked the damn steps over. I grabbed and steadied them.

'Is Thea all right in there?'

'She's gone, Dad. *Gone.* There was a flash of light – and a kind of rushing wind – and . . . She's beyond the Windows! She's on the other side.'

'Get down the steps! Let me up!'

Quickly Danny descended and I climbed to the top. I leaned inside to look.

The golden desert: Thea stood staring about her in horror. She was breathing – she hadn't fallen, poisoned or insensible. She began to wave aimlessly in one direction then another. She couldn't see me; or see any Window. The sun beat down.

The savannah: Thea was also standing there, thigh-deep in grass. Some of those flamingo-gazelles were bounding away in the distance. She gazed around, white with shock, rooted to the spot.

The third Window . . .

Thea again. She was *in a city.* A city not of Earth. Columns of many-coloured lozenges soared upward, pierced by black spires, towards a cloudy grey sky. Perhaps the lozenges were fastened to the spires, the way a lupin flowers. She was standing by a broad, brown street. Opaque bubble-vehicles rolled along on squashy tyres. Creatures were approaching her, and she was screaming. The creatures were upright grey tubes – eyes and other organs at the top – with tiny waddly legs and thin whip-like arms. Walking worms, that wore sashes and boxes and clusters of small silver balls.

This was the alien jackpot.

The pay-off was instant transportation to that alien city. And to the desert. And to the savannah.

A jackpot of horror.

How could Thea be in that city, and also in two other places?

I wrenched at the Windows. To see more clearly and easily? To bring Thea back; to rescue her?

The Windows snapped apart. The triad became three separate Windows, leaning together.

I backed quickly down the steps, disposed of those on the lawn, and manhandled the Windows to stand separately so that we could all see Thea, three times over. And the city, with its inhabitants.

'Why did you do – ?' Denise gasped.

'*Aliens*,' I said.

Danny pawed the savannah Window as though he could follow Thea through. He couldn't.

'How is she in three places?' Denise asked me numbly.

In the desert, she was beginning to trudge up a dune.

In the savannah, she was stamping down the grass as though to make a nest for herself, a safe place.

In the city, the aliens were forming a discreet and curious circle around her. Their whip-arms pointed at her, waggling and wavering.

'Windows multiply themselves,' said Denise, 'And they multiplied her too . . . Is one of those the *real* Thea? Are the others only images? She looks real in all three.'

'Doesn't she?' I agreed. 'But where's she going to go in

a desert? Or in a savannah? She might find food and drink in the savannah . . . but the desert. My God.'

In the city she had stopped screaming. She was shaking as she faced the aliens.

'You broke the triad,' Danny accused me. 'You smashed it, Dad. Now she's stuck on the other side. She can't get back!'

'I didn't break anything. We have to be able to see! What makes you think she could get back?'

'I might have been able to follow her – to be with her.'

'In that desert, where you'd die?'

'So that's the score,' Denise said quietly. 'You didn't want to lose your son. You bastard.'

'I . . . That isn't why. How would you be able to follow her, Danny?'

'Not now, he can't,' said Denise. 'You tampered.'

The aliens were opening a gap in their ranks. A large bubblecar had stopped near by. Thea was herded by waving arms towards the transport.

Danny took a deep breath, shut his eyes, and threw himself at the city-Window; as though with eyes closed tight he might pass through.

His whole weight crashed against the Window. The Window toppled over. It fell upon the steel edge of the barbecue, with Danny sprawling after.

The Window cracked across. The view vanished.

In the desert – and in the savannah too – Thea jerked around as if she had heard a sudden explosion, or had felt something twang and snap. For a while she searched about in puzzlement. Then in the savannah she gave up and continued stamping grass. In the desert she resumed her climb up the golden dune.

The city was gone, the broken Window blank.

'You utter fool,' I said to Danny, as I helped him up.

'Fool? Fool?' He shook himself free.

'You've lost the city.'

'Lost *her*, you mean.'

'Yes, yes. I'm so sorry . . . that you broke the Window. If I hadn't separated them you wouldn't have been able to break it.'

Looking at the expression on Danny's face I felt the same cold, hollow suction that I'd felt when Ruth was killed. A feeling as if I was being emptied out. I feared that I'd lost my son, after all.

Also, we'd blunderingly lost the alien city, jackpot of millions of Windows. No one else but us three had seen it. Us four, if you counted Thea. How could I count her? She was no longer on the Earth.

Yet of course I *could* count her.

Thea One, there in the desert, disappearing over the dune crest in search of water, life.

Thea Two, on the savannah, also getting under way. I realized now why she had been trampling the grass. That was to mark the spot where she had arrived, so that she could locate the place again. How long would it take the grass to right itself?

Did each Thea think that she was the only one? She must.

What kind of mad transportation system was it which gave rise to two extra, doomed copies of the traveller?

Never before had Windows transported anything other than views. And likewise, never after? This once, a Window had transported a person, and we had broken the Window.

'Danny! What was it that triggered the Window? What did you two do in there?'

He stared at me bitterly.

'Did you kiss? Did you do more than that?' I spoke with urgency. 'Did you – ?'

'You're being crass,' Denise told me.

'I'm trying to work out how it happened.'

'She's going to die,' said Danny.

'They might treat her well in the city,' I said. 'They might even know a way to return her.'

'Through a broken Window?' asked Denise.

'What about the other Theas?' my son asked.

'Maybe those are phantom images. How can a person become three persons?'

'I thought God once managed that trick,' said Denise. 'The Holy Trinity, hmm?'

I smiled. I said, 'We'll have to report what just happened.'

'Why should anyone believe us?' she countered.

'We have to, because poor Thea has disappeared. Gone missing. And also because we've just glimpsed an alien civilization – which Windows can transport us to!'

'Where's our proof?'

'If we all swear blind – '

Denise nodded at the two surviving Windows. 'The rest of the evidence is busy walking away.'

'She'll surely come back when she can't find – '

'I wouldn't,' said Danny. 'I'd carry on walking.'

I groaned. If only I'd thought to rush and bring a camera. Too late now. Thea had disappeared over the dune. In the savannah, in the distance, half-hidden by grass, she might have been any kind of creature.

Danny began to cry. And then he started to curse. Denise made a fine show of consoling. However, Danny wouldn't let me even try to console.

'Listen,' I broke in at last. 'She has disappeared, damn it all! We can't pretend that Thea walked out of the house, and maybe somebody kidnapped her. We have to tell her parents the truth. We have to explain to the police. We have to be honest!'

All of which was perfectly true, as Danny and Denise were forced to acknowledge, by and by.

Accordingly we confessed; though not to any crime.

Parents came. Police came. Government scientists came, and took the broken Window away for tests, along with the other two Windows. News reporters and camera teams arrived; and went.

In their wake, a couple of days later, came Donna-Jean Scott; and for a few confused moments I thought she had flown in specially from Mars.

'Honey,' she said to me on the Windowless patio, 'I'm heartbroken for you. I had to come, because in a sense I blessed your Window. Will you tell me every little bitty detail of what went on?'

I knew then that this was no private visit. Nevertheless, to her I told every last nuance of the incident; including my failure to call out Thea's name. Maybe a woman from Mars might understand my feelings of separation. I'd certainly lost Denise, which perhaps was no disaster. But I'd also lost Danny, though he still lived in the house.

'I might be tempted,' said D-J, 'to speculate that a heightened state of consciousness – erotic, right? – can trigger a Window –'

'Danny got out fast,' I interrupted, 'and he was fully dressed.'

'Even so. That doesn't prevent excitement. But the fact is, the alien city was already showing when the pair of them climbed down inside. It was, wasn't it?'

'The tundra was showing on the outside.'

'Are you positive the worm city was on view before-hand, *inside*? This is kind of important. If not, maybe the kids' excitement triggered *that*, as well as transporting Thea.'

'Danny has been a bit reticent with me; as I've told you. Those investigators asked enough questions.'

'I know. And no one challenged that particular assumption. Because everything happened in a flash. I'd like to speak to Danny, if I may?'

'Go ahead. He respects you. He's upstairs, brooding.'

* * *

D-J descended from Danny's room twenty minutes later.

'The ladder was facing the savannah,' she reported. 'So that's all he saw, as he climbed down. He admits to feeling sexually aroused, as well as filled with a spirit of venture. Thea was just busy turning round. They were jammed together. Danny was still on the bottom rung. He fondled her ass, and there was a flash. She screamed. He looked; he saw the city. Next there came that rushing sensation. And she vanished into the Windows.'

'If Danny had stepped off the ladder, I could have lost him too?'

'Possibly. I'd say what we have here is a repeatable experiment.'

'How do you work that out? The Window's broken.'

'Take another newly formed triad. Don't sneak a look at the final view – the one you won't have seen. Don't dangle mirrors. Climb down inside with someone who excites you. Caress, and turn round. The alien city might flash on, and grab you. Or maybe a different civilized destination.'

'Plus two others where you could wander till you die. What sort of transport system is that? It's crazy.'

'It's one that operates. It delivers. I don't think Windows are pre-programmed with zillions of views. I think each new Window locks in on a view at random by some kind of action-at-a-distance. And it's always a view of a planet or moon, isn't it? Never mere empty space. A mind in a heightened state might direct the random search to a world where there are also thinking beings.'

'Plus two other worlds. Who would take part in an experiment like that?'

'I would. I've already visited Mars. I'd kind of like to visit another star system – no matter what the outcome. I guess you need a partner with a hefty emotional charge in them. Preferably one who also has a fierce emotional link with Windows.'

'*Danny*?'

'You, my friend. I read you. You're charged with guilt and self-contempt and loneliness and lust.'

'Don't flatter me so much, Donna-Jean.'

She grinned. 'When you're cooped up with ten other guys in a tin can for two years you get good at reading people's hearts, and accepting what's in them with love. Otherwise none of you survive.'

'What you're proposing doesn't sound like much of a strategy for survival.'

'There's a time to survive, and a time to make sacrifices. And to take risks. A time under heaven. How are you going to carry on facing Danny's contempt and anger if you don't try to follow his girl?'

'And two years in a tin can makes you an expert at pushing the right emotional buttons?'

'Could be.'

'Where would this experiment of yours be staged?'

'Why not Sam Jakobs' place? He's going on a business trip. We'll install a new Window and let it grow.'

'We?'

'Me and some acquaintances. I'd like your son to be there.'

'So he can watch me head off into an alien wilderness?'

'So he can admire his old man once again.'

The night before the experiment was scheduled, Donna-Jean came round to my place for an intimate dinner. She almost seduced me; but didn't. Danny was away for the night, by arrangement, already at Sam Jakobs'. Deliberately D-J took me up to a peak of desire and abandoned me there, frustrated. She showed me herself and denied me herself. Had I been a caveman, I would have reached for my club. But we aren't cavemen, are we?

'This is naked exploitation,' I complained, with an effort

at wit. (She was mostly naked at the time.) 'You're exploiting yourself shamelessly.'

'Now who's exploiting who, Honey?' she purred.

'You're exploiting me. Your bosses are exploiting you.'

'I'm increasing your charge, darling; should that be what's needed. *You* should complain about exploitation, with your nymph showers and nude basins and your bestial baths.'

'I plead guilty,' I groaned.

'Just you increase that charge of guilt, too.'

'You're a remarkable lady, Ms Geology Specialist. I think I'm falling in love with you.'

'No, you ain't. But feel free to imagine it.'

It took me a long while to get to sleep that night (alone).

The newly completed triad was planted in a small rear garden of tubbed shrubs with high brick walls around it, not totally dissimilar to my own patch of patio and lawn at home. My very own pair of steps was set up adjacent to the triad, with the same aluminium ladder at hand – no expenses spared. D-J's fellow specialists had hung video-cameras overhead to record the scene inside the triad and the view from the final Window upon tape. As yet no one knew what, if anything, that sixth Window showed. Nobody was kibitzing just in case the consciousness of the observer should interfere with the functioning of the Window prematurely; hence the video-recorders, left unmonitored.

The outer views were of an alien swamp infested with creepy-crawlies; a yellow, surf-lashed beach backed by coconut palms; and a plain of bubbling mud.

I'd been shown videos of the first two inner views. I'd seen an alien forest with rutted barrel-trees sprouting enormous parasol leaves and dangling yellow fruit, the ground covered with velvety purple fuzz. I'd also viewed a sloping rocky terrain with a few stiff growths reminiscent of stag's-horn coral.

D-J's colleagues were maintaining a low profile indoors, so as to keep out of our hair; and Danny was with them.

Both inner landscapes looked survivable, for at least a while. Presumably if one of those views had been of an airless moon or of molten lava we mightn't have pursued the experiment.

Which commenced with my telling Danny, inside the house, 'I'm going to search for Thea, Son,' then my stepping outside, to be deeply kissed by Donna-Jean. D-J and I were both kitted out in stout boots, tough trousers and hooded weatherproof jackets incorporating numerous pockets crammed with survival essentials, even including little high-powered radios and a pistol each. We both wore Reactolite sun-glasses. All courtesy of D-J's team. This was equipment left over from the returning Mars-ship – in case Venturer Two had come down in the Amazon or Arctic. I felt ludicrous to be standing in that little city garden dressed this way.

'Okay, let's go. Catch me if you can.' D-J climbed. I followed up and pushed the ladder high so that she could manoeuvre it over and slide it down.

She took care not even to glance at the view which was as yet unrevealed, both while she settled the ladder firmly and while she clambered down inside. We'd agreed that we should face the barrel-forest – until the moment when I caressed her and we both turned round.

'Come on in,' she called up softly. 'Water's fine.'

So I started down the ladder. Five rungs more to the bottom. Four. Three. By now I was squashing against her. Her breasts pressed my thighs, my back. Two.

One foot on the soil now. The soil of Earth: the human humus.

'Okay,' I said.

'Both feet, Buster.'

'Both,' I confirmed.

'Let go the ladder. We're going to both turn round together, and you're going to fondle me.'

Here we were, two fancy-dress-ball explorers stuck in a tight glass elevator . . . the situation was absurd, but damn it I felt excited.

'On the count of six. If you know some Latin, that's English for *sex*.'

'Oh very droll.'

'One. Two. Three. Four. Five. Sex.'

We both squirmed round together, and I placed my hands on her jacket over her breasts.

The 'target' Window was blank – for only a moment. Suddenly it flashed, and the view was . . .

To our surprise radio communication through the Windows is no problem at all, just so long as there are radios on both sides.

There are two radios in that rocky terrain.

There are two more radios – *ours* – in the alien forest.

And there are two in the alien civilization where the 'successful' Donna-Jean Scott and I arrived. (Plus a spare with the team at Sam Jakobs' place.)

We can all chatter to each other, and to those back home on Earth.

Our jubilant twins in the civilization have great tales to tell: of the sparkling city they arrived in, and of its saurian-descended inhabitants who haven't torn them to pieces but who have proved hospitable and brightly curious. Those two are already learning how to talk to the natives.

Our other twins are slogging down an endless rocky slope, hoping against hope to find somewhere less stark. At least it's cool there, though they're being burnt by the naked rays of a white sun.

And us? We've been hiking through these barrel-trees for a couple of days now, wondering how soon we should drink from a stream or test the fruit or even shoot one of the miniature dappled 'bears' to try the meat.

It's odd talking to your own self on the radio and hearing your own self answer.

'Hullo, Donna on the rocks,' says my Dee-Jay. 'Hey Honey, you're the Madonna of the rocks!'

'At least it's better than Mars,' comes the parched reply. 'Not much. A bit. And it's downhill all the way.'

'We're going to test a barrel-pear tomorrow morning. One of us. Doesn't matter which. If one of us gets poisoned, the other one's days are numbered too.'

'We can eat the food here,' calls D-Jean from the saurian city.

'Some folks have all the luck,' remarks my Dee-Jay.

I don't talk to my own twins very much. Can't stand the sound of my own voice.

It's evening under the parasols. The purple fuzz is soft beneath our feet. Time to bed down for the night. We'll build a camp-fire of barrel-tree bark and branches, though we haven't seen any sign of predators. There ought to be some predators, otherwise the mini-bears would overrun the forest. But perhaps the mini-bears aren't too hot at breeding.

'Call a halt here, Dee-Jay?'

'Yep. Over and out, Earth and elsewhere. We're gonna gather kindling.'

Later, as we sit in the dark by our camp-fire listening to assorted distant croaks and twitters – none of them notably menacing – the radio beeps.

'This is Earth. You guys all listening?'

Dee-Jay and her twins acknowledge.

'On account of this radio business we've figured that Windows must be some kind of transmitter device after all. They're a type of galactic phone directory. Something's obviously screwy about the way we've been using it – I mean, multiplying millions of the things. Also, the idea must be to transmit equipment, not personnel. Because of the tripling factor, right? There has to be a way to trigger a sending without sending people in the process. We're really going to work on this. Maybe if we could somehow send a Window *through* a Window, we'd have us a two-way door. Don't know as yet how we could fit a Window inside of a triad. . . but if you guys can hang in there long enough there's a chance we could haul you out.'

'Haul three copies of us out?' enquires Donna of the Rocks.

'Yeah, there's that to consider too. Maybe you'd all three fuse back together again. Maybe three copies are meant to be routed variously and fused at destination – as a checking system – in case of signal loss.'

'Personally I'm in no wild hurry,' chips in my twin from Saurian City. 'I want to see if I can interest our hosts in some new home designs. I appreciate that it's difficult for D-Jean and myself in that stony place – '

'You ain't kidding,' says that other Donna. 'Four or five days, and we've had it. Unless a miracle occurs.'

'And here in the forest,' says my Dee-Jay, 'we just don't know. If we can live off the land without poisoning ourselves, I guess we could last out.'

I hear the voice of my twin with incredulity. He's me – yet he isn't me. I find it hard to accept that I exist elsewhere and that the elsewhere-person is myself. Or that he's sure he's the real me. Which, of course, he is. If Windows can make copies of people, are people no more than complicated biological machines? Perhaps! It's futile to pursue this line of thought.

Yet curiously it isn't futility which I feel right now – though I'll accept that my twin on that stony slope may be feeling terminally futile. Sitting here in the firelight under the alien trees I feel oddly content at last. Finally

I've arrived somewhere, even if I don't know where it is. I have even found a true friend.

I put my arm around Dee-Jay and she nestles against me.

'Goodnight, Earth.' I thumb the radio off. 'Let's make love,' I suggest.

'Yes,' she agrees.

Today we reach the edge of the barrel-forest. We have eaten alien pears and not fallen sick. Ahead, across a shallow river, stretches a blue pasture land with scattered groves of umbrella-trees. And there's a crude village or encampment. With dappled dwellers who have two legs and two arms and knobbly, tufted heads. We watch them through our binoculars.

'They look fairly primitive,' murmurs Dee-Jay.

'Maybe they weren't so primitive once. And maybe a lot of Windows have wandered off focus since they were first designed a million years ago; or whenever. Or maybe climates have changed. Forests have grown. Deserts have shifted. Mountains have heaved up. Maybe Windows can be drifted across a landscape to a good destination. If only we knew how.'

'A million years ago those villagers might still have been animals.'

'They might have some more sophisticated cousins a thousand miles from here.'

'Compared with animals, they look sophisticated. What do we have to lose? Let's try them.'

'We have ourselves to lose, Dee-Jay. Though really I don't feel lost at all. Not any more.'

So we paddle then wade across the river.

Evil Water

The vicar, Hubert Smythe, pointed to the humpy field beyond Pook Pond where Charolais cows were grazing. Those cattle were as large as rhino; they seemed closer than they actually were, and the daffodil-bordered lawn fading into wild garden, less extensive. Yet there was no menace in the beasts. Frisky they might be; their tufty woollen coats, reminiscent of the mushroom-coloured carpet in the lounge, were visually cuddly.

'Easton Hampcote was sited there in the Middle Ages, you see,' the vicar told Paul and Alicia Philips. 'That was once the village duck pond. After the Black Death laid us waste – '

'*Us?*' echoed Alicia, and Paul smiled at his wife. Alicia was an agnostic, and the quaintness of this visit by a vicar amused her. Just so long as it did not become a regular practice! Paul continued smiling, appreciating Alicia. Reasonably slim, long honey hair, challenging blue eyes, fine small breasts, good tanned legs. The bloom of pregnancy was on her, not yet the distortions. He realized that he was undressing her mentally, and his smile died. It had been several weeks since they last made love. Morning sickness, headache at bedtime, a touch of back pain, womb pain; whatever else.

'One soon feels oneself part of the community. I hope you will too.' The vicar, who must only be in his early forties, was greying, almost haggard. A poor diet for clerics, on their salary; and he wore cheap clothes. He wouldn't undress in his mind any female members of his flock.

'I'm sure we will,' said Alicia. 'Paul especially. He's a real chameleon.' She darted him an (affectionate?) glance.

'A chameleon, Mrs Philips?'

'Private joke, Mr Smythe. Or should I call you Reverend?'

'Whatever you wish. The younger people sometimes call me Hubert.'

'We've had such a string of welcomers,' Paul intervened. 'Betty Nichols from the Women's Institute, Harry Dale hoping for a gardening job . . .'

He realized he was doing 'it' again: unconsciously mimicking, in this case, Hubert Smythe's accent which was clipped and unctuous, with a strong hint of Midlands. 'It' must have begun as a means of ingratiating himself. 'Speaking the other fellow's language.' The beneficiaries hardly ever seemed to notice, or resent, the subtle parody. So: a useful talent for an insurance manager.

A few times lately, now that he was driving ten miles every morning to the office of Life Mutual in Lederbury, on his own in the Saab he had spoken aloud, trying to overhear the real Paul without success. He would crane his head to glance in the driving-mirror at a face – under neat brown hair – which was at once mobile and vacant, as if awaiting expressions to imitate. A pint of water, which would take on whatever shape it was poured into.

Puzzled, the vicar resumed. 'The survivors abandoned the old site and rebuilt the village half a mile to the north. Of course, in the nineteenth century and then with Birdland, Easton Hampcote has spread down here again.'

'Birdland!' Alicia grinned. 'Is that what the locals call the development?'

Nightingale Close, Pigeon Drive, Owl Close, Wren Close, Magpie Close: the private housing formed an ingenious maze, or jigsaw, packing the maximum number of barely detached residences and pocket gardens into the minimum acreage. Owl Close, highest ranking in the price spectrum, favoured repro brass carriage lamps in the Georgian-style porches. The Philips' own house, Holly-hocks, was near the ten-year-old development, but definitely not of it. Hollyhocks was two artisan cottages knocked spaciously into one. A steep tiled roof. (Who but a snob wanted a thatch? Rethatching every seven years. Double the fire insurance.) A fine spread of land at the back ran down to Pook Pond.

'It fits,' the vicar said with a smile of complicity. He didn't live in the sprawling old vicarage – the Church Commissioners had sold that off to a car dealer – but nor did he live in Birdland, half of whose residents seemed comically ambitious to graduate upwards to Owl Close and carriage lamps.

'Amazing,' said Alicia, 'how they had the energy after a plague.'

'They would wish to escape a revisitation of the evil. Rat fleas in the straw. Though they didn't know that.'

'So why move? Why not stay put and pray?' She was needling the vicar, gently.

Hubert Smythe shrugged. 'As it happens, they chose providentially. After a fashion, the new village prospered.'

'Praise be.'

'So those bits of ruins beyond the pond are medieval cottages?' asked Paul.

'Oh no. The little that's left is all under soil. The ruin, such as it is, features on old maps as Barton's Folly. You know Barton Farm over the hill? Owned by the Langleys now?'

Paul nodded. 'We've met. Briefly.' The tubby, red-faced man with the ethereal wife. They farmed pigs, in intensive housing. When they mucked out on to the concrete, and the wind was in this direction, you certainly knew it.

'Humphrey Barton was a gentleman farmer. Eighteenth century. He travelled around Britain and even in Germany just before the Napoleonic Wars. He conceived a passion for spas, and saw Easton Hampcote as putting in a bid to rival Harrogate or Baden-Baden. He began building on the old village site. Plenty of stone buried there. Pook Pond was to be a centrepiece – deepened, marble-floored, roofed over. With statues of nymphs and grottos. A fantasy! He hired a sculptor. He was going to heat the spring-water. He was a man possessed by a vision.'

'Why is it called Pook Pond?'

'*Spook*, Mrs Philips. It's a way of saying "spook".'

'Have people seen ghosts, then?'

'I haven't, in ten years. What I've seen is mist coiling up from the water. Quite wraithlike, till I shone my torch.'

'What a shame. I could fancy a ghost at the bottom of the garden. Ought to be worth another thousand on the price, eh Paul? "Large delightful modernized period cottage, the rear laid to lawn and wilderness and ghost."'

'This *is* a lovely house,' agreed the vicar.

'I suppose people in the past thought your mist was the souls of plague victims.'

'Drunks thought so, I expect. In the nineteenth century Easton Hampcote boasted five pubs, would you believe? The strongest ale cost but a penny a pint. The old records say that farm labourers used to lie paralytic in the lanes. Roaming pigs sometimes chewed a finger off, or bit through an ear. But the drunks thought they were seeing the ghost of Humphrey Barton. When his spa scheme foundered he went mad and drowned himself in Pook Pond, you see. Apparently he roped himself to one of the stone nymphs. Dived in clutching her. She, mm, dragged him down.'

Alicia had pursed her lips. 'No, I don't see. Why did he go mad?'

Smythe spread his hands. 'Why? Disappointment. Obsession. He must have been unbalanced to begin. Easton Hampcote was hardly a likely candidate for a fashionable spa. What, a rustic village with a rutted road? Where were the promenades and parks and lodging-houses? The concert-hall, the library, the assembly rooms?'

'If he was mad to start with,' Alicia said logically, 'madness can't be why he killed himself.'

'Progressive madness, Mrs Philips. There has always been a lot of madness in the world.'

The vicar was staying too long, eking out his cup of Earl Grey tea, hoping for additions to his congregation.

'Yes,' said Paul, 'all sorts of people have been calling on us. We can hardly get fixed up. I have to repoint the kitchen wall.'

'Oh, do excuse me.' Smythe rose.

'For instance,' said Alicia, 'just before lunch there came an emissary demanding Paul's presence at "Boys' Night".'

'But there's no youth club, Mrs Philips. I tried my best. The club collapsed after a year.'

Alicia laughed. 'Boys' Night is every Friday night at the White Hart. Wives apparently excluded.'

During the next couple of months Paul became a *habitué* who looked forward to Boys' Night, though this kept him up late and involved drinking more beer than quite suited him, to judge by his head next morning. He'd never lived in a village before. Back in Lederbury, which was almost a city, whenever Alicia had switched on the radio soap opera about the daily lives of country folk Paul had scoffed at the way the characters never ordered more than half a pint at their local; this seemed like health education propaganda. Now he understood the reason. Unless you always ordered halves, given the number of rounds you'd never get through the night.

It was gregarious Matthew Davies who guided Paul into the Friday-night ritual commencing around nine, concluding when the White Hart's patrons felt so inclined. Since there was no police house in Easton Hampcote, at drinking up time landlord Ronnie Wilson simply latched the front door of his pub and closed the curtains. He rarely draped towels over the pump handles, of Everard's, Fuller's, and Bass, till half-eleven, not always then. The record was half-past midnight.

Gangly, freckled, and red-headed, Matt Davies was a biochemistry graduate of twenty years vintage, an executive at Whitney's, the agricultural research centre on the northern fringe of the village, which Paul drove past every morning and evening. A high chain-link fence surrounded the offices and labs but not the pastures and livestock sheds. The barrier at the gatehouse was generally left in the up position, though guard dogs patrolled at night. Whitney's was researching new antibiotic additives for feed, and hormone boosters. The centre employed several villagers as cleaners, gardeners, and canteen staff; its salaried staff tended to live in Birdland – as did Matt, who often wittily mocked life in the aviary.

Matt was no more a native of Easton Hampcote than Paul or the vicar or most of the other inhabitants. A couple of 'aboriginal' families survived – the Tates, the Dingles – but Paul and Alicia had been surprised at what a melting-pot, or crossroads, the village was. One rural odd-job man proved to be a wartime evacuee from the East End of London. Another rustic gaffer hailed from the south coast, via the merchant navy.

A melting pot – or a rich stew, after the blandness of Lederbury . . . A lot of oddities lived in this village: a hippyish book illustrator, a professional conjuror, a retired submarine commander who had visited the North Pole, a retired, half-Russian lady gymnast, a lady potter, an expert pot-holer, a Dutch herbalist, an Australian husband and wife who ran a mail-order lingerie business.

People still fell into sets, with a certain amount of crossover. There was the church-going fraternity, the 'smart set', the farmers and Young Farmers, the Tories and foxhunters, the Council House people, the Birdlanders, the beer and darts mob, and the Americans – two American families lived off base in Birdland, both white, both pilot grade.

Paul supposed that Matt and he belonged to a mixture of smart set and beer set. Along with Bill Morrison, planning officer for the District Council; Conrad Golby, antiques exporter; and Adrian Waller who farmed in the village.

In the White Hart of a Friday night there was farming talk and property talk, school talk and car talk, sports and beer and food talk, and misadventure talk.

'Stuck his car in the ditch Tuesday night. Slept in the back. That's the third time. Don't know how he gets away with it . . .'

'Took the family to the Boatman. Steak as big as my plate, I couldn't finish . . .'

'Bass? Needs to stand for three days before you tap a barrel . . .'

'So the rain came down, and the centre court was a waterfall . . .'

'Pearces are asking eighty grand.'

'No, Becky got a "B" in German.'

'Wimbledon.'

'Beef in Guinness.'

'*Ninety* thousand? They'll be lucky.'

'It's going to auction.'

'Just a recall for the seat-belt mounting.'

'Steroids for steers, as our Texan friends might put it. Lowers the fat content of the beef. We're working on some pretty potent . . . Put a drop of that in your baby's bottle! Deoxycorticosterone.'

'Who?'

'Water balance regulator.'

'Bloody discos! Had to call the police to Fardley village hall last week. One lad got *stabbed*. You just can't have a

ticket-only do. Word gets round. Your Young Farmers
want to raise funds but they don't want the responsibility,
do they?'

'Whose round is it, anyway?'

The White Hart was also the hang-out for the older
boys and girls who had spurned the vicar's youth club.
They gossiped in whispers, giggled, sat in silence, cud-
dled, drank shandies, played the STOWAWAY gambling
machine in the hall. The girls tended either to be over-
weight or punkishly, anorexically skinny, but one or two
were attractive, particularly Sally Dingle who had left
school and worked in the canteen at Whitney's. Paul didn't
see her in the pub as often as the others, of a Friday night
or Sunday lunchtime, though he spotted her wandering
about the village solo and managed to say hullo several
times.

She was perhaps a bit on the buxom side, emphasized
by tight jeans, and her breasts were ampler than he really
cared for, but she had an air about her of . . . what? Not
exactly sophistication, though she applied blushers and
shaders to her pert oval face (with sparkling eyes of rain
on slate) and highlights to her straw-blonde hair to good
effect. Not exactly sensuality; she appeared to have no
boyfriend (any more than she had a close girl-friend), nor
much interest along those lines. Far from making a beeline,
the local boys seemed to shy away. Perhaps, thought Paul,
her potential challenged them beyond their present adolescent capacities.

Yes, that was it: Sally Dingle had potential, and she
knew it, but withheld it from her peers, who therefore
resented her faintly. It was as though she was waiting, and
despising. Waiting for what? Maybe she read romances
and her head was fogged with illusions.

Paul was more aware of Sally – only casually, to be sure
– because Alicia still refrained from making love for one
reason or another. One night she even said, 'I can't. I feel

we're being watched. Listened to. They're so nosey in this village. They need to know everything. It's all very well for you, away in Lederbury every day. If I wash my nightdress, someone's staring at the clothes-line next morning looking for stains. I'm sure Mrs Badgot has X-ray eyes and can see through walls.'

'Don't you like it here, then?' he'd asked.

'Oh yes. It's idyllic after Lederbury.'

What could he say to that?

Another night she cried, 'What's that? Someone's prowling in the garden.'

No one was, though he went outside in his pyjamas with a torch. Alicia had gone to sleep when he got back.

Sally Dingle. She did look at Paul with covert interest, as though she knew him. Well, obviously she *did* know him. Yet not exactly 'know' in the ordinary sense. As though she . . . expected something, and despised whatever it was. Did she expect Paul to . . .? It was ridiculous even to imagine.

At the Life Mutual office Paul found himself paying compliments to one of the typists, then suggesting a lunchtime drink. She accepted; and over vodka and lemonade, plus smoked salmon sandwiches, the girl told him casually about her union's stand on sexual harassment in the work place. His own secretary remarked pointedly that she and her boyfriend had nearly saved the down payment on a flat.

Paul was working down in the wild garden, from where it looked to be a long way to the house. He was sorting a pile of ironstone which had been overgrown with nettles. Down at soil level he had just uncovered a perfect ring of stones neatly dovetailed together. He was trowelling rubbish out from inside the ring when a voice said close by, 'You going to open the well up? You shouldn't, lightly.'

His heart jumped. Sally Dingle was standing behind

him in her jeans and floppy muslin blouse which sunlight shone through, outlining her.

'Is that what it is, an old well? Did you want to speak to me, Sally?'

She smiled. 'That's what I'm doing. Speaking.'

'Did you want something special?'

'What would be special then, Mr Philips?' She eyed him. 'I'm just passing through, by Pook Pond.'

'Excuse me, Sally, but aren't you sort of trepassing on our property?' (Had it been *her* that Alicia thought she heard that night?)

'There's a right of way. Across this corner of your garden, round the pond, over the fields.'

'A right? There was nothing in the deeds. There's nothing on the district council's large-scale map. It shows every *tree*.'

'The right's ancient.'

'Why don't the Ramblers use it? They were tramping by last week.' A party of giant garden gnomes in their laced-up boots, knee socks, green and red anoraks, and woolly hats. 'I thought they made a point of crossing any scrap of land where there's a right.' Adrian had told him so; a disputed right leading through the Wallers' farmyard was a bone of contention between him and the Ramblers Association.

'Too old for them to know.'

'You aren't ancient, Sally. So how do you know?'

'How old am I, then?' She smirked. 'Old enough.'

'What did you mean, I shouldn't open the well lightly? Why not? It should look romantic.'

'Romantic, is it?'

'Rebuild the sides; put a pitched roof on. Bingo: wishing well. Cast-iron grille across. Use it as a barbecue.'

'Use it for water-wishing. Water don't like fire.'

'Don't it?' He realized that he was falling into her speech

patterns, adapting to her, like peas in a pod, like the wedded in bed. 'What?' he barked.

'Dip a babe in the right water, wish; it'll never die a natural death of body rot, only violence and treachery. Like a stab in the heel.' Obviously she was repeating something half-remembered from school about Achilles, whose mother dipped him in the Styx. 'You got the water-touch; I know. Our bodies are mostly water, see? Ninety per cent or more. We're walking bags of water. When the right water shifts itself, it shows you what's underneath. You got the flow, but it's dammed.' (Or did she say 'damned'?) 'Your water-sight's pent up.' (Or did she say 'site'?) 'Some water's alive, and dissolves illusions. Juice of the earth.'

'You're having me on, Sally.'

'Am I? Come down to your well on Lammas at midnight, if you've dug it out, an' you may see something; or may not.' She nodded towards the house. 'On Lammas you keep her out of the way. An' I'll keep out of hers.'

Paul looked towards the house, thinking that Alicia was watching them talk; but she wasn't. When he turned back Sally was already by Pook Pond, outside of their boundary, staring at the muddy water which a Charolais had stirred up. She must have run away on tiptoe.

'Who was that over by the pond earlier, Paul?'

'What? Oh, the Dingle girl, what's she called?'

'Sally Dingle.'

'Right. *Listen*, I've made a discovery – and I've an absolutely wonderful idea. We have a well down in the wild area . . .'

Lammas proved to be the first of August, several weeks away.

'That's the old name for harvest festival,' Adrian told Paul on Boys' Night. 'Smythe and the faithful might still call it Lammas, for all I know. When all arable farmers give thanks for subsidies from the Common Market, and the grain mountain, and oil-seed rape that paints our English fields bright yellow like Italy.'

'Bit early for a harvest, isn't it? End of July? I thought harvest festivals were in September.'

'Wonders of technology,' remarked Matt.

'I think Lammas was more to jolly the harvest along. Pagan thing. They probably fucked in the fields.'

Paul's heart beat quicker.

'Personally,' Adrian went on, 'I haven't been inside a church for years. Bunch of hypocrites. It's the bitches and gossips that go there. They need forgiving.'

'Give thanks, too,' chipped in Matt, 'for growth hormones. Steroids. Antibiotics. Oops, I believe my glass is empty.'

'We can take a hint.' Conrad Golby drained his own mug, and waved it through the mob at a harried Mary Wilson. An out-stretched arm was the closest he could get to the bar. Young Farmers packed it out, while in the other half of the room the rubber-matted pitch leading up to the dartsboard was deeply cordoned by team members and spectators; Easton Hampcote was playing a friendly with Fardley. A shifting of bodies briefly revealed the full frontal calendar on the far wall, published by a car accessories firm. Above hung the joke clock, where the hands turned anticlockwise.

'I heard on the radio,' said Bill Morrison, 'that all these antibiotics we eat in good old meat are knocking out our resistance to flu.'

'Load of bollocks, Morry,' said Adrian.

'Bullocks' balls,' agreed Matt. 'Heard this one? How do you get an Irishman to climb on the roof? . . . You tell him the drinks are on the house!'

'There's something I did want to ask you,' Paul heard

himself saying to Adrian. 'Is there anything funny about the Dingle clan?'

'What kind of funny?'

'Oh, inbreeding. Paganism. Madness.' Paul grinned loosely. 'Usual rural stuff.'

Matt dug him in the ribs. 'I wouldn't mind breeding with that Sally Dingle.'

Paul did his best not to twitch. 'I expected a village at least to boast a spot of ancient devilry.'

'You'll be lucky. Old Ned Dingle's a Baptist. So's his missus. When they bother.'

Baptist? Was that how Sally got her strange notions about the power of water?

'Funny thing *did* happen ten, twelve years ago,' said Adrian. 'When my oldest had just started school. We had our own primary school in the village then, before the kids got bussed. Commander Potter's place: that's the old school house. Bought it for twelve and a half. We thought he was crazy.'

'What do you reckon it's worth now?' asked Morry.

'Ooh, a good ninety.'

'What type of funny thing?' Paul reminded Adrian.

'Some playground brawl. They said that little Sally Dingle spat in a lad's eyes – he wanted her to show him you-know-what, and she did, but then she spat – and he went stone-blind. The Merricks' son; they moved soon after, to get near a special school.'

'She blinded him by *spitting*?'

'Hospital said it was hysterical blindness, since they couldn't find anything physically wrong.' Adrian tapped his temple. 'That's why they needed a special school.'

Conrad began hauling fresh half-pints of Everard's shoulder high from the bar, like an angler reeling in his catch.

★ ★ ★

By the end of July Paul had finished building the wishing well-cum-barbecue. The well had proved to be blocked off with spongy old timbers under a few inches of soil and rubble. He'd easily torn the rotting rubbish out, revealing a deep shaft. A torch lowered on a string showed the stones to be large and unmortared. The soil in Easton Hampcote, even in their own garden, varied wildly. Here it seemed to be solid yellow clay, which could explain how the shaft had been cut and had survived – for goodness knows how many centuries – without collapsing. To Paul's surprise a bucket on a rope brought up water clear as gin. He felt relieved once he had completed a stout circular curtain wall and had fitted a heavy iron grille over the top, removable so that he could water the garden in the event of drought. A dovecote-style roof on rustic poles followed. Next year, when the wilderness had been further tamed, they would throw an outdoor party for the Wallers, the Davies, the Morrisons, the Golbys, whose wives Alicia had met through the Women's Institute.

Her pregnancy – their pregnancy – followed its course, and her belly was plumping. The foetus had been scanned acoustically, a needle had been poked in to her womb to sample the water; no abnormalities apparent, though she did complain of back pain and a varicose vein. In the circumstances she didn't wish him to lie on top of her, nor did she fancy squatting impaled on him.

On the first of August Paul brought home a bottle of fine champagne and insisted on a celebration.

When he refilled her glass for the third time she gave him a peculiar look. 'What are you trying to do, souse the baby? Get it drunk in charge of a womb? I'll be all acidic in the morning.'

In fact two-and-a-bit glasses were ample; Alicia slept soundly.

Paul stayed awake in bed by meditating about mortgages. At quarter to twelve he slipped from the sheets, from the room. Downstairs he pulled a raincoat over his pyjamas and climbed into rubber boots.

It was a hot, still, dark night with a yellow sickle moon only intermittently visible through cloud. He debated taking the torch, but knew the way and had no wish to signal his presence. Walking down the lawn, through the wild garden to the well, he kept his eyes peeled. He waited.

A movement in the field? One of the cows?

The moon broke through, no longer meagre yellow but forged of white-hot steel that silvered Pook Pond. Sally was standing on the far bank, also dressed in a raincoat, not that any rain threatened. She opened the coat, let it fall. She had been naked underneath.

As she stepped nude into the pond, he was no longer seeing a muddy watering hole and a fringe of ruins. He saw a large bath with gleaming stone steps, stone surrounds, marble benches, sculptures of nymphs and satyrs, a hint of pillars rising. Sally stood thigh-deep, water lapping at her pubic hair, gazing across at him expressionlessly. His erection pushed at his raincoat, having thrust through his pyjamas. Then she submerged herself.

Cloud ate the moon, and for a few disconcerting moments he could see nothing; was blind. He clutched at the larch pole of the well for reassurance, felt the rutted cracking bark. When his night vision returned there was only the dim outline of the pond, no bather evident.

Trot along Sally's 'right' to the bank? Discover her standing ankle-deep in mud among the cow pats? He doubted it. Find her coat cast down on the grass as bedding? Hardly.

It seemed so dark now. No one could possibly see him, even from a few feet away. His erection was almost painful.

He loosened the coat; held himself. Sally's after-image lingered. Almost immediately he ejaculated into the well.

He went back to the house, and up to bed. Surely he had experienced a waking dream, a hysterical vision, a sort of self-hypnotism.

Alicia stirred, and groaned.

When he returned from Lederbury the following evening, Sally was loitering near the open five-bar gate of Hollyhocks. Paul swung the Saab in on to the shingle fronting the house and got out.

'Hullo, Sally.' He felt himself flush.

'Enjoy yourself on Lammas night?'

'Um,' he said.

'See somethin'?'

'Saw what I saw.' That sounded like a good country answer.

'An' you gave yourself t' water,' she said, and walked away.

Gave himself to water? He remembered how he had ejaculated into the well. She couldn't have seen that; even if she had been there in the first place.

After greeting Alicia briefly he hurried down the garden and stooped over the iron grille. Any stains which might have been his doing were indistinguishable from other marks. Suddenly he gripped the grille and wrestled it free. The bucket was still upside-down beside the well, with the rope coiled underneath. He dropped the bucket down deep and hauled water up, emptied it over the grass. Absurdly he felt that it was urgent to recover himself – his substance – from the well. He had hauled up and dumped a dozen bucketfuls without any sign of hitting bottom when Alicia walked up.

'Funny homecoming! Did you lose something down it?'

'Damn fountain-pen. Fell out.'

'Isn't *that* your fountain-pen?' Her ring finger pointed at his breast pocket.

'Different one. Borrowed it from Tom at work. Now it's gone.'

'Are you sure it fell down the well?'

'Course I'm sure!'

'When? Just now?'

'Ye . . . No, yesterday.'

'Hence your sudden dash down the garden? Well, a pen would probably sink. So it's lost. Better buy Tom a new one.'

After that he could hardly continue trawling. Why was he trawling anyway?

'Why guard dogs?' echoed Matt. 'Look, Paul, if any idiot – burglar or vandal or industrial spy – broke in and breached the safe-handling area – '

'Safe-handling?'

'For experimental hormones. The tailored ones. We have to dump some concentrates in the furnace. Can't have chickens sprouting four legs. Much as the poultry trade might appreciate it!'

'Are you serious?'

Matt paused before replying, 'Course not. Drink up. My round.'

'I think we ought to have our baby christened properly,' said Alicia.

Paul looked up, amazed, from his plate of beef bour-guignon. 'You're joking.'

'It seems vaguely appropriate, in an old village. Doesn't commit us – or the baby – to anything. I was speaking to Hubert the other day.'

'So the vicar's been working on you?'

'It wouldn't do any harm. Picturesque ceremony. Grandparents would like it. Take snapshots.'

'You wouldn't get old Adrian trotting along.'

'Do we want to? But you might be surprised.'

'Astonished is more like it. You don't believe the nonsense. It's almost an insult to our child.'

'Hardly. It's part of belonging to the community. It'll do us good.'

'We already do belong.'

'What you belong to, I don't necessarily belong to. Late nights at the pub while I'm –'

'Okay, okay. I've no bitingly radical objection. Mind, I think it's disingenuous.'

'Fancy word, that be,' she mocked in a broad accent which no one local actually used.

'Okay. I give up.'

'Good. Hubert will call round to chat to us.'

'We don't need to go to church for weeks on end, do we?'

'Only the once.'

The baby was due in late October. Autumn was an Indian summer with warm still nights, the temperature only dipping two or three degrees. In the garden of Hollyhocks, hollyhocks reared high their spikes of rose and burgundy flowers, blooms made out of crêpe paper by slightly clumsy children.

On the first Friday in October Paul was in the White Hart as ever, though he had promised a terminally pregnant Alicia not to stay too late. Sally wasn't in the pub; he hadn't spotted her since the day he had tried to bail out the well. Glancing at his watch, he found to his surprise that it was going on for eleven.

'I'll be off, Matt. I'll just win a fortune on the way out. I'll bust its guts.'

'Give the bugger hell, boy.'

The gambling machine in the hall had been changed.

Odd that he hadn't noticed this on his way in. He recalled how earlier the village lads had been clustered round it.

No wonder; the new machine was named STRIPTEASE.

Each letter in the word overlayed a woman in successive states of undress. Numbered fruits on the win line caused that number of letters to light up. Instead of a query mark to signal a random chance there was a sinuous nude with one hand across her breasts, the other clutched between her thighs.

He fed in coins, hoping for a hold so that he could complete the word and light up the flashing option features allowing him to 'stroke' or 'grope' or 'thrust' his way towards jackpot.

Ronnie had already doused the hall lights, leaving the STRIPTEASE machine alone lit up, bright and pulsing. As Paul played, racking up nine letters of the word before losing them again, the stripper's face began more and more to resemble Sally's. He won minor prizes and fed them back, then more change from his pocket. His pulse was racing. He must succeed in stripping Sally, to be able to stroke or grope or thrust his way to victory.

A query-nude popped into place. Lights ran along the STRIPTEASE panel, inviting, denying. He thumped the button; the word lit as far as STRIP. The nude held, and he scored fruit worth two apiece. He couldn't lose. He thumped the START button. T-E-A-S-E lit up. The machine played an electronic fanfare. Lights flashed from 'thrust' to 'stroke' to 'grope'. He punched 'stroke'. Softly softly catchee monkey. Reels clicked up and down. Three nudes appeared. The machine played 'Kiss Me Tender'. A hitherto blank panel came to life, showing Sally lying stark naked, spread-eagled on a bed. The pay-out slot began to ejaculate tokens.

'Triumph, eh, boy?' Matt poked his head round the door.

Hot – yet why should he feel guilty? – Paul stared back at the machine.

It was the same machine as last time: STOWAWAY. The glass frontage showed a sailing-ship with an angry captain and sailors chasing a stowaway who was trying to reach the jackpot hold. There had never been any such machine as STRIPTEASE. Yet he had played it for ten minutes. He had believed he was playing it. He must be drunk, so drunk that he was seeing things. He didn't feel specially drunk. The flashing lights in the dark of the hall must somehow have mesmerized him, put him in a trance in which he hallucinated. He staggered against the heavy box in shock – as if embracing it. He realized he had an erection. Turning to hide this, he fled towards the door to let himself out into the protective darkness.

'Hey! How about your winnings?'

'Cash them in for me, Matt, will you? Have a drink. A short. I just remembered I'm expecting a phone call.'

He stared up at the flood of the Milky Way. The big dipper pointed the way back home.

Diamond-frost stars, those! However, the night was much milder than those sharp stars diagnosed. No need to zip his coat. On the contrary, he felt overheated, sought the caress of the breeze.

He tried to forget about the striptease machine but couldn't. An electronic succubus, all of his own imagining . . .

At Pook Corner, a shadow detached itself from the bushes.

'Ev'nin', Mister Philips.'

'Sally!' He smelt musky perfume. She was wearing that raincoat, buttoned up to the neck; boots on her feet.

'Did you get a jackpot, then?'

'What?' he gasped. He often played the machine in the pub; the good old STOWAWAY. She would know that.

'Oh I knew, Paul. I could feel your fingers on the buttons, couldn't I? Touching and pushing. Holding and stroking. I'm sensitive, remember?'

Telepathy, thought Paul. Unless somehow Sally *caused* his hallucination.

She bumped up against him, and he began to kiss her. His hand roved down her back, circulated around her buttocks. He was sure she was wearing nothing under the coat. She ground her loins against his, groaning faintly, as a cat growls over a mouse it has caught. He seemed to hear liquid running from her, down her legs. Juices, from the excited wetness in her. No, it was the stand-pipe near by . . . That was still leaking vigorously despite the Parish Council's efforts at volunteer repair.

She resisted. 'Rose Cottage is empty. I have the back-door key with me.'

'How's that?'

'I've lots of old keys, Paul. Keys going back for centuries. Come with me.'

So he went.

She tugged him by the hand, up twisty pitch-black stairs which she seemed to know well. Only a carpet and open curtains remained in the starlit room she drew him into; plus an abandoned single mattress lying by the wall.

She kicked off her boots, dropped her coat. Naked Sally began to unbutton him, unzip him, stroke him and lick him. His body was someone else's – hers. It was behaving as *it* wanted to behave. As she wanted it to behave. His muscles and nerves rippled like harp strings, playing water-music. Soon he had entered her, upon the mattress; soon he pumped himself into her.

Sally was whispering. 'Blamed her for the Plague, bloody fools. So they ducked her. That's what they did to women as they thought was witches. Or as they *knew* to be. Not that witches did 'em harm. Helped 'em. Kept

their waters sweet. Trussed her up tight, they did, and
tossed her in Pook Pond with a rope to haul her out again
if the fancy took them. If she sank, she wasn't a witch,
see. They might pull her ashore afore she drowned; or
after. She was guilty if she floated.

'Huh. A girl with water-magic floated on Pook Pond all
right. What did they do then? Well, what?'

'Built a bonfire?' Paul asked reluctantly.

What was she telling him? That she, Sally, had been a
witch in an earlier life? That she'd been reborn – into a
family which could well have lived here ever since medieval times? A – how appropriate – a Baptist family. When
she was barely knee-high she'd rediscovered her affinity
for certain water . . .

'Naw. Witches weren't burnt in this country. Just
heretics was. Ord'narily they hanged witches.'

'So they hanged the poor girl.'

'Naw. They had a bright idea. Boiled me alive in a
cauldron. Till I scalded to death. Till the flesh floated off
me bones. Then they fed the stew to the hogs.'

'You . . .'

A thought crossed his mind. Could those ignorant
peasants of an earlier epoch have guessed that the boiling
of water killed off any harm in it? Any germs, or imps?
Was there something in the spring-water? Down the well?
And in Pook Pond? Some sort of collective microscopic
life? Some . . . spirit? Yes, like those spirits which the
Greeks believed had haunted pools. An ancient force
which could enter its devotee and permeate her waters?
This was a spirit which, in Sally's saliva when she wished
ill, could blind a boy . . .

'That was their mistake. When they ate those hogs, they
ate me. So I come back. An' I keeps comin' back. As I
came to Master Humphrey.'

'*What?*'

'Humphrey Barton. When we made love, him and me,

he promised he'd build me a temple for our water. Ours.
Later on he said he'd *heat* the water. He'd boil it. I
remembered how I'd been boiled alive; an' I hated him for
that. I'll never drink tea, you know. Or coffee. Only milk
and fruit drinks. An' spring-water.'

Paul felt afraid. He had to leave, get away.

'You can bail me out from this bloody boring village,'
she murmured. 'I've waited. I've watched out. You're the
one. Knew you'd turn up. Water showed me.'

'Sally, I'm just an insurance manager, not a millionaire.'

'That'll do. Lots of money in insurance.'

'Cheques; not cash. Electronic money. I don't have any
safe I can rob, and run off with the loot to South America
or whatever mad idea – !'

'Never asked you to. I'm not a fool. Think I'd want to
be Mrs Paul Philips the Second for years? I deserve more.
You're going to sell my Mum and Dad insurance. Lots of
it. Hundred thousand. To look after their little girl in case
of accident. Instead of "Let's trust in the Lord"! The water
in their tea'll persuade them. Next it'll poison them, same
as it poisoned those dumb buggers once before. I've the
power, you know. You saw on Lammas. Want to watch
the other scene? Where those bastards dunked and boiled
their wise girl? I could arrange it.'

'I don't want to. No.'

'While it happens I'll go away for a week or two. I'll be
staying with me aunt in Scotland. You'll not make any
fuss about the claim.'

She was deranged. Dangerous. But he believed her. No,
there wasn't a 'spirit' in the spring which fed Pook Pond.
Couldn't be. There was a spirit in her. A talent. A terrible
power. A knowledge.

In Rose Cottage that night he'd given his substance to
her – his living fluid – far more directly than he'd done at
the well on Lammas midnight.

'I suppose you fancy living it up in London? Or is it

Monte Carlo? Or New York? You'd be leaving your pond, your source. A . . . priestess surely can't do that.'

'Think so, Paul? I carry me water with me. In me bladder, in me veins. In every watery cell of me body. And think! You'd have me out of the way. You could live tame again. Maybe you don't want that, eh?' Her hand aroused him, despite all. 'An' I'll be *wild* if I don't get what I want. Wild.'

Yes. And he would be an accessory to murder, as well as a partner in fraud.

Finally he escaped. He didn't arrive home till two o'clock, creeping in quiet as a mouse. As usual Alicia had left some lights on. Hastily he killed those in case she woke and spotted the alarm clock.

She did stir. 'Paul? That you?'

'Me.'

'Wha's time?' Already he could hear that she had turned over again.

'Bit after twelve,' he murmured. 'Night.'

He dreamt he was heading down the garden towards the well. A fierce suction drew him against his will; a powerful, dragging draft. If only he could break free, run back to the safety of Hollyhocks, slam and bolt the door. When he looked desperately for reassurance the house was no longer there. Other cottages loomed in the night, rough stone hovels thatched with straw. In vain he dug in his heels; he seemed to slide over the grass – till he came up against the wall of the well, which he gripped limply. His hands were jelly, meat boiled off a bone. How the mouth of the well dragged at him, the air current kissing and sucking. The deep dark well: down in its black-water depths was death. And something worse; something pre-human and vile that would swallow his mind and play with it, during gibbering, insane eternity.

Terror woke him, sweating. He slid from bed, hurriedly felt his way to the toilet (somehow avoiding the hands of darkness), switched on the light. He sat a long time, reading a travel magazine.

Finally he dared turn off the light and creep back to bed.

He was woken, what seemed moments later, by inhuman nasal screaming. Hogs were fighting over the swill of the witch's boiled flesh and guts. It was still dark. Then he recognized the grind of a truck engine, the groan of springs and chassis.

Pigs on their way to be slaughtered.

Pigs crowded on to two tiers of Sam Langley's huge old truck, which was cornering, heading up the village.

The pigs were fighting because they were packed in with strangers. And were shit-scared. They'd been driven from hot, wallowing, smelly sleep in their intensive-rearing shed into another world, a chilly, tight, roaring, swerving alien world where they could only scream; but their desperate panic shrieks wouldn't help. The rumble of the truck and the squealing quickly receded. How much more hygienic – for the human inhabitants – than in the nineteenth century when the pigs roamed free, and might bite a paralytic peasant boozer's hand in half.

He lay thinking about witchcraft. A witch needed you to *believe* in her powers, wasn't that so? And it helped if she owned some part of you. A hank of hair. A nail-clipping. Semen, blood. Or else nothing would happen. Unfortunately he did believe in Sally Dingle. Since Lammas night. Since the STRIPTEASE machine.

Those 'experiences' had been caused by auto-hypnosis. By his own mind. Surely.

Begin to disbelieve, then! Command yourself to be a sceptic!

How?

* * *

He spent the next few days exercising his sceptical faculty. He rehearsed a certain inevitable encounter.

As he was driving back home through the village a week later, at six-thirty, the headlights of the Saab picked up Sally walking towards the White Hart. He stopped the car beside her, beneath the illuminated inn-sign.

He spoke harshly. 'Now you listen to me. Your parents won't be taking out any policies with Life Mutual, *ever*. That's the end of it all. Understand?'

Her eyes moistened. She didn't seem to be crying, exactly. Her voice was as cool as the evening had now become.

'The end, is it? Maybe you need some more . . . incentive.'

'No, I don't.'

'Didn't say what kind of incentive, did I? Wasn't necessarily offerin' you another night in Rose Cottage.'

'You can no more threaten me than you can bribe me. I'd deny everything. Wild fantasies of yours.'

'*Wild*, yes.'

'No one would believe that we had, well . . .'

He oughtn't to have halted under the lit-up sign. He could always say, if challenged, that Sally had recently been accosting him in a totally silly way. He hadn't told anyone, so as not to upset Alicia at a critical time. So as not to lose face with the Boys. They too would have refused Sally's advances; but you had to pretend otherwise.

'Suppose they mightn't,' she conceded. She did seem remarkably self-possessed.

He nodded, gratified. 'So any sort of blackmail is out.'

'Any mundane sort.'

'Mundane, eh? Fancy word, that be.' He imitated Alicia imitating a joke yokel. 'What's the other sort?'

'You know.'

'No, I don't. I don't believe in you, Sally, not one scrap. Medieval witches boiled in great big cauldrons? Blah.

Medieval peasants never owned a witch-size cauldron.
That's straight out of fairy-tales – or Disney. Magic water?
Ho-hum.'

'A few bottles of *that* in church, the way the vicar carries
on!'

Paul sniggered. 'Constipated water.'

'Different kind, though,' Sally said. 'Much weaker.'

He shook his head. 'I don't believe the least little bit.
You and Humphrey Barton? Bollocks.'

The pub door opened, and Mary Wilson stood framed
there.

'Hey, Paul!' she called. 'No time for a drink. Your
Alicia's waters broke half an hour ago, real sudden. Pains
only just came on. Mrs Smythe drove her in to the
Maternity.'

Paul revved, and mounted the tarmac outside the pub,
to turn. Sally dodged away. 'That'll show her I mean
business,' he thought, with a twitch of satisfaction.

How did Mary Wilson know so soon? As Alicia said:
people in Easton Hampcote knew what you were eating
for dinner before you knew it yourself. Except, they didn't
know about Sally and him; of that he felt positive.

He sped towards the hospital, back the way he had just
come. He must have passed the Smythes' old Ford en
route earlier, and not noticed. He had been planning his
encounter, and practising scepticism. Well, those had paid
off.

The birth was remarkably rapid, however the presiding
surgeon inflicted an unnecessarily vigorous episiotomy to
enlarge the opening, requiring a number of stitches. Alicia
murmured that she had heard through an anaesthetic fog
his assistant protesting at this. No doubt it was inconsider-
ately late in the day for a mother to give birth; maybe the
surgeon was going out for supper? Alicia had refused her
consultant's persuasions to check in a few days early and

have the birth induced with a prostaglandin drip, labour thus commencing in the morning and concluding by late afternoon. Here was the pay-back.

To himself too, Paul reflected. That cut in Alicia's vagina would delay the renewal of love-making by weeks. Or longer. A woman could stay sore for months.

Yet he wasn't thinking too much along those lines. He was a *father* – of a well-formed baby boy. He and Alicia were parents, of David Gordon Philips, Alicia's choice of names. A solid, handsome ring to them.

The nurse on duty also forgot to bring Alicia a milk-suppressant tablet – she wasn't planning to give suck – but Paul sorted that out.

He stayed while he and she fed David Gordon his first bottle; then the baby was carried off to its plastic bubble-chamber in another room. Alicia would need to stay in hospital for a week to ten days. Likewise baby. The medical profession expected him to develop post-natal jaundice, and were already removing test samples of blood from the ball of his poor little foot as if to deplete his supply of the red stuff.

Exhausted, Alicia faded out; and Paul drove home a second time, vaguely cursing doctors.

He visited every evening, using up the intervening couple of hours by working late at the office then catching an early pint and a pub meal: hot pie, cheeseburger and chips. A pint, in Lederbury, yes. He wouldn't arrive back at Hollyhocks till nearly ten.

On the third night, Sally was waiting in the shadows.

'Sorry and all that,' he told her definitively, 'but bugger off.'

That night after he had climbed into bed alone he saw again the after-image of her, nude in Humphrey Barton's fine spa bath.

Fair enough. This at least was no nightmare of falling

down a well, disappearing into darkness. He could cope
with that particular image easily enough; and he did, then
went to sleep.

Next night was Boys' Night, so he went directly from the
hospital to the White Hart. It was only a short drive home
afterwards, unmonitored by police.

Matt didn't seem his normal jokey, chipper self. Brooding into his beer?

'What's up, Matt?'

Matt contrived a grin. 'Up? Don't talk dirty.'

'You seemed preoccupied.'

'I was thinking about the magpies of Birdland. Wondering which ones would like to fly from Whitney's to a
better feathered nest overseas. Migrating to the sunny
dollar.'

Conrad Golby was quick on the uptake that night. 'Why
magpies? Why not owls or nightingales? Has somebody
nicked something?'

Laughing, Matt dealt Conrad a friendly cuff. 'You'd
know all about nicking in the antiques bizz! When was the
last time the boys in blue turned you over?'

'*Has* someone? Stolen? Secret formulas? Inside job?'

Matt shook his head. 'Nope. Heard the one about the
stripper with the artificial leg . . .?'

They hadn't.

'Hath this child been already baptized or no?'

What a stupid question, thought Paul. If it was already
baptized, why would we be here?

'No,' replied Alicia. The baby was limp in her arms,
half asleep.

Standing by the font, she was a radiant madonna.
Madonna with child, in a long robe of Victorian lace.
Surely that was the true symbolic aim of the christening

ceremony: to transform every mother into Mary, every infant into Jesus (or his sister).

A bitter thought intruded: David Gordon's might as well have been a virgin birth! And now that wretched cut and those stitches. Paul itched. Guiltily he glanced along the aisle, however Sally wasn't lurking anywhere that he could see.

The vicar began to pray. Quite a gathering was standing to attention. Two godparents by the font: an old school chum of Alicia's, Maggy, and Raymond Thwaite, their ex-best man. Two sets of grandparents upright in the front row, looking proud. Maggy's husband Bob, and Mrs Thwaite. An aunt and cousin of Alicia's, and her younger sister Antonietta. Paul's older brother, Daniel, with whom he never really saw eye to eye. A scattering of the church regulars, Mrs Badgot prominent: and the Boys' Night indomitables (including, wonder of wonders, Adrian) plus wives and kids. No Sally. Thank God.

He'd been a fool, and his folly would likely find him out; though not today. If he itched, he should scratch that itch well away from home. Easier said than done. No, he shouldn't have scratched it at all.

Hubert Smythe raised his voice, as if in an attempt – unsuccessful – to capture Paul's attention.

'*None can enter* into the Kingdom of God except he be born anew of water – '

The old stone church only possessed one stained-glass window, and that was out of character: a First World War memorial in rose and violet with several soldiers being exhorted by an angel – their company commander – to go through the barbed wire to heaven, surely a rapid route. Several marble bas-reliefs dating from the sixteenth and seventeenth centuries were inscribed with pious encomiums praising gentlemanly charity and valour, ladylike sweetness and forbearance. Black-painted plaques from the pragmatic nineteenth century specified the amount of charity: five pounds willed to furnish bread for the parish poor. Nearer the font, in an enormous flagstone, a brass inlay of a local knight had been worn by centuries of tread till it was a featureless golden puddle. Yellow chrysanthemums crowded vases.

'. . . Suffer the little children,' the vicar was reading. Alicia glanced sharply at Paul; an angry madonna.

'Praise be – ,' the congregation chorused raggedly; just as Alicia had quipped to the vicar months ago, apropos the village's recovery from the plague. Now she was uttering the response with feeling.

Would Sally tell, out of venom? If so, he too could tell a tale! About how Sally Dingle had planned . . .

. . . for her parents to take out substantial life insurance? Unprovable.

How she aimed to poison them both? 'By witchcraft, sir, is that so?' Already Paul could hear the scornful tones of the imaginary policeman.

'*I demand therefore* – ' Hubert Smythe was staring directly at Paul. 'Dost thou, in the name of this child, renounce the devil?'

Oh absolutely. I already renounced Sally Dingle.

The service droned on, via the Creed, to the blessing of the water.

'. . . beloved Son Jesus Christ, for the forgiveness of our sins, did shed out of his most precious side both water and blood – '

Did he, indeed? What kind of water was that, then? Dilute acids from the stomach? The Church didn't make quite so much of the water, did they? The blood, yes. Buckets of blood split down the ages; and cup after cup of communion wine. Communion water wouldn't have quite the same cachet. Couldn't baptize someone in blood, though.

Paul wished that *he* could lose some water out of his side. These days the waistband of his trousers was uncomfortably tight. In fact he felt positively obese. All those cumulative half-pints at the White Hart? Maybe too much salt in his food of late was the culprit. Convenience meals and pub snacks were making him retain water. Gas shifted in his intestines, pressed by water-laden tissues, and he squirmed so as not to vent a sulphurous stink in church.

Smythe accepted the white package that was David Gordon from Alicia; lace hung down like a dwarf's bridal train. Consecrated water spilled from the vicar's fingers upon the baby's bald head. 'I baptize thee – '

Smythe received David Gordon into the flock, painting an invisible cross of water on his brow next, and handing him back to Alicia. Then he read the Thanksgiving followed by another prayer. He instructed the godparents on their duties – fluffing his lines now, as if distracted – and finally opened his mouth to pronounce the blessing.

The baby shrieked like a cat caught in a snare.

Smythe cringed, then he too cried out, brandishing his right hand – the hand which had baptized.

The vicar's index finger was swelling obscenely. More a phallus than a finger.

Alicia screamed too. The wailing baby's brows were swelling visibly, bulging. Its whole face was puffing up, compressing its eyes tight, inflating its lips to block the mouth, closing its suddenly misshapen nostrils. The howling stopped, from lack of air. The body in the lace robe convulsed. At the same moment Hubert Smythe's huge finger burst open at the tip, spraying blood and water at the font.

In a congregation frozen by horror only one person moved. Matt Davies jumped up. 'No!' he shouted. 'That's impossible!'

At eleven that same night Paul sat in the kitchen of Hollyhocks with the lights off and the curtains open, watching the garden by moonlight, trying to think. He felt ragged and dog-tired.

Alicia already lay upstairs, tranquillized then put to sleep by barbiturates, dead to the world. Paul would take some sleeping pills presently, tired though he was, to give himself the alibi of chemical unconsciousness. He'd turned the lights off because village eyes would be scrutinizing Hollyhocks tonight. He sipped some whisky. Haig. Drops of fire. They'd bought it because he didn't like it, so it would stay longer in the bottle, reserved for visitors.

His memories of the past nine or ten hours were chaos. Mrs Badgot – formerly a nurse – trying to force the empty tube of a ball-point pen down David Gordon's throat to ventilate him. Fast thinking, that. But useless. The vicar rocking from side to side like a drunk, bleeding all over his vestments. Matt insisting that the font should be covered immediately and that no one should touch the remaining water, or empty it.

Then the useless, screeching drive in Matt's BMW with a hysterical Alicia and the bloated, asphyxiated baby to hospital. Dead on arrival. Matt burbling, on the way, about allergy shock, or something. Matt phoning urgently from a pay-phone in the hospital. Other arrivals by car: godparents, grandparents, Mrs Badgot driving a bandaged Hubert Smythe, sallow with shock, and his wife. The emergency doctor's questions. Matt taking the doctor and Paul aside while a nurse was giving Alicia a sedative injection – because she was screaming at Matt, 'Why was it impossible? Who were you phoning? Why were *you* so bothered about the font?'

According to Matt, a bottle of experimental synthetic hormone concentrate appeared to have vanished from the safe area at Whitney's. Or rather, the bottle in question had proved to contain tap-water; *if* it was the same bottle. No, the police hadn't been told – just the security officer – because Whitney's weren't certain that there had been a theft. There may have been a stupid error in the lab. When? Hard to say; some time during the previous fortnight. Pointless to stir up publicity. Counter-productive. *If* this was a theft, it indicated industrial espionage, and the spy was still about. Some chemist or other staff member who lived in Birdland. A magpie.

One of Whitney's analysts – whom Matt trusted – would be taking a sample from the font right now. It was quite unlikely to be the missing hormone (if any was actually missing). Why put *that* in a font before a christening? It couldn't have had such a lightning effect. The effect was wrong, anyway.

Paul said nothing. He knew. In his mind's eye he clearly saw Sally standing in the empty church pouring clear liquid from a bottle into the font and murmuring water-words to it.

He said nothing about this even after the hospital notified police and coroner; even to the inspector and constable from Lederbury who called at Hollyhocks that evening. ('Does anyone local have a grudge against you, that you know of? Mrs Philips? Mr Philips?' 'No.' 'No.')

Of course he said nothing. The liquid in the font might well turn out to be the stuff stolen from Whitney's, where Sally Dingle worked; but *it couldn't have done what it did*, on its own. Unaided by enchantment. ('Enchantment, Mr Philips? What *do* you mean?' Fall into that trap? Not likely!)

It might even prove to be harmless water, after the event. ('So a chemical can be told to turn into water miraculously, like water into wine, is that it, sir?' Hmm, bring on the men in white coats with needles and strait-jacket.)

And their son was dead. Not just blinded. Dead.

It was too late to tell anyone about the water-witchery. No one would manage to pin this on Sally like the tail on the donkey. She wasn't a fool. If he blurted out the truth, there'd be nothing to connect her with the theft. Nothing, nothing, nothing.

Besides . . . how could she break into a safe room and know what to take? She was only canteen staff at Whitney's.

Maybe she had stolen nothing – but had hexed the holy water waiting in the font; spat into it, cursed it. The missing hormone might be a huge red herring. Yes, that was it. The more Paul thought about it, the more he felt that the theft – if any – was sheer coincidence. Matt had been keyed up, nervous about the possible lab error in labelling. The horror at the church had triggered his anxieties about a missing chemical.

How could Paul accuse Sally of hexing plain water without confessing how he had . . . had it off with her? Guilt made him fantasize; that's what anyone sane would say. What a fool he would have made of himself, all to no effect – except personal disaster.

And their child was dead, vilely.

He hated Sally; and feared her. And desired her.

As he stared down the garden the moon suddenly illuminated a misty Pook Pond and the rumply field rising beyond. The scene . . . shimmered. He saw not Charolais cows but distant cottages, hovels facing the village duck pond. An uncouth crowd clad in smocks, sleeveless surcoats, and hose were gathering. Paul started to his feet, gripping the window-sill. She was doing it again! The crowd milled, braying soundlessly. Three men dragged a silently screaming woman towards the pond, started to tie her wrists and ankles. This vision was worse – clearer – than his glimpse of Barton's half-built spa. This time it was populated, by the spectres of dead peasants.

She must be near by, as he had guessed she might be!

He opened the kitchen door, ran down the lawn in darkness – the vision had vanished – and stalked through

the wild garden, circling soft-foot towards the well. A
black figure loomed by it.

He hissed, 'Sally Dingle!'

''Bout time you came. I've been missin' you. Will you
fix that insurance now? An' I'll reward you, way you like
it.'

Painfully his foot struck a stone left lying in the grass.
Immediately he knew what to do. Stooping, he hefted the
stone, and struck at her head. She sprawled against the
wall of the well. He couldn't see what damage he had
done but she was certainly still alive, groaning in pained
confusion. Discarding the stone, he cast about for the
bucket. He freed the rope, tearing a fingernail back on the
rough fibre. He trussed her ankles, trussed her wrists, just
as the vision had shown. Then he heaved the iron grille
aside.

'No, no,' she moaned. 'No use. Too late. No.'

'Too late, is it?'

'Yes, yes,' she gasped. For a moment he thought she
was encouraging him.

He upended her over the edge by the legs, let her drop
head first. Heard, moments later, a single sludgy splash.
Then he vomited on the grass.

He restored the heavy grille and walked back to the
house, to take two sleeping tablets and go to bed.

It rained morosely the next day. Paul phoned his office to
take several days' leave. Grandparents and Antonietta were
staying at the White Hart which had some bed-and-
breakfast rooms. They soon arrived at Hollyhocks to
console morosely. Matt had put up Raymond and his wife
overnight; Adrian had done likewise for Maggy and her
husband. They also came round to the house; then Mrs
Badgot with Ruth Smythe. The vicar was still house-
bound, in no fit state. The gathering resembled the after-
math of a funeral except that the funeral hadn't yet taken

place. Daniel Philips had excused himself – unforgivably, said Maggy to Paul, as though Paul was to blame for his brother. Maggy and Amanda Thwaite took over the kitchen, to brew cups of tea and cook a large lunch.

David Gordon should be cremated in Lederbury, Alicia decided. She couldn't bear to enter St Mark's, Easton Hampcote, again. 'Not so soon, Ruth. Do you understand?'

'Hubert will . . . understand, I'm sure.'

Maggy invited Alicia to come home with her for a few days after the funeral. 'A change of scene? You too, Paul,' she added. Alicia shook her head, unable to decide.

After a buffet lunch Paul carried plates to the kitchen to escape the conversations. The window was steamed up; raindrops ran down the outside. Occasional beads of condensation slid down the inside of the glass, clearing thin strips of view like those in a mirrored security window. He watched the race between blobs of moisture, betting on one, then another. Tiny pools lay on the inside paintwork.

He poked a pool with his finger. Drops of water began to run from it, up the glass. *Up*. The beads wrote raggy letters in the steam.

SAL WELL.

Trembling, he seized a tea-towel and wiped the window clean. He must have written the message himself with the tip of his finger. Some part of his mind had directed his hand without his knowing, without his seeing it happen.

'Sal well.' What kind of 'well'? She still survives? Or, she's *down* the well?

He fled from the kitchen; but found himself returning every ten minutes to check the window. A few times he wiped fresh condensation away, then quit doing this, realizing that he was creating a porthole on the rain-sodden garden and the distant well.

He ought to tip rubble down the well. Old stones and

broken bricks. Buckets of rubble to cover the body! Alicia might spot him; someone might. What excuse could he have? Nobody would go near the well all winter long, and it was almost winter already. Long wet grass, rain, chill, mud.

'Better leave well alone! Wait till spring.' He shivered at the confusing ambiguity of his thoughts.

Later, the same Inspector Horrobin called with his constable driver. The post-mortem on David Gordon, performed early that morning, had produced no adequate explanation other than a massive allergy reaction. Though to what? And why had Hubert Smythe also been affected so dramatically?

'I gather you're aware of the possible theft of a dangerous substance from Whitney's, sir?'

'Mr Davies told me.'

'I wanted to reassure you – not that it's any consolation, sir – that there's no conceivable connexion. The liquid in that font was ordinary water. Whitney's and the police lab both tested it.'

Ordinary: Paul had known it.

Not ordinary, no. Evil water. Witch water.

He nodded.

'In view of Mr Davies' suspicions, we'd prefer to avoid ungrounded speculation.'

'Softly, catchee monkey; is that it? If there *is* any monkey; or magpie.' Really, Paul ought to keep his mouth buttoned.

Horrobin frowned. 'Between you and me, sir, one of the village lasses who works at Whitney's has gone missing. Probably she's staying with some friend; didn't bother telling her parents. Or else she's skipped it to London with a lad. In view of Mr Davies', hmm, allegation we're making some enquiries. I'm sure, after the lab analysis, you'll appreciate there's no link between that and your – tragedy.'

Ought he to ask, 'Which girl?' Would that lead naturally on to Horrobin asking Paul's opinion of Sally Dingle? Policemen liked to accumulate information, didn't they? So Paul refrained from asking. He tried simply to look numbed by the whole business. After Horrobin and Constable Cresswell left, Paul hurried into the kitchen, where the window remained a blank.

The funeral took place two days later at the crematorium in Lederbury. Alicia had decided against going to stay with Maggie and Bob for a few days, though Paul urged her to; nevertheless Maggie and her husband drove back to Hollyhocks, along with others of the family, so that the house would be comfortingly full for a while . . . before it became empty.

It was dark by four, and the curtains were closed. At six, Maggie and Bob were in the process of leaving. Light flooded from the front door over shingle and parked cars. The moon was up. Mrs Badgot bustled in from the road.

'I don't mean to intrude! I saw you all at the door.'

'Thank you for what you tried to do for David Gordon,' Alicia said.

'Think nothing! I don't want to upset you but . . . have you looked at the bottom of your garden?'

Paul froze.

'I hope it's still there. I'd feel a fool.' Mrs Badgot took Alicia by the arm. Footsteps crunched the shingle as everyone walked along to a vantage point. A couple of hundred yards away Pook Pond glowed mistily by moonlight. Somewhat closer – where the well was – a white foggy figure writhed.

'Isn't it just like a soul dancing in paradise?' whispered Mrs Badgot. 'An angel!'

To Paul's aghast eyes the luminous shape looked more like a soul in torment.

'I think,' said Mrs Badgot, 'it's a sign from your poor baby – not to grieve, because he's blessed. The wee mite did die baptized.'

'That's mist,' Alicia said sharply. 'Mist drifting out of our well. Hubert already told me about all those oafs who saw ghosts down by Pook Pond. Mist, Mrs Badgot, mist!'

'*I* never saw the like of that.' Mrs Badgot sounded offended. 'I've looked down your garden lots of times through that gap in your hedge.'

'I believe you have!'

'A well, is it?' said Bob heartily. 'Why don't we take a gander? Meteorological oddity, eh? Does look a bit like a faceless apparition. Got a torch handy?'

'No,' croaked Paul.

'Got one in the car.'

'No! Can't you see how this is upsetting Alicia? Go away, Mrs Badgot, please! I don't know what you were thinking of.'

'But it's there,' she insisted. 'It's a sign.'

'No, it damn well isn't. It's a trick of the moonlight.'

'Fair enough,' said Bob. 'C'mon, Maggy, time we went.'

In any case, the wraith above the well had already started to fade.

What would Alicia see if she went down to the well the next day? If she had the wit to take the torch to shine down into the depths. A pair of heels? Legs? As soon as he could, Paul emptied the good batteries out of the torch by the back door and hid them. In their place he put used ones which he hadn't bothered to throw away. The bulb produced but a poor glow now.

It was a week later, a Saturday. Paul had witnessed the wraith once more, dancing for a while upon the well. Alicia hadn't mentioned seeing anything.

At half-one he arrived home from Lederbury to find a white police car parked outside. He ran indoors. Alicia and Constable Cresswell were talking in the sitting-room. Relief welled up.

'Darling, Inspector Horrobin called – '

'Where is he? I don't see him.'

'He's in the garden. Mrs Badgot must have been gossiping about that funny mist we saw; though the Inspector wouldn't say who. He asked to have a look at our well.'

'In connexion with that theft from Whitney's,' Cresswell overrode her, 'which Mr Philips knows about. Someone may have dumped the stolen whatsit down your well – it's close to the field. A gas may be leaking.'

'A gas – from a bottle of hormone? That preposterous.'

'I'm no chemist, sir. Are you?'

'You make Whitney's sound like a weapons factory!'

'You seem agitated, sir. Relax. The Inspector knows what he's doing.'

Very likely. Theft from Whitney's. Baby killed in church. Local girl goes missing same evening. Spook spotted in bereaved parents' garden. *Is there a link?* Ignoring Cresswell's advice, Paul hastened through to the kitchen and stared out. It had started raining. An expressionless Inspector Horrobin was treading back towards the house. His overcoat pockets could hold half a dozen torches. Paul wrenched the back door open.

'Ah, Mr Philips. There appears to be a body down your well. Wouldn't have any idea how it got there, would you?'

Paul said nothing.

'Ankles look to be roped together. Body's upside-down, you see. That should expedite recovering it, with a grapnel and winch. If the knots were properly tied. Were they, Mr Philips?'

* * *

Rolled-up drainage piping lay on the field the police car
was passing, looking like huge millipedes which would
presently burrow into the soil, sucking at its black water.
The segmented, flexible pipes, now slicked with rain,
seemed alive, about to uncoil and squirm.

At university a friend had once persuaded Paul to drop
half a tab of acid with him – the way they persuaded you
to drink halves, and halves, in the White Hart. Paul hadn't
enjoyed the experience; the LSD had invaded him, taken
him over for hours like a parasite, a bright monkey sitting
in his brain. Now, slumped in the back seat beside
Horrobin, he felt that he was undergoing a worse drug-
trip.

Except that he had taken no drugs. He realized that he
had become insane. Now that he was mad, the world was
much sharper and clearer than ever it had been when he
was sane. Before, the world had been fuzzy; he hadn't
needed to pay full attention, could take reality for granted.

The sodden verge along the roadside glowed lumi-
nously. Tree skeletons etched against the sky were bodies
whose flesh had rotted away, leaving branches of naked
nerves. A ploughed field was ten acres of chunkily knitted
brown wool; or dog turds.

No drugs. Something had reached into him, flooding,
touching every cell in his body, invading and corrupting
them.

Now he understood the why and wherefore of witchcraft: it was to gain this clarity, this power of vision, this
immanence. He was roused from everyday slumber,
awake to existence. Other people only acted the role of
being alive – of driving a car, of behaving like a proper
police inspector – grotesquely and clumsily.

Horrobin leered at Paul. 'Mrs Dingle thinks her daugh-
ter ran away because she was pregnant.'

'What?'

'Mrs D used to restock the girl's towels. Kept a count.

Not enough got used last time. Sally must have missed her period and didn't flush enough clean ones away to put her mum off the scent. I'll wager the autopsy'll show she was pregnant, once she's hauled out of your well. Someone killed her because she was having their baby. She'd have made big trouble for you, Mr Philips. That sad business with your other baby put us off the trail.'

'She was what?'

'In the family way. Bun in the oven. We'll soon know. How surprised you sound. Shame you never went on the stage.'

'How many months did her mother think?'

'Consulting your mental diary? Wondering if anyone else had a poke?'

'No!'

It was only a few weeks since they'd made love. She would hardly have known yet. Unless some young farmer *had* knocked her up, previous to that, at a disco . . . Unlikely; she didn't go in for boyfriends. Mrs Dingle must have been talking rubbish. It was just the kind of thing that would appeal to a policeman. Houses of cards formed and collapsed in Paul's head.

Rain dotted the windows, running jerkily across. The wipers swished. The car halted at a junction to let a bus race by on the main road. Drops changed direction, downward. Beside Paul's face a single fat raindrop was climbing smoothly *up* the glass.

Sally was dead, but the water remained. Anywhere in this area! In the sky, in the fields. It cycled round and round, pervading the neighbourhood over the centuries like a blot spreading outward, always refreshing itself from the source. From Pook Pond, from the well. There where the witch had been boiled alive; where Humphrey Barton had clung to a stone succubus and drowned himself; where other events must have happened too – all of them increasing the evil power, no, the *primeval* power,

that visionary power which awoke its devotees from the
rubbery idiocy and banality of the everyday world.

As the car speeded up in the traffic stream bound for
Lederbury, that single drop continued to march defiantly
up the window, which was slightly open. Paul shrank
from the glass.

But of course the water had already entered him long
since. It sought a human presence in the world. A view-
point. A raindrop was quite like an eye. Perhaps it had
found Sally deficient.

Insane thoughts.

Being proved insane in court was his only escape route
from an ordinary, brutalizing prison where 'sex offenders'
weren't at all popular. So: a psychiatric lock-up? Basket-
work therapy, drugs, indefinite detention rather than an
eight- or ten-year sentence? Even so, that might be pref-
erable. Now was the time to choose.

Paul said to Horrobin, 'Sally was a witch. I mean that
literally; she was a reborn witch. A *water*-witch. I think
they all were, really, in ancient times. On the Continent
they burnt witches to get rid of their wicked water, to
convert them into dry blazing husks. Because God created
the solid earth out of liquid, and a witch sought to dissolve
what was solid and ordinary and reform it magically.
Make reality more fluid. So that you could master it
directly. They didn't burn witches here; they hanged them
with rope. Maybe afterwards they burnt the bodies or
buried them in lime. It was a mistake to boil Sally in the
cauldron, when she wouldn't drown in Pook Pond. Afterwards the water was poured like greasy soup on to the
green, into the duck pond. The ducks laid eggs; cows
drank their fill from the pond, and their udders swelled
with milk. The boiled loose meat of Sally was fed to
screaming hogs for their supper. Thus in many ways she
re-entered the village.'

'So he's a fucking fruitcake,' Cresswell commented over his shoulder.

'Or else he's trying to con us that he is,' replied Horrobin.

Witchcraft wasn't only the ability to *see* the world; it was also the capacity to alter the world with one's will, one's desires, one's imagination. Paul concentrated on the errant raindrop.

It changed direction, began creeping stubbornly against the wind towards the front of the car. How would it cross the gap between the doors? Paul imagined a raindrop-size bridge. The drop reappeared on the driver's window, which was also open slightly. That was the same raindrop; he knew it well. He sensed its wetness, its liquid tension, the swarm of animalcules swimming inside it, eating molecules of suspended chemicals – and eating each other. Mating, giving birth, dying. He intuited the life in the water, the spirit which was mirrored in himself. He urged that bead of water to climb the window towards the inch of ventilation.

Briefly the drop hung at the very top of the glass. It gathered, and launched itself. In slow motion he saw the drop fly at the driver's face.

Cresswell screamed deafeningly. He clapped a hand to his eye. His other hand leapt free of the wheel, clawing at that blob of boiling water which was eating its way like molten lead into his tear duct. Horrobin grabbed over the back of Cresswell's seat for the wheel, but the car was already careering, skidding, over the centre line, and a bulk flour truck – oncoming, giant-size – was only yards away.

He was a puddle of rainwater on the verge, reflecting a small patch of blue sky. He was an eye which stared up bleakly, an eye in which reflections formed: of rain-clouds, and of crows. Crows were clever scavengers of roadway carrion who never let themselves be clipped by traffic no matter how late they left it to flap out of the way of wheels. What carrion were those black birds eyeing now? A dead driver, thrown through a splintering window? Cresswell had stopped screaming.

In fact there was absolute silence. What sounds could a puddle hear? That's all he was: a pool of water which would presently soak into the turd-like soil.

No. '_I won't dissolve!_' He couldn't feel anything because he had broken his neck, snapped his spine, when he was thrown clear; that's why he couldn't turn his head away from the sky. His eardrums had ruptured; that was why he couldn't hear the hiss of air-brakes, horns, voices, a distant ambulance siren. Ambulance men would load him carefully. He would spend the rest of his life – long or short – in a bed unable to bat an eyelid or twitch a finger, while inside his body all the waters would pulse with secret, dark activity . . . '_But I shan't dissolve!_'

Paul shook his head. The car was still driving along the road. Cresswell muttered, 'Bugger it,' and rubbed his eye, carrying on steering casually, expertly. The wipers swished.

To alter things . . . meant to see an alternative event with a vision so compelling that the event became entirely real; at least for a while. The insane dwelled in a world where alternative events continued on and on forever. Possession by evil – by primeval vision – must be very like possession by madness.

Paul stared into his lap at the twin bracelets he wore. One was surely a stainless steel watch strap. The other, a chain and shield inscribed with his allergy to penicillin. For some reason chain and strap had fused together, bonded by powerful magnetism. He couldn't move his wrists apart.

Now he knew why those ignorant medieval powers-that-be had been able to torture and execute witches; why a demon never came to the witch's rescue. That was because a witch saw the demon coming to her aid so vividly it was as if this had already occurred – until the hot iron tore her flesh, or the faggots blazed, or the water began to bubble. Until she suddenly lost faith and screamed. It was that loss of faith in her vision which was fatal.

Sally's vision sustained her while she floated on Pook Pond. It failed when the peasants boiled her. Had it failed her again when he hit her and drowned her? Perhaps. But perhaps the vision had passed from her to Paul, given away gladly. Why, she hardly had struggled. Had grinned up at him from underwater. Or was that an alternative event?

People were made of water. In their organs, glands, and limbs. In the brain. Because of all the vulnerable water in them, people could be controlled by a master or mistress of magic. Could be made to dance to the song of water – as he had danced to Sally's tune. Now she was free of the fierce, luminous vision, in which you must either believe totally or be destroyed.

Since she had come back from the dead, why so would he. He had drunk the water of immortality.

The car sped into the outskirts of Lederbury.

The cell, with its single light bulb protected by a grille, was bare apart from a bolted-down bed and the toilet bowl which lacked a seat: a china cauldron.

As Paul sat on the cold ceramic rim he stared between his parted legs into the water.

Sally had immersed herself on Pook Pond, baptized herself, drowned herself. Her flesh had dissolved in the water of the cauldron. She had drunk the well into her lungs. Dying was dissolving, was it not? He had fought against dissolving. That had been his mistake, when he sat handcuffed in the police car. His failure of faith.

Paul reached a hand down into the bowl where his diluted urine swam. He re-established contact with his water. He imagined himself dissolving: his body fluids, the overwhelming percentage of his person, flooding into the china toilet bowl, by way of sewage pipes out of the police station, via a treatment plant to discharge in a river not too far away.

He imagined furiously – '*I believe!*' – and began to melt away from his surface down to deep inside himself; and the bright light in the cell started to fade.

All these books are available at your local bookshop or newsagent, or can be ordered direct from the publisher.

To order direct from the publishers just tick the titles you want and fill in the form below.

Name _____

Address _____

_____

Send to:
Grafton Cash Sales
PO Box 11, Falmouth, Cornwall TR10 9EN.

Please enclose remittance to the value of the cover price plus:

UK 60p for the first book, 25p for the second book plus 15p per copy for each additional book ordered to a maximum charge of £1.90.

BFPO 60p for the first book, 25p for the second book plus 15p per copy for the next 7 books, thereafter 9p per book.

Overseas including Eire £1.25 for the first book, 75p for second book and 28p for each additional book.

Grafton Books reserve the right to show new retail prices on covers, which may differ from those previously advertised in the text or elsewhere.